DARK HORSE

A DEMON'S GUIDE TO THE AFTERLIFE

BOOK ONE

KEL CARPENTER

AURELIA JANE

Dark Horse

Kel Carpenter and Aurelia Jane

Published by Raging Hippo LLC

Proofread by Dominique Laura

Cover Art by Malice and Mayhem

Discreet PB ISBN: 978-1-957953-51-9

Discreet HB ISBN:978-1-957953-52-6

 Created with Vellum

ABOUT THE AUTHORS

Kel Carpenter and Aurelia Jane are the hilarious team behind the international bestselling series, A Demon's Guide to the Afterlife.

They pride themselves in being absolute weirdos, spending hours on the phone coming up with detailed worlds, and laughing about crazy ideas for torturing characters. While they believe they each have the personality of a rabid badger, people still seem to like them okay.

They share a love of coffee, snarky t-shirts, and tacos, and they've made some adorable tiny people with their equally weird husbands. Best friends and work wives, Kel has the audacity to live in Maryland while Aurelia lives in Texas, but they try to see each other as much as possible.

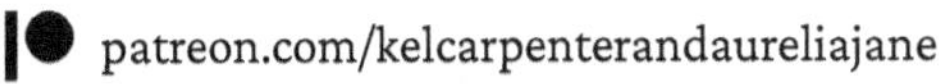 patreon.com/kelcarpenterandaureliajane

To Maegan,
You're to blame for the asshole crow. You're also pretty spectacular.
— Kel

To Patricia Browne,
It took eighteen years, but I kept my promise. You are missed.
— Aurelia

Hell is empty,
    And all the devils are here.

— William Shakespeare, *The Tempest*

CHAPTER I

"Dinner time, Huck," I called out, tapping my fingers next to the bowl.

A forty-year-old man came around the corner on all fours. His naked skin hung flaccid, and his knees stuck to the crappy linoleum floor. The tags on the dog collar around his neck tinkled.

Hate-filled, shit-brown eyes stared up at me. I grinned.

"You call that dinner—" he started.

I grabbed his face by the jaw and squeezed tight. "No talking back. Bad dog."

Indecision warred on his face. He wanted to hit me. Kill me, if he could. But he was thinking back to the last time he had made those attempts. It didn't end well.

For him, at least.

A moment passed, and he lowered his eyes. I dropped my hand away and patted his head mockingly. "Good mutt," I said without any of the positive inflection I'd use on a real dog.

I left Huck McKinley to his dinner of dog food covered in

hot sauce, not feeling the least bit bad. Some would say I was more than a little fucked up. Cruel.

They were right, of course.

But I was a demon by trade. It was sort of in the job description.

A hundred years ago, I died. More accurately, I was murdered—by my ex-husband, to be exact. He was a piece of shit too, but that was a whole other can of worms I didn't often like to open.

The point was, I died and came to the Afterlife.

Because I wasn't in the bottom forty percent of humans that had to serve punishments for their transgressions on Earth, and I wasn't in the top one percent that automatically went through the proverbial pearly gates, I had to get a job. That's how I became a demon.

My time in the realm of the living had mostly held pain. It was what I knew. What I was good at. I took that pain and I turned it on assholes like Huck McKinley. He had also died, except he was a wife beater, and he ran dog-fighting rings that had killed hundreds of animals.

That was how he ended up here under my tender loving care.

Where is here? Hell.

Huck took a bite of food and gagged. He spat it out all over the floor, grasping at his throat. Murder shimmered in his eyes.

How cute.

"You bitch—"

"Ah-ah." I wagged my finger back and forth. "We talked about this. Dogs don't speak—"

He let out a growl that might have scared me a hundred years ago. Now?

I cracked my knuckles and grinned. He launched off the

floor, saliva dripping from his lips, hot sauce mingled with bits of dog food staining his chest.

As he came up, so did my knee. I struck him square in the face. A crack echoed in the room. He flew through the air, crashing into the wall with a loud bang. He dropped to the floor, an indent of his disgusting body left in the drywall.

I tsk'd.

"Now you've done it, Huck." I walked over and picked him up by the back of his neck. My demonic strength was a godsend in moments like this. I tossed him in a wire metal crate and latched the door.

He groaned.

I hummed under my breath as I lifted my Apple watch to my face. "Play 'Baby' by Justin Bieber."

Huck let out a slew of profanities that were drowned out by the tween's obnoxious singing. I bobbed my head along to the music as I started for the front door.

"Wait—wait!" he yelled out for me. I paused at the exit. "You can't leave me like this. Please—" He cut off when I grinned maniacally.

"Should have thought about that before you were a bad dog."

With that, I stepped outside and closed the door.

All along the street sat ordinary cookie-cutter houses. They spanned miles. Every house was actually a prison containing a bad soul that had fallen into that lower forty percent of the human race that needed to be punished. How long each person served before being recycled and sent back to the realm of the living differed, but the houses didn't. The only thing separating each of them was the number on the door. Each one was special to the soul inside it. I was currently in charge of a dozen or so. People that ranged from pedophiles, to Huck McKinley, to emotionally manipulative twats that stole from their kids.

Each of their crimes were different in act and severity, but the outcome was not. They'd landed themselves in Hell, and it was my responsibility to punish and rehabilitate them before they were wiped clean of all memories and sent back to try again.

Two houses down, Malachi the Dreaded stepped out of a door. He let out a low sigh of exhaustion and straightened his blood-soaked tie.

"Long session?" I asked.

He took one look at me and wrinkled his nose in distaste. I knew what he saw. A twenty-something-year-old body with leather pants and a black corset. I wore knee-high black boots with a chunky heel. My red hair hung loose around my shoulders and not a weapon or speck of blood was in sight.

"Very," he said after a pregnant pause. "You?"

"Not terribly so. I'm enjoying this case. I've already got another fifty years planned out for this guy." I hooked my thumb toward the door behind me, and Malachi's eyebrows inched up in barely discreet incredulity.

"Hmm."

I had to give it to him. He didn't say what he was clearly thinking. Must have learned from that asswipe, Karen. It wasn't exactly a secret that my methods of punishment were unusual. On the contrary, it made me an oddity for a demon.

It also made me the best at our job.

Anyone could hammer nails in a kneecap or shove bamboo under someone's nails. I was a true master of torture. A connoisseur, of sorts.

Not every demon saw it that way, though. Our profession generally attracted people that barely came in just above the forty percent. Shitheads that liked the idea of taking out their daddy issues on other people. People like Karen the Horrible.

A couple of decades back, I got assigned a case she wanted. Thinking she could get it back, she had openly challenged me to a duel. She and the others like her assumed I chose the punishments I did because I was weak. How wrong she was.

Malachi must have been there, or at least heard the stories. Then again, almost every demon had. The open snipes stopped after that day, even if the wandering eyes didn't. Oh, I heard the whispers through the grapevine, and over the years, several of the newbies had started to wonder. New demons always had something to prove. A bone to pick. It came with the territory. The demon guild was one of the most cutthroat in the Afterlife, and they had a tendency to judge or maim first and think later.

In that lay the problem. That behavior had broken way too many souls before their punishment was up. They weren't fully healed, and then those souls went back to the living realm to make the same shitty life choices that led them right back to Hell. Talk about a broken system.

Malachi idled warily, as if waiting for me to decide what I wanted. He likely didn't want to seem openly rude and run the risk of winding up on the other end of my legendary temper. Taking pity, or rather tired of my own mind games for the day, I waved at him and hit the home button on my watch.

My body de-materialized as I teleported into the demon dorms.

Several people took notice. I walked past the reception area where Diego the Dastardly was on duty. He gave me a wink and a sexy smirk, flirting shamelessly despite me having turned him down twice now. Still, I smiled back and inclined my head toward the gawking new girl next to him.

"Fury," she said in a low whisper.

"In the spirit," I chimed as I went by. Diego chuckled, his deep voice following after me.

Some of the oomph left me as I climbed two flights of stairs, but I kept my shoulders back as people passed me in the hallway. Some idolized me, like the girl downstairs. Usually that worshipping phase wore off after they had a few years to settle in. Right about the time the punishing and their new reality finally got to them. She was as green as they came, but that wouldn't be the case for long, and when life after death became the new norm, it wasn't so easy for most.

There was a reason over seventy percent of our new recruits dropped out in the first six months and transferred to a new guild. Everyone was earning their way toward one of two things: retirement, or the chance to be recycled. Most wanted to be recycled.

In the Afterlife, everything was what you made of it.

On Earth, you get what you get by happenstance, but either way—you get it.

Money. Opportunities. Race. Ethnicity. When you were recycled, your circumstances and start to life were all completely random, and it was utter bullshit.

One thing I learned in dying was that most people preferred the bullshit. They'd rather play the lottery and hope they got an easy ticket in the next life, and maybe an easy ticket into Heaven.

I was never one for believing in chance. Whenever fate had a choice, it fucked me over. So, I opted to take the hard route.

Become a demon. Earn my spot.

My own little piece of heaven.

Literally.

I sighed at that thought as I opened the door. A full-size bed, half kitchen, and tiny bathroom. Everything I needed was in these four walls. By this point in my career, I could have left the dorms. Moved into my own little place in one of the lower circles of the Afterlife. Settled down with another demon and lived in . . . boring blah.

I refused. Instead, I was biding my time, saving every single second I earned for the big ticket. A place behind the golden gates.

On Earth, I'd been no one, but here—here I would be someone. Here, I already was.

Sort of.

It was an ongoing process.

I started for the bathroom, ready to strip out of my badass (and uncomfortable) outfit, run a nice hot bath, and drink a few beers.

Maybe whiskey instead.

It could really go either way after dealing with Huck all day.

I was just reaching for the zipper on my corset when my watch started to ring.

Incoming call from . . . Jake.

I threw my head back and groaned. Why? What could Jake from Afterlife Resources possibly want?

I weighed the merits of ignoring his call till tomorrow, but my curiosity got the better of me. I wanted to know what reason my resources officer would have for calling me this late in the evening.

My thumb hit accept before I could think it over more,

but instead of a voice picking up on the other line, my body de-materialized once more.

I had only just registered that I was teleporting when I appeared in the hallway outside his office. His personal assistant, Francine, blinked in surprise.

"I'm sorry, but Jake is not available right now—"

"Well, I hate to break it to you, Francine, but I didn't come here by choice." I motioned to myself, happy I hadn't stripped first. I was so not feeling an orgy tonight.

Francine adjusted her glasses and picked up the phone on her desk. "Let me just call and see," she muttered, dialing his extension. Never mind that she could have just knocked on the door, or yelled, or better yet—Jake could have just given either of us a heads-up. I leaned against her desk and tapped my fingernails impatiently on the shiny veneer surface. "Your name is . . ." She left it open-ended, waiting for me to answer.

I gave her a hard look. You'd think I hadn't seen her once a month for the last thirty years.

"Fury."

She sighed. "Which Fury? Fury the Great? The Awful? Oh, I know—"

"*Just* Fury," I said, pinching the area between my brows and closing my eyes. A hundred years ago, I'd been an angry, murdered dead girl when I chose my name and profession.

How was I to know that Fury was essentially the 'Jessica' of the Afterlife?

"Oookay," she drawled passive-aggressively. We both waited for Jake to pick up. When he did, Francine said, "I have a 'Fury' here for you. She said you summoned her."

"Which Fury?" I heard him ask.

If my eyes could shoot fire, I would have melted the

phone. I leaned forward over the edge of the desk and said into the receiver, "*The* Fury. The one you called after—"

The line went dead, and my lips parted.

Why that piece of—

His door opened. Jake stood there, wearing a wrinkled suit and chipper smile that always made me a little stabby.

"Hey Fury, why don't you come in and take a seat?"

I shook my head, heading into his office. The door closed behind me right as I sat in the metal-framed chair. Outside, the second sun was setting.

"Why did you summon me?" I asked, cutting to the chase. He hummed to himself the whole way to his chair and then took his sweet time sitting down. I waited expectantly.

Finally, Jake said the last thing I ever expected to hear.

"I want to send you back to Earth."

CHAPTER 2

I heard the words, but I couldn't fully register what he'd said. I stared at him, blinking, finally processing some sort of response.

"I'm sorry, what?" Okay, so it wasn't the most brilliant response, but it was all I had.

He pointed at me. "You." He pointed up. "Earth." He turned his hand to his desk then made his index and middle fingers walk across the surface imitating a tiny person. "I want you to go there."

I narrowed my eyes and my nostrils flared. "Right. I got that part—" I started.

"Then why did you ask?" he interjected, a slight sparkle in his eyes.

My head fell back, and my groan filled the room. If I were being honest, it was probably heard down the hall . . . and possibly the entire floor. I didn't have the patience for conversations like this.

It's not that it was a time issue. I had all the time in Hell. But that didn't mean I wanted to waste it going in circles with Jake—who liked to screw with me for the fun of it. It was different when I did it to him. That was funny. But right now I could've been in my bed, binge-watching something I borrowed from the Current Affairs department.

"Oh, you can piss off if you think I'm going back there."

Why would I go back? I mean, why in the *hell*—literally—would I go back to Earth? I'd been gone for so long I wouldn't recognize the place, even if I did keep up with the changes . . . the culture shifts . . . and the technology. Okay, I couldn't use that excuse.

But that didn't change the fact that Earth was where my ex-husband killed me, and I wasn't exactly excited to take a joyride back to the crime scene.

I knew it wouldn't be the same. Anyone and everyone I'd ever known was long gone. I'd heard about them when they crossed over. I'd looked for some of them. Found a few of them too.

I'd kept tabs on the only one I'd truly cared about, and that was really all that mattered. The rest of them were getting what they deserved, for the most part. I shook my head, clearing those thoughts and pushing them aside.

"So I'll take that as a maybe?" he asked, that stupid grin still on his face.

"Look, Jake, it's been a day, and as much as I love these shared moments between us, it's getting a little old after, what? A hundred and three years now?" I crossed my arms in front of my chest. "Spit it out. Why do you want me on Earth?"

He met my eyes but didn't answer.

I uncrossed my arms, moving them to the sides of the chair to push myself up as I said, "Okeydokey, I'm out—"

"Wait." There was something about the way he said it that had me pausing. "Just wait. Sit back down."

So I did. He had my attention. In the century I'd known him, he'd never once had a tone as serious as he did now.

Back when I first met him, he was falsely kind. Not in the human-backstabbing-drama kind of way. In the way you have to be when someone is newly deceased—his words, not mine—and you have to break it to them. Then you follow that gem up by telling them they have to get a job. With a pleasant attitude, he'd walked a murdered young girl through her options in the Afterlife. That had eventually morphed into the banter we shared as we laughed at each other's expense, more often than not.

But this? He wasn't pleading, but if I had to put a word to what it sounded like, that would be the closest thing I could come up with.

"What's going on, Jake?" I sat back down completely. "Answer for real this time. A bottle of whiskey and a bath were calling my name before you did."

He sighed. "Upper Management has a problem that needs to be . . . addressed." He twirled a pen around on top of a file I hadn't noticed before. "Ultimately, it ended up on my desk. So here we are."

"Upper Management?" I asked, raising my eyebrows a little. He nodded, lips pressed together. "Well, that's intriguing. You going to tell me more about it, or . . .?"

"There are some basics you need to understand first."

I cocked an eyebrow. Even after all these years, he was underestimating me. Still, I dipped my head, motioning for him to continue.

"Okay," he said with a sigh. "So as you know, there are hundreds of departments in the Afterlife. Lots of dead people, lots of roles to fill. It's simple enough once you accept it." I scoffed. Murdered, and I still hadn't been able to rest in peace. "One of those departments is Risk Management—"

"You mean the fortune-telling department. Future affairs. The risk witches—"

"They aren't witches," he cut in. I shrugged. "But yes, that department. I wasn't aware you knew of it. Most don't . . ." he trailed off, waiting for me to fill in the blanks with how and why I knew of the highly secretive group.

"I get around," I said suggestively, and he raised his brows.

I grinned, not bothering to correct his train of thought.

He pursed his lips and nodded. "Right. Anyway, so the fortune-telling department, as you called it, saw the possibility of something happening. It's big. Like, *end of the world big*."

"Okay," I said. "I'm not sure what that has to do with me. I mean, if the world ends, that means our workload doesn't even increase because no one gets recycled, right?"

"We're talking about the entirety of the living realm extinguishing. Imploding. You do know what 'end' means?"

"You mean how my life 'ended'? Ceased to exist and then I got dumped here?" I deadpanned. "Yeah, I'm familiar with endings, Jake. Get to the point."

He pinched the bridge of his nose and scrunched his eyes shut. "Listen. The living realm needs to exist, just like we need to exist. It's a symbiotic relationship. A cycle. Upper Management doesn't want this happening, Fury. It *can't* happen. They've sent countless angels to try to redirect this situation, but each of them has failed. Hell, none of them even made a dent."

"Wait," I drawled. "You want *me* to go back to Earth to fix something that the angels can't?" He nodded. "That doesn't even make sense. That's basically their entire job, isn't it? To go fix shit on Earth and deal with problems before they become bigger problems—"

"Fury—"

"I mean, that's what they do. They don't hate Earth. They like it. They like the people and the hope and the . . ." I grasped for a word that encompassed the bullshit way angels spoke about Earth, "the goodness of it all—"

"Fury—"

"And I don't. I don't like anything about it. This isn't my job. I'm a demon. That's the job I picked. Of course I could've taken some pencil-pushing job like you—no offense—but that just didn't suit my needs because I was *really* fucking angry at the time, and now I'm fine with it—well, mostly—but I'm earning my way to retirement because I just want to rest, for fuck's sake—"

"*Fury!*"

I stopped my rant, looking at him with wide eyes. I took a deep breath, cleared my throat, and clenched my teeth. "What?"

"This is different. The angels have failed. They don't fail. Not like this. The men they're trying to alter aren't the usual cases that end up on their desks."

I shook my head. There was something about this story I was missing. Something he wasn't telling me. Whether he knew and was keeping it from me, or he was in the dark too, I wasn't sure. But there was more to it. "I'm not sure how I can make a difference if they couldn't? I'm just a demon."

"That's actually *why* we need you on this," he said, slowing his speech as though he was searching for the right words. "The standard practice didn't work. This needs a special touch. A demon's touch."

I cocked an eyebrow and smirked.

He groaned. "Not *that* kind of touch, Fury." He leaned back in his chair, not taking his eyes off me. "You have the highest reform rate we've seen in eons. The other demons can say what they want about your methods, but they can't touch your success rate. Whatever it is you do, it works. And that hasn't gone unnoticed."

I sighed again and shook my head. "I hate Earth, Jake. I'm not going back. For a century, I've saved for retirement. I'm almost there. It'll be modest, but that's all I want. I just want to be left alone. For the rest of eternity. I don't think that's too much to ask."

And I meant it. He'd asked me before if I was content settling down by myself. The answer was always yes. I was fine on my own. I preferred it that way. Being with someone had landed me here. I barely had a chance in life. It was taken away from me. Taken by the person that was supposed to 'love me until the end of my days.' Hmpf.

When the time came and I moved out of the dorms, I'd go get myself a nice little unclaimed stray that crossed the rainbow bridge. Rest peacefully. Alone. It was true that animals had unconditional love to give.

"No," I said, breaking my train of thought. "I won't do it. Find someone else. Earth sucks." I got up, ready to walk out of his office so I could just materialize home. I touched the doorknob—

"You do this, and you retire when it's over."

I turned around and stared at him.

"Go on."

"You finish this job, successfully reform them where the angels have failed, and you get whatever you want. Full retirement, full benefits, anywhere you choose."

You choose.

Those words pinged back and forth in my brain.

This was too good to pass up. He had to follow through with his offer. That was how things worked in the Afterlife. I sighed, looking out his window. Not a bad view for Jake. I could have a view. Anywhere I wanted.

"All I have to do is reform these assholes, and I get whatever I want in retirement? That's it?" I asked, looking back at him.

He pressed his lips together and nodded. "That's it."

"Am I being recycled? Demons don't get to go to Earth. How would it work?"

He laughed. "No, you won't be recycled. Call it a special pass. From Upper Management, of course."

Of course. Upper Management could really do whatever they wanted.

"You'll go back as you. Your memories, your body, your charming demoness qualities. We need *The* Fury. No one else."

I gave him a deadpan look. "Laying it on kinda thick now, Jake." He shrugged. "Fine. I'll do it. For immediate and full retirement, I'll do it."

"Here," he said, handing me some files. "You leave tomorrow. You'll need to read up on current affairs and the intel we've gathered on your targets. It should help you locate them and get started on . . . whatever it is you do to fix people."

I grabbed the files and turned to walk out. "Pleasure as always," I said, shutting the door as he grumbled a response.

I glared at Francine as I prepared to send myself home, but a body materialized, and I stumbled back as someone plowed past me.

"What the—" I shouted. "Watch where you land, you wanker."

The girl was flustered, red in the face, and shouting at Francine. "I need to see Jake, *now*! When I said I'd take the job at the rainbow bridge, I *did not* agree to escorting spiders or snakes!" she squealed, her body shivering and squirming as she ended her sentence.

I busted out laughing.

Francine smiled at her. "People have pets of all sorts, Carly. Wait for the cockroaches. Entomologists love their pets too."

Newbies. I snorted as she screeched, reaching down to pick up my files and put them back in order.

A picture caught my attention, and my mouth dropped open a little. Three gorgeous men, each uniquely different from the other, stared back at me with piercing eyes. It was time to go home and study. Earth had just gotten a little more interesting if I could play with the likes of them.

CHAPTER 3

The Department of Earth Affairs was bustling when I teleported in, but that didn't stop a few of them from staring. I wasn't sure if it was my blacked-out sunglasses and flask in hand that did it, or simply me. I was The Fury, after all. My trademark red hair and resting bitch face were unmistakable, even in the Afterlife.

So was my hatred of Earth.

"Fury," the front receptionist said, stumbling over herself to scan her appointments for my name. "I wasn't aware you were—"

Silently, I pulled a silver plate no bigger than a business card from my back pocket and dropped it on her desk.

The etchings that read *special pass* were unique. As was its holographic iridescence. Stardust, an extinguished soul, and metal harder than anything that existed on Earth went into creating them. It was the signature of Upper Management, and it was the greatest hall pass of all time.

"I see," the receptionist said, as understanding settled over her. "Come with me."

She stood and walked around the back of her long desk. Several people noticed as I took another swig of whiskey from my flask and followed her. We went through a set of double doors, down a long hallway, then cut in front of a line of people to approach another desk. This one was smaller, less showy. Like the high school teachers' desks I'd seen in movies.

"Excuse me—" the girl first in line started.

Duke, the controller who handled all comings and goings between Earth and the Afterlife, lifted his hand to silence her. "Fury," he said with a soft smile. "How's it going, baby girl?"

I smiled back at him and lifted my flask. "About how you'd expect."

His smile turned a little sad. He knew.

Duke was one of my friends in the Afterlife. Hell, he was the first friend I'd made, and over the years, he'd turned into more of a father figure of sorts.

We'd bumped into each other that first day as I was leaving Jake's office. Turned out, we'd died a whopping half-second apart. Except where I'd succumbed to my ex-husband's fists, he'd been taken out by a brain aneurysm at the ripe old age of thirty-eight.

Duke and I had absolutely nothing in common. On Earth, I'd been a pretty housewife kept in a dollhouse cage. He'd been a steelworker with a wife and two little girls. If there hadn't been life after death, we never would've met, separated not just by the distance between our homes but by the color of our skins.

But here in the Afterlife, we were both dead and lost in our own ways. While I took a job as a demon and rose in the ranks through skill, he took a job with the Department of Earth Affairs, and his trustworthiness had led him to being the man in charge of the only way out of here and back to the realm of the living.

That job made him quite popular with all the wayward souls hoping to cheat the system. When he was alive, people had lifted their noses at him. Here, they fell over themselves to please him.

The receptionist flashed my hall pass. "*The* Fury has been assigned a job by—"

"I know," he said, waving her off as he stood up. "I was briefed when I came in this morning." Turning to the line, he said, "I'll be back in a few."

I saluted the crowd and followed him to a door marked with his name.

He motioned for me to take a seat, so I did. He had a comfortable couch, and I always enjoyed lounging when I came for a visit.

"How's the fam?" I asked.

He smiled. "Henrietta's good. The girls are still adjusting to the Afterlife. It's only been twenty years for them, and you remember how hard it is to get used to this place." He looked away, almost nostalgic. "But we're all together again. I'm happy about that."

Duke was maybe the only person I knew that meant something to me, and having his family together in the Afterlife was a big deal. People usually moved on in the living world. Humans weren't made to be alone, and the idea of soulmates seemed stupid. Call me jaded. But his wife had never remarried. Never looked for another partner. She loved him in a way that was rare and beautiful, and she'd waited to be with him again. Of course, she'd been expecting to be reunited in Heaven. But even though that wasn't exactly what had happened, she was still with him, and that was all she'd wanted.

"I'm happy for you, Duke. I really am. Not everyone gets the same ending you have. Not when we kicked it so early."

He laughed at me. "Always a way with words." I shrugged. "And yes, we're lucky. But it's not the ending."

"Isn't it, though?"

Duke shook his head. "You know it isn't. It's just the next step in our existence. Endings are permanent. Like the end of a book. You turn the last page, and the story has been told. We don't have that. We're still reading, waiting for the next chapter."

I couldn't help but scoff. "C'mon, Duke. The story *has* been told. At least mine has. My story is just sitting on the last page. There's no happily ever after for me. I'm just stagnant, waiting to retire from this life-after-death."

He frowned, looking sad. "Retirement is overrated. You're making a difference as a demon." It was my turn to frown. "Which brings us to why you're sitting in front of me today . . ." He trailed off, staring at me.

"What?" I asked. I knew where he was going; I just wanted to avoid it.

"Cut the shit, Fury," he said. "What are you doing? Going back to Earth," he huffed. "You said you'd never go back. Never be recycled. And I don't blame you. Life screwed you over pretty badly. So what's the deal here? Why did I get a memo this morning about sending you to the living realm with a special pass? They don't exactly hand those out often."

I sighed. "I know, I know. I swore I'd never go back. But they offered me retirement, Duke. Full benefits. Anything and everything I want when I finish this job."

Duke raised his eyebrows slightly. He nodded his head, thinking on what I had just told him. Finally, he let out a deep sigh. "I can see why you took it, then."

"Right? I can't turn that down. Even if it does mean going back to that shithole." I fidgeted with my hands. That wasn't like me, but I needed to know what he had to say. I respected him. His was the one opinion that mattered.

He looked worried for me, as though he was thinking carefully about his words before speaking again. "Are you going to be okay up there?"

I smiled at him, appreciating his concern. "Yeah, I'll be okay. The file said I'm going to Houston. I never went there when I was alive, and it's been a century since I've been *anywhere*, so it can't be that bad."

I honestly wasn't sure who I was trying to convince. No, I wasn't going to run into anyone from my former life. I wasn't going to even recognize a lot, and if it weren't for the Department of Current Affairs, I wouldn't know about all the technology and advancements that had been made. I wasn't even going up north. No memories should be dredged up in the process. But it was still Earth. With humans. The same pieces of shit that found their way onto my roster. I got to deal with them day in and day out, but now I had to see them in the flesh. So to speak.

He looked at me like he knew I was full of it. "Mhm hmm," he muttered. "I read the file too. I won't talk you out of it, Fury. My role in this is to get you there. I'm your go-between. So that being said, do you have any questions?"

"Wait, you said you aren't going to try to talk me out of this?" I asked, surprised that he'd just moved the conversation forward.

"No one can talk you out of anything," he deadpanned.

I barked a laugh and smirked at him. "You know me better than anyone." It was true.

"I know," he said matter-of-factly. "So? Questions?"

"What's my timeline?"

"Dunno, actually. The risk witches have been having visions about this for a long time. Tried to take care of it, but nothing has worked long-term. With each attempt and failure, the visions increased. None of which are good signs. It was about twenty-five years ago that it altered so drastically that they haven't been able to adjust accordingly since."

"What does that mean exactly?" I asked.

He twisted his lips. "It means the frequency and the intensity of the visions increased exponentially, and the attempts they've made to correct it have only made it worse."

I sighed. "So you're basically saying the end of the world could happen tomorrow or a year from now. It's just a bomb waiting to go off, but there's no clock on the detonator."

He nodded slowly. "Pretty much."

"Great. No pressure," I muttered, shifting myself in the seat. "Okay, so the file isn't specific about information in regard to me. What about powers? Do I get to keep all of mine while I'm up there? If I'm going up against three supes, I need to know what I'm working with."

He nodded. "You do. Full capabilities. Just do me a favor and try to keep it under wraps as best you can. The living can't handle much in the way of what they call paranormal. They get weird and make TV shows out of it."

"Noted." I snickered, thinking of how they reacted to the poltergeists that worked in Current Affairs. "What can you tell me about this assignment? How I could go about getting this started, maybe? I can't just show up and go knock on their front doors."

He shook his head. "I can't help you with that. I've read

the same file you have. As you move along up there, I'll know more, and then I can help you where I can."

It was my turn to deadpan. "Well, aren't you just immensely helpful."

He shrugged. "I do what I can." He reached into a drawer and pulled out a backpack-styled purse, handing it to me. "Here. You'll need this. It has the information you need to get around. ID, wallet, cash. We had an apartment set up for you and your access card is in there too."

I opened the bag, reaching in for the wallet and fished the ID card from its slats. "Wow, you really thought of—" I stared at the card, narrowing my eyes. It was my face, all right. Birthday that made me twenty-six human years old. But . . . "Really, Duke? You made my name *Jessica* Fury?"

He snorted. "You have to have a first name up there. You can't walk around telling people you are *The* Fury."

"Oh, come on. It's not my fault—"

"You picked the 'Jessica' of the Afterlife," he finished for me. "I know, I know. I've heard it for decades. You still needed a name, and I may be dead, but my sense of humor isn't."

"Fine," I grumbled to myself while he laughed. "How do I get in touch with you? You said you're my go-between."

"Ah yes . . ." He got up, crossed the room, and opened a door I'd always seen but never knew what was in it. It had markings scribbled on a plaque in a language I couldn't read. He disappeared inside while I waited. I didn't know what the hell I was actually waiting for because he hadn't said anything to tell me what was going on.

The silence was deafening. Awkward. I tapped my foot, looking out his window. He had a nice view. It made me question what Houston was going to look like. When I'd been alive, I'd heard it was filled with cowboys and horses.

The file said it was a big city now. Like Los Angeles. I knew about L.A. I had a lot of charges from that pit. Everyone had sin. That place was teeming with it. But the most I'd read about Houston was that it had a lot of people, and most of those people didn't wear cowboy boots unless they were trying to complement the bedazzled asses of their designer jeans. I would not be dressing anything like that. That was a firm no. Sparkly wasn't my thing.

My thoughts were interrupted when I heard a loud squawk and Duke came back through the mystery door, a large black bird on his shoulder.

My mouth fell open. "What in the hell is that?" I yelled as it screeched at me again.

Duke reached up, stroking its feathers. "He's a crow. And he's yours."

I shook my head. "Um, thanks, but no. You know I'm more of a dog person . . ."

The crow snapped his beak at me, and Duke laughed. "It wasn't really an invitation for pet ownership. He's your go-between. This is how you will reach me."

Of course it was. A fucking bird. A big one, at that. I groaned and nodded, knowing that nothing I could say would matter, anyway. You couldn't really negotiate in the Afterlife.

The bird flew in my direction, and I scrunched my eyes shut as he landed on me. I turned and looked at him. "Shit on my shoulder, and I'm sticking you in a cage. Got it?"

He ruffled his feathers, lifting up a leg like he was thinking about testing me. I narrowed my eyes at him, and his body vibrated like he was *laughing* at me. This had to be a joke.

I looked back to Duke, scowling. "Right. So the plan is I send the bird back to you when I need something . . .

because with our infinite wisdom and phenomenal powers, we can't find some better form of communication between realms. So we're just gonna jump back a few centuries and send the pigeon."

Duke opened his mouth to say something, but all I heard was an ear-splitting scream. My eyes crossed at the sound.

"I was going to suggest maybe not calling him that, but I think he already shared that with you," he said, chuckling.

"Yep. Got it. Thanks for that," I said, thankful living in the land of the dead didn't include getting tinnitus. "Anything else?" If I hadn't already resided in the Afterlife, I would've said the excursion I was about to embark upon was going to be hell.

He smiled at me, but it didn't reach his eyes. He wasn't saying something. I'd known him long enough to know his tells.

"What aren't you saying, Duke?"

"Nothing, kiddo," he said, smiling a little more. "I just worry about you, but I know you can handle going back. I'll miss our chats while you're gone." He jutted his chin out at the bird. "Send him if you need anything. I'm usually here, and he knows where to find me when I'm not."

Silence spanned between us.

He clapped his hands, grabbed my bag, and headed for another door in his office. "All right, let's get you out of here."

With the messenger crow sitting on my shoulder, I followed him silently, not having a clue where I was going. As a demon, my job was here in the Afterlife. I didn't leave. I hadn't been back to Earth since the day my life had been cut short with one final blow to the head. Down a white hallway, down another hallway, and finally to a single blue door at the end of a long corridor.

"This is it?" I asked, expecting something cooler. Like a portal. Not a freaking door.

"This will take you there," he said, handing me the leather backpack. "You've got what you need, and you'll manage to acquire the rest once you get there."

I took it, tossing it over my birdless shoulder. "Thanks, Duke," I said, throwing him a little salute. "Beam me up, fucker." I snickered. I'd wanted to say that since I'd watched a show years ago. Of course, I added my own little touch.

Duke laughed and shook his head. "Take care."

I walked through the door and saw a portal. Ha! Finally something that didn't feel so disappointing. Galaxy colors shimmered in a circular pattern, the edges moving like waves.

I held my chin up and stomped through, mustering the confidence I needed to go back. I was a motherfucking demon. I was The Fury. I had this. Do the thing. Save the world. Retire.

Then I stepped through.

I squinted as a blinding light assaulted my eyes. I felt disoriented, unsure of which direction I was facing. And it was loud. I was blasted in the face with steam. Jesus, was that *the weather*? Oh my god, where was that awful heat coming from? I felt like I was drinking the air. Where the hell had I ended up? The fucking sun?

I groaned, my senses adjusting and my eyes focusing. Being a demon with much more heightened senses than a normal person actually made the process take a second longer. I looked around, taking in my surroundings. Concrete. A lot of it. Incredibly tall buildings on all sides. And people walking and seemingly talking to no one in particular. I didn't see any steam, so the heat was the actual weather.

It was literally hotter than Hell. I'd know.

"You've got to be kidding me," I muttered under my breath. Why hadn't I been teleported to where I was supposed to be?

I pushed a button on my watch, looking at my notes. I needed to be somewhere cooler than this. I knew air conditioning was a thing. I'd read about it. And now I wanted it.

"Ah . . . okay, I need to be here," I said, tapping the watch and talking to the bird like he knew what I was saying and could help me.

I turned my head, twirling my body around to get an idea of my surroundings. I couldn't teleport unless I knew where I was. I needed both locations.

I saw some lights and signs, so I walked toward them and looked up to read. I was on Texas Avenue. How original.

A loud honking startled me, and I saw why. I quickly hit my watch to teleport myself, but nothing happened.

"That's not going to work," the crow said.

I turned my head quickly, looking at him. "Did you just talk?"

"You should move." He spoke again, flapping his wings and flying off my shoulder.

I jumped out of the way of the oncoming vehicle . . . and into another lane of traffic.

Tires squealed, and I looked over to see a massive bus . . . and I met it head-on.

Literally.

Fuck my afterlife.

CHAPTER 4

BAM.

My body landed on the tiled floor in a tumble, like I'd been a laundry pile dumped on the ground.

"Ugh," I groaned. I still felt pain, though it was generally a heavily muted form of it. More like a slight discomfort. This? It felt more like I'd been dropped off the side of the building.

"Fury, what are you doing back here?" an exasperated voice said.

I jerked my head toward Duke.

"You failed to mention that I can't teleport, and I got hit by a fucking bus," I grumbled as I stood and dusted myself off. "You said I would have my powers."

He pinched the bridge of his nose and then chuckled. "You do have your powers. Teleporting isn't one of them. That's a perk of being in the Afterlife, but it's not a power that demons have." He laughed again and shook his head. "But now you know. You die, you end up back here, in my office. I'll regenerate you and send you back up."

I stared at him wide-eyed as he tried to keep his

laughter contained, but he was failing miserably. I threw my bag at him, nailing him in the face. That cut him right off.

"What the hell, Fury?"

"No, Duke," I said, pointing my finger up, "you mean what the Houston? Have you been there? It's ridiculously hot. The air is thick. How can air be *thick*?"

He busted out laughing again, throwing my backpack to me in return. "That's called humidity. I'm from Louisiana. I'm aware of what July feels like down south."

I caught it and then pointed at the crow sitting on Duke's desk. I gestured at him, raising my voice. "And you didn't say feathers over there can fucking talk, Duke. He *talks*."

"I know he does," he said.

"You didn't tell me that either," I shouted.

He shrugged, getting up and stroking the bird's feathers. "You didn't ask."

I groaned in frustration, long and loud. *It's fine. Everything's great. It's good.*

I straightened my shirt, picked up the bag, and tapped my shoulder. "You got a name, or do I just call you pigeon?" I asked the crow.

He flew over and landed on my shoulder, his claws pricking my skin a little harder than I thought was really necessary. But now I knew when he pissed me off, he would henceforth be known as pigeon.

"Hades."

"Cool, Hades," I said. "Try being more helpful about oncoming traffic next time, will ya?"

I looked at Duke, peacing out as I walked to the door behind his desk. "I know my way back to the portal. I'll be going now." I stopped, turned, and looked at him with a cocked eyebrow. "Is there anything I need to know about going back?"

A little twinkle appeared in his eye. I fucking knew it.

"Yeah, when you go back, you regenerate into a new body."

I nodded in understanding and sighed. "So I'm being sent back to the same place and there's a dead version of me lying in the road right now?"

"There is," he said, cracking a smile. "So don't go confusing people by sticking around too long."

Incognito it was then.

This time when I went through the portal, I was prepared for the god-awful heat and humidity. Last time, I'd been so assaulted by the weather and my surroundings, I hadn't noticed the instant frizz in my hair, or the way sweat slicked the undersides of my boobs.

I wrinkled my nose in distaste.

That was when the screaming registered. I flinched, side-eyeing the growing mob of people in the street. The man that I could only assume was the bus driver was sweating bullets as he spoke loudly about how I'd run into the road, others comforting him and saying they saw the whole thing. Sirens were going off left and right. That was my cue to get out of Dodge.

I pushed my sunglasses back on my nose and started down the sidewalk in the opposite direction. When I went to take another swig out of my flask, only bitter drops coated my tongue with disappointment.

Empty. Damn.

I sighed, stuffing it in my backpack.

This expedition to Earth was quickly proving why I wasn't a fan.

I needed to find my targets and nip their little apocalypse in the bud ASAP.

But where to start?

I looked around, peering up and down the street. My eyes lifted to a flashing neon crescent moon. Ugly pink letters that read *After Dark* triggered a memory. I'd read that name in the file last night.

A slow smile curled up the left side of my mouth.

"Take the afternoon off, birdie. I got a lead," I said under my breath to the crow still chilling on my shoulder. He let out an indignant squawk before flying off in a blur of black feathers.

I sauntered down the sidewalk and across the busy streets, careful to watch for cars this time. My boots clicked on the pavement as I approached the double doors. Two bouncers stood on either side, wearing full suits despite the awful heat. A carpet led off to the side of the building, like they were used to having a line.

There was no line now. Yet two bouncers were stationed here.

Hm.

I flashed them a pretty little smile as I approached the doors, tossing my shiny red hair over one shoulder. Both their stoic faces softened, becoming more approachable.

Bingo.

"Hey, big boys," I purred seductively. They puffed up their chests a little and internally I rolled my eyes but kept the smile plastered on my face. When I reached for the door, though, the one on the left stepped forward, crowding the entry.

"Club's closed," he said.

I might've believed it if I didn't know that was their

standard line to non-supes. Little did they know, I had the password.

"Whiskers."

He blinked, stepping back. His hand dropped from the doorway he was trying to block. "You don't smell like a wolf," he said. He eyed me curiously.

"That's because I'm not," I retorted, smiling like I had a secret.

"Ears aren't pointed either," the other bouncer said with a jut of his chin toward me.

"You got a question there?" I said softly, leaning forward.

"What are you?"

"I'd tell you," I whispered to both of them, "but then I'd have to kill you."

His eyebrows drew together as if he was confused. The one on the left let out a barking laugh.

I flashed them a smile as I reached for the door again, and this time, they didn't press it. "Be safe now in there, little lady," the one on the left said. The bouncer on the right still seemed a bit unsettled as I opened the door.

I'd have to remember that for next time. Less smiling. Not so close. Demons carried an aura about them, similar to angels. While our holy counterparts typically handled business on Earth in all manner of ways, their goal was to make things better. Keep the world turning. As such, part of their charm was that people gravitated toward them. They couldn't help themselves. Human or supernatural, everything wanted to be close to divinity.

Demons weren't the opposite, but we sure as shit weren't the same.

Around us, emotions ran high. Chaos ensued. An unsettling sensation touched everything we breathed on. The bouncer's reaction was to be expected, and I would need to be more careful.

The glass door closed behind me, and the painfully bright sunlight winked out as a more muted atmosphere took its place. Blessed air-conditioning fanned my sweaty skin, and I extended both arms out and tilted my head back.

An unexpected and loud cracking sound broke the silence and made me tense. I loosened up quickly, taking a look at my surroundings.

A burly man was bent over a pool table, just shooting the shit with his buddies. They clinked their beers and walked with an air of confidence.

No, not confidence, I realized, after a closer inspection.

Arrogance.

There were a few others in the bar, men and women alike, but they gave these fellows a wide berth. I found that intriguing, given they looked like your run-of-the-mill chumps. In my time, these were the good ol' boys. They'd wear loafers and smoke cigars while making demeaning jokes about their wives and mistresses.

The more times changed, the more they stayed the same.

I sauntered toward the bar.

"What'll it be for ya?" a short woman with a killer afro asked. She wore a yellow bandana as a headband and a black T-shirt with a graphic that read *Nine Inch Nails.*

I liked her already.

"Gin Rickey," I said, leaning against the counter. "Make it a double."

To her credit, she didn't give me a dubious glance. She just got to work.

Thirty seconds later, she set a drink down next to my hand. I took a sip and sighed almost blissfully.

One of the patrons sauntered up beside me. "You're new," a nasally male voice said.

"Yup," I replied without looking at him. The four men at the pool table were being loud and obnoxious as they placed bets. I knew it wasn't really *them* that was bothering me. Just what they represented. Still, I couldn't help scrunching my nose.

"What's your name?" the nasally one continued, not taking the hint.

"Not interested."

Was it bitchy? Probably.

Did I care? Not one bit.

"Are you sure—"

A feminine laugh behind me drew my attention. "You heard her, Paul. Take a hike."

I glanced sideways at Paul. His thin lips twisted into a frown. "This doesn't involve you, Roxanne."

The bartender came up to the other side of the bar and leaned forward. "It does when it's in my bar. I won't have you harassing paying customers."

His face blustered as he huffed. "I was hardly harassing the girl—"

"Woman," I interrupted. "Don't call me a girl. It's rude."

Paul looked between Roxanne and me, as if weighing whether he still had a chance. She made a shooing motion. His fingers tightened into a fist, but he balled it up at his side and walked away.

Guess he knew a lost cause when he saw one.

Or Roxanne was a bigger badass than she looked.

Either was possible with supes.

"Let me know if he bothers you. I don't tolerate that shit in my bar," she said, wiping down the counter with a white rag.

"He's harmless," I said, turning back to the boys at the pool table. I jutted my chin toward them. "What's their deal?"

"You must be really new if you don't know them."

I cocked an eyebrow. "Am I that obvious?" I asked, taking a swig, and setting it back down on the bar top.

"Yes," she said flatly. "Try not to draw attention to that fact."

"I'll try to work on it." I leaned toward her. "Any tips you want to give me, then?"

She chuckled. "I'm the one who gets tips around here, in case you haven't noticed."

So that was how it was going to be. I pursed my lips and nodded at her, reaching into my backpack of magic tricks, and pulling out my wallet. I grabbed a twenty, and stretched over to a tip jar, ready to drop the money in. She quickly covered the top of it with her hand.

"Whoa, there," she said, shaking her head. "That wasn't me looking for a bribe. That was me being a smart-ass."

"Well, you made it sound like—"

"If I wanted you to pay me for information, I would tell you to pay me for information." She took her hand off the jar and leaned her elbows on the bar.

I smirked. "Straightforward. I like it. I can work with that." I looked around, glancing back at the guys. "So, if I were a new girl in town, what do you think I should know?"

She took a moment to appraise me before dipping her chin and nodding toward the pool table. "Those guys? They're the Dawsons. Shifters. I swear to everything holy that each one of them is an alpha because they all walk around like they have the biggest dicks in the locker room."

I snorted. "Anything to back that up?"

She huffed a laugh. Keeping her voice low, she said,

"The one with the black hair is Taylor. He's technically the alpha. They run some territory south of Houston, but not Houston itself, and that pisses them off. Some of the packs are rivals, but most of them just bark. There are two packs that have a powerful bite."

"Let me guess. Another pack with big dicks in the locker room?" I repeated her phrasing. I was pretty sure I understood the context of it. I'd have to look it up later to make sure.

"Yes." A smile curved on her lips. "But they can back it up."

My eyebrows shot up. "I want that information next."

She busted out laughing, drawing attention from some other patrons. She cleared her throat and leaned toward me again. "At any rate, the Dawsons have hot tempers. They come here to intimidate supes and gamble. They're good at it too."

"Intimidating or gambling?" I asked.

"Both," she answered. "The local packs leave them be. If it's all for show, there's no reason to start a pissing contest over territory and shit. But don't play cards with them and don't drink with them. Just don't bother with them, honestly."

I was still scanning the room when I heard a sniff by my ear and turned my head to see Roxanne uncomfortably close to me. I could have sworn I heard her inhale my hair.

"Did you just . . . smell me?"

She shrugged. "Your hair smells nice. Good shampoo. Not something I've smelled before." She turned around to grab a bottle of gin and started mixing me another drink. "Where did you say you were from?"

"I didn't." And I wasn't planning on telling her either.

She raised her eyebrows and stopped pouring.

"But if you're asking, I'm from Indiana," I supplied, not actually lying.

She resumed pouring. "Never been up there."

"Not missing much," I mumbled, wanting to change the subject.

She topped off the drink with some club soda and handed it over. "So, woman-who-has-no-name, what brings you down this way?"

"Fury."

"I'm sorry, what?"

"My name is Fury."

"Is that your first name, or your last?" she asked, slight confusion coloring her voice.

"It's just Fury. I don't go by my first name," I said, trying not to grit my teeth at the idea of having to say what was on my ID.

"All right, Just Fury," she said, cracking a smile. I don't know what she thought was so damn funny. "So tell me. What brings you down here? I can't quite place you, and I'm pretty good at my job."

"I'm just here to have a good time. Make some friends, see the sights." I kept my features calm, and she studied me. I could tell she wasn't sure if she should believe me or not.

Finally, she nodded. "Okay. Well, I can't do much about the sights. But I like you, and you can have a good time in my bar. Darts that way, if you're so inclined." She cleaned out a glass, dipping her chin and nodding to a dark corner. "Cards are upstairs—buy-in depends on the supes you're playing with."

"And pool," I said with a mischievous grin.

"Mmm hmm. And pool," she repeated.

"So liquor and gambling. What else do you sell here?"

"I sell anything I want to. Humans don't regulate us, but I draw the line on what I will and won't have here. Why? What exactly are you looking for?" She eyed me with suspicion.

"Just something to eat. Whatever your favorite thing is."

"Oh. Sure, that's no problem. Anything else?"

An idea formed. "Yeah, do you have cigarettes?"

She wrinkled her nose and reached under the bar, slamming a pack of smokes and matchbook on top. "Knock yourself out. Away from me, though. My bar, my rules. It stinks."

"Fair enough." I grabbed them and my drink and stood. "I'll just go have one over there. Keep my tab open." I gestured vaguely and started to walk away.

"That shit will kill you," she called after me.

I looked over my shoulder and said, "So I've heard."

It had been over a hundred years since I'd had one. In the Afterlife, I'd taken to drinking my sorrows since cigarettes were banned. Go figure that I'd kick it during prohibition just to end up in another one after I died. I didn't know why I couldn't smoke in Hell. I didn't make the rules. I'd often wondered if there was contraband somewhere . . . I wondered if Duke could get me some. I'd never ask him, though. I didn't want to abuse his position or our friendship. He deserved better, and Roxanne was right. It stunk. Still, old habits died hard.

I walked over to the corner, swaying my hips just a fraction as I passed by the pool table.

"Hey, baby, you need a light?" Taylor said, stepping in front.

I grinned in a way he probably thought was flirty. "That would be great," I purred. Once upon a time, I would've been disgusted by his attention. The barely hidden predator beneath his leer would've set me off in a blind rage.

Luckily for him, I took anger management seriously and had gotten my shit together. Forever was a long time to suffer from PTSD, and I wasn't giving my piece-of-shit ex any more of myself after he killed me.

So instead of ripping his cock off and then choking him with it, I leaned forward as he pulled out a lighter and I cast him a demure look.

He lit the cigarette, and I took my first long drag.

Fucking perfect.

The only thing I needed to complete my day was an introduction to my first target.

"Heard you're new?" the man in front of me said.

"Mhmm," I hummed softly, blowing out a steady stream of smoke.

"What brings you to town?" he continued, ignoring his buddies who had stopped playing altogether to listen.

"Oh, you know. Same ol', same ol'. I needed a change of pace," I answered vaguely, gesturing with the hand holding the cigarette.

His black hair was oily from using too much gel to slick it back, like a shitty impersonation of *Grease*. The dark jeans and leather jacket didn't give him that badass vibe I suspected he was going for. Not when he talked shit about having a girl back home and already banging two random chicks while he was in Houston for the week. Someone should've told him to speak a little quieter in public places if he was hoping to pick up another hot piece of ass.

Fortunately, though, these types had a tendency to be ignorant of their own obvious faults, and they were far too arrogant to believe they weren't god's gift to the world.

"Change of pace, huh?" he asked, while looking at his pack. "You like pool?" He motioned to the table.

"I've played a few times," I said mildly, lying through my teeth. He didn't need to know that just yet.

"Wanna play a round with us?" he offered.

I turned to look at the other three pack members but kept an eye on him in my peripheral vision, not missing the way his gaze dipped to my cleavage before he licked his lips. Gross.

"I suppose I could . . ."

A pool stick was thrust into my hand. From across the room, a perplexed look crossed Roxanne's face. I would have apologized in advance if it wouldn't have fucked up my little plan. The unfortunate thing for her was that while she ran this bar, she didn't own it. Not really.

They went the rounds telling me their names, but I only partially listened while finishing off my cig. One of the Dawson boys racked up the balls. They lifted the triangle, and Taylor motioned for me to break. Internally, I snorted, suspecting he just wanted an excuse to look at my ass.

Giving him a show, I stubbed the cigarette out in the ashtray then leaned over the table, positioning the pool cue between the gap of my index finger and thumb. Taylor put the cue ball on the table, and I lined up the shot, but tipped it when I went to break. The ball rolled to the side, and I grimaced.

"Oops," I said.

One of the boys chuckled and said something under his breath about me being a woman. My back hand clenched the pool stick before releasing, as I stood up and shrugged.

"It's okay. Let me show you how," Taylor said gruffly. His pants were tenting like a twelve-year-old boy looking at his first porno. Talk about awkward.

This next part was my least favorite.

I acted like a shy little supe as I let him bend me over and cop a feel while pretending it was to help my stance.

Seriously. What a pig.

I was happy I'd picked these guys. They deserved what was coming.

He put his hand over mine, jerking it against the wooden pole like it was a hand job. "Not too tight now," he said in my ear. His breath smelled like sour whiskey and Cheetos. A disgusting combination. I actually had to work to keep the frown off my face as he took way too much time to hit the damn ball.

As soon as he did, a crack went through the club once more, followed by the pings of the others bouncing off the side. Two went in pockets by pure luck.

"See?" he said, reluctantly letting me up even if he was standing close enough to press his cock into the crack of my ass.

"I think so," I murmured. "Let me try again. Am I supposed to hit the striped ones or the solid ones? I never can remember."

A round of derisive chuckles followed my airheaded question. I let them mock me, pretending to be oblivious.

"You sank two stripes, so you're supposed to aim for those," Taylor said with another not-so-subtle lick of his lips.

"Oh, okay," I said softly, going to hit one that should've been an easy shot and then barely making the pocket. At least it looked believable.

"That was better," he said, grinning like a fiend as he went on to sink one solid then narrowly missed on the second. "How would you feel about a little wager?"

"Wager?" I repeated like he'd stuttered or something.

"Yeah, let's say if you win, I'll buy you a drink," he said.

Inside, I was smug as hell, but I simply said, "I'm listening."

"And if I win, you give me a kiss."

"Hmm," I murmured, like it was a tempting offer and I was playing coy. "What about your friends? Doesn't seem very nice to them if it's just me and you."

"You're right," he said, not at all surprised, though he acted like it. "How about—"

I stepped forward and ran a black-painted fingernail down his chest. "Let's speak plainly," I said in a deep, husky voice. "You're hard as a rock, and I'm here for a good time. You win, I'll suck your cock."

His eyes dilated. A smug grin turned up the corners of his thin lips.

"And if you win?"

I grinned right back. "I watch you suck one of theirs," I said with a thrust of my chin toward the other three.

"You're into that?" he asked, a little dubious.

I shrugged. "I'm into a lot of things. Mostly being straight forward. I don't like beating around the bush, and we both know where this is going. Now do you want me on my knees in the bathroom in ten minutes or not?"

He licked his lips once more and picked up the cue.

I was going to enjoy this.

CHAPTER 5
ROMAN

Two knocks on my office door made me pause. I lifted my head.

"Yes?"

The knob turned and in walked my beta, second-in-command, and closest thing I had to a friend. "Alpha," she said with a dip of her head.

"Caitlin," I replied. "Is there a problem?"

"I'm not sure . . ." she started. "One of the boys down at After Dark just called. Said a pretty little thing not from around here just showed up at the club." I lifted my eyebrows, silently asking her if she was really bothering me for this. Her cheeks darkened. "He said he couldn't identify her as a supe. She didn't smell like a wolf or have fae ears and her heart was still beating."

I tilted my head, waiting for more. It seemed that there was none.

"Please tell me you didn't just interrupt me when I asked for quiet to talk about a woman who showed up at one of my bars and could be any kind of supe. Witch. Succubus—"

"I know," she said. "It sounds like nothing, but Will doesn't call me for nothing. He said she has an air about her. Something not quite right. It reminded him of last time . . ."

I froze.

Last time.

She was talking about the creature that had killed my mate and unborn child.

I swallowed and then took a slow, steady breath. Thinking of them was painful, even three years later. I'd survived, and that was more than most wolves could say about losing a mate. I was here physically. But part of me hadn't made it. That part was buried in the same coffin. Six feet under and never returning.

"Pull up the video feed for After Dark," I said.

She gave me a tight-lipped, apologetic smile as she tapped a few buttons on her phone and then plugged it into a wire on my desk. A new screen opened, showing a live feed of After Dark.

I knew who they were talking about instantly.

Everything about her, from the flaming red hair to her full, luscious mouth, screamed trouble. And currently she was bent over one of my pool tables with that prick alpha from the Dawsons feeling her up.

My blood heated as something primal surfaced that I hadn't felt in a long time. My wolf looked out at the screen and found himself curious about the creature he saw there.

"How long has she been there?"

"Ten minutes," Caitlin said. "Maybe fifteen. You want me to send in—"

"No," I said, too sharply for what was warranted, but I didn't apologize. Alphas didn't apologize to anyone but their mate and parents. The former because they wanted to remain mated. The latter because it was owed. Caitlin was neither. "Let me make a call."

Caitlin hummed in acknowledgement. I pulled out my cell and hit speed dial two. Roxanne picked up on the third ring.

"What's up, loser?" she answered. The sounds of the club filtered through the speaker. From the muffled noise, I could tell she was holding the phone against her shoulder while wiping down the counter.

"Rox, what have I told you about—"

"No one can hear me. It's fine. What do you need, seriously?"

I sighed, my gaze still lingering on that unnatural red hair. I'd never seen a shade quite like it. While it was unmistakably red, the color was so dark it almost looked black when she moved around the table and into the shadows. She wore a devious little smile, and there was a wicked glint in her eyes.

"Tell me about the woman," I said.

Roxanne sighed. "She's new. Came down from the north, although her accent isn't quite right. She doesn't smell like a shifter, and I heard her heartbeat."

"So I've heard. You know what she is?" I asked, eyes narrowing on the loose hands that kept touching her slim waist. She touched a hand to Taylor's chest, and I had to work to keep my breathing normal.

That realization was alarming.

As was the recognition that my wolf wanted me to get up and go find her.

"No idea," Rox said. "She's got a weird aura . . ." My sister trailed off as if thinking. I breathed a little easier when the mystery woman and the Dawsons went back to playing pool.

Taylor went first, sinking a couple balls before missing. That bastard's greedy eyes roamed her body the moment she bent to line up a shot.

"Weird?" I repeated, mostly to keep myself focused on the conversation and not heading down to After Dark myself. It was only a fifteen-minute drive—

She aimed at nothing striped, and I frowned. When the cue ball bounced off one side and hit a striped ball, then pinged back and hit another, knocking them both into pockets, an uneasy feeling settled over me. Taylor's shocked expression confirmed it as she proceeded to clear the entire fucking table in one turn.

She never missed.

Holy shit.

"Roman?" Rox asked, coming back into clarity. Shit. I'd spaced.

"Yeah?"

"I said she feels like anticipation. Chaos. It's like there's a buzz of energy surrounding her."

"Uh huh," I murmured as the woman on screen turned to a slack-faced Taylor and then motioned to one of his men. He turned ruddy and started speaking in hard tones I couldn't make out.

She smiled scathingly and pointed out something in a quick motion that had him clenching his fist. She turned to walk away, and he grabbed her roughly by the arm.

Whatever Roxanne was saying was instantly lost on me as red-tinted my vision. Blood pounded in my ears.

Taylor put his other hand on hers and then placed it on his cock.

Then my wolf lost his fucking mind.

CHAPTER 6

"You either walk to the bathroom and get on your knees, or you do it right here," the sleazeball alpha growled.

I cupped my hand around his balls, fisting them tightly. I used my fingernails to dig into them.

He tensed, doubling over. "Bitch," he hissed.

"A deal's a deal," I said. "I was going to walk away, but then here you go, trying to force a girl. Is that how you got laid twice in the last week? You like throwing around those big, bad alpha vibes?" I asked him in a mocking tone.

Supes had a highly increased heal rate, but my demonic strength was definitely putting it to the test on his balls. "Logan. Owen," he wheezed.

A pack member appeared on either side of me.

I took a step back, releasing his family jewels, and my free hand went behind me.

They tried to grab my arms right as I closed my fingers around the pool cue.

Big mistake, boys.

"Hey, no fighting in here," Roxanne yelled.

One of them sent her a scathing look and walked over to the counter in a way clearly meant to intimidate. The other two holding me just straight up ignored her.

"We got her," the one on my left said.

Taylor lifted his head, and anger mixed with lust shone in his eyes. "I was just going to get what was owed," he said, taking a step forward, "since you hustled me. But now . . ." He looked around, ignoring Roxanne, who was currently dealing with the fourth dude in their little gang. The rest of the club scattered like roaches. "I think I want a taste of it all."

"That's cute," I said. "I got a better idea."

"Oh?" he asked.

I smiled.

Then I headbutted him.

His nose crunched, and Taylor stumbled back, bleeding everywhere. Good god, he was a bleeder. I'd disemboweled people with less mess. The two holding me froze like idiots, which made it easy for me to tear myself away from them and turn around. I brought the pool cue up and smashed the thick end into one of their groins. The other rushed me, and I whipped it around to slam it into his temple. The sound echoed through the club like a gunshot, and he dropped right there.

"Lights out, motherfucker."

Two down. I turned back to Taylor, who launched himself at me. His anger made him sloppy. Dumbass. First rule of fight club was don't get mad.

Not unless you wanted to take a nap.

I cackled, and he stopped, completely confused. "I just came up with the funniest joke," I said, shrugging, then jabbed the pointy end into his kidney. "But you wouldn't get it. Inside joke, I guess," I added, laughing again.

I loved being a demon.

"Now," I mused, kicking his legs out from under him. "How about that bet, buddy boy?"

I was probably going a tiny bit overboard.

But, again, I was a demon. This was what I did.

I punished the guilty motherfuckers and made them repent for their sins.

Or something like that.

Taylor's knees hit the sticky floor. I tapped under his chin with the end of the pool stick, making him lift his head.

"I believe you promised to suck a dick if I won," I said, grabbing his jaw with one hand and prying it open. "I guess you can suck mine if you're so insistent on getting a little action."

I shoved the butt of the pool stick between his lips and let it slide back until I hit the tight barrier of his throat.

Taylor coughed, and his eyes watered.

"Uh huh," I singsonged, "I like it deep-throated."

I was still shoving the pool stick in and out of him when the door to the club opened.

A tingling awareness spread through me. Goosebumps lined my arms. I turned to look at the fourth member of the Dawsons, only to find him unconscious on the ground, bleeding from a head wound. Standing over him, a grim-faced Roxanne held a shattered Jack Daniels bottle and a phone to her ear.

Ah, that meant my first target was here.

Time to meet the big, bad Roman Mikaelson.

I dropped the pool cue and slammed my elbow into Taylor's temple. He slumped to the floor, lights out. I turned around, then placed my hands on my hips.

Ten feet away stood the man whose picture was in my file.

He was massive, built like a god—if there were any. Easily six and a half feet tall and all muscle with proud shoulders. His dreadlocks were pulled back, but a couple weren't playing nice and fell free around his face. They looked wild and fist-worthy. I could easily imagine his short beard brushing over the sensitive skin of my inner thigh. A tingle went through me that I shook off.

There was only one thing that really struck me as odd.

His eyes in the picture had been a warm brown.

Right now, they were ice blue and glowing.

The temperature in the room spiked a few degrees as he looked at me, and then in the deepest, most pained and husky voice, he said one single word that changed everything.

"Mate."

From the sidelines, Roxanne let out a low whistle. "Well, this just got interesting."

CHAPTER 7

Mate.

Um . . . no.

The word echoed in my head. The tingling electricity I'd felt moments ago buzzed along my skin in awareness. It traveled the length of me, leaving shivers in its wake.

Roxanne stood by her bar grinning like the cat that got the canary. Bitch was just missing feathers sticking out of her mouth. Another woman with ebony skin and curly brown hair streaked with silver halted at Roman's side. Her deep brown eyes were wide, and her mouth hung open slightly.

Then there was Roman.

I cleared my throat.

"You mispronounced Fury," I said, finding my voice. I had to get control of this situation again. All it had taken was a single word for me to lose the upper hand.

His hands were tightened into fists at his sides, and I heard a deep rumbling in his chest. The sound did things to my body that I wanted to ignore.

"Nice place you got here." I looked around, surveying

the damage I'd done. "I'd be lying if I said I'm sorry about the douchebags I left on your floor. You really should be more careful about who you let in."

Roxanne barked a laugh and waved her broken bottle at me.

"Boss . . ." the other woman next to him whispered. She carefully placed a hand on his arm, and I found myself not liking that she'd touched him.

What the fuck was wrong with me?

Whatever sway she had, it must've been big. He turned his head ever-so-slightly, never taking his eyes off mine. The intensity of his stare weighed on me. I liked it, and every physical part of me wanted it. Except the rest of me didn't.

"Tell Will we're closed," he ordered.

The girl I could only assume to be his beta nodded, then turned to walk out the main door.

"You," he said. "Sit. We have to talk."

I narrowed my eyes and crossed my arms. "What's the magic word?"

Roxanne snickered, turning and walking back behind her bar. I watched her as she shook her head. "I'll get that food you asked for, Fury." She went to a door on the side, calling to Roman as an afterthought. "Regular for you, brother?"

Fuck me, did she just say brother?

This entire scene was catching me off guard. I was losing my touch. Flustered and heated by his mere presence. And frankly, that picture in his file didn't do him justice. Parts of my mind told me he looked like he'd be fun. That I'd like to lick him, maybe punish him a bit too—and not in the way I was supposed to. I scolded myself silently.

He grunted in response to her question, but I was still

waiting for him to speak to me again. I raised my eyebrows at him expectantly.

His fists shook, and he said through clenched teeth, "Sit." He inhaled deeply. "Please."

"Now was that so hard?" I said, moving to a table that wasn't knocked over. I sat down, crossing my legs, and leaning back in the chair.

Roman covered the distance between us in a few large strides. His presence was imposing. Then he took a seat across from me and I almost felt like we had an even playing field again.

Almost.

"Who are you?" he asked. His deep voice was strained, and it called to me.

"Fury," I repeated. "I believe we already established that part."

"Not your name. *Who* are you? What are you doing here?"

I cocked an eyebrow, leaning forward and putting my elbows on the table. "That's not the same question . . ." I trailed off, waiting for him to give me his name. He just stared at me fiercely. "I'm sorry, I didn't catch your name. I'm assuming I shouldn't call you brother or boss."

"Roman," he answered. "But I wonder if you already knew that."

"Roman," I repeated, ignoring his slight. A rumbling sound vibrated in his throat as soon as I said his name. My core tightened at the sound, and I dug my nails into my arm. I schooled my features as best I could. "I'm from up north. Looking for a change. Something new to hold my interest." The tenor in my voice wavered as I aimed for snark but came closer to seduction.

"And have you found anything to hold your interest?"

"You could say that..." I responded.

"You're my mate," he said matter-of-factly.

A part of my body hissed *yesssss*, and it sent a bolt of electricity to the apex of my thighs. The rest of me said to get that bitch in check.

I shook my head. "I, uh, I don't do the mate thing. Polite pass."

His brows furrowed. "It wasn't a request."

I looked at him in surprise. "Mmm," I hummed. "I'm not exactly down for that kind of commitment." My stomach rumbled, and I looked away, wondering if Roxanne was coming back. It would seem my body was betraying me in multiple ways.

"You aren't really aware of how mates work. It's not a request, nor is it an order from me. It just *is*, Fury."

Holy shit, I liked the way he said my name. Sin and seduction and images of sweaty nights rolling in sheets flashed in my mind. I coughed, choking on the want that filled me.

"But I don't know what you are, and neither do the people who work for me," he continued. "So . . . what are you? You're not a shifter, and you aren't fae..."

"I couldn't tell you if I wanted to," I said cryptically. "I was born human. Then at the age of twenty-three, I changed."

"You . . . you were born human?" he asked, clearly shocked. He looked like he was conflicted, trying to make sense of what I'd said. His eyes raked my body.

I nodded.

"How old are—"

"My turn," I said, cutting him off. He growled. The motherfucker *growled* at me. I raised my eyebrows at him. "Tit for tat, Roman. You're calling me your mate—"

"Because you are." His hands were wrapped around the edge of the table on either side. He gripped it harder, struggling to keep his calm.

"So, it sounds like I'm entitled to ask some questions of my own."

I'd played out so many scenarios in my head. And this was never one of them. I was in completely new territory, and I wasn't quite sure which direction to take it.

Wing it. That was the best I had.

"Well, I've told you who I am. Where I'm from," I started. "What about you? Who are you, exactly? You just walked into the room, acting like I'd done something wrong when all I was doing was handling some unwanted attention."

"You beat four shifters in my bar—"

"Three," I interrupted.

His eyes flew open, seemingly shocked that I'd spoken over him again.

I pointed to the dude on the floor in a puddle of blood and whiskey. "I didn't do that. That was your sister." I shrugged one shoulder. "And let's get something cleared up here. You really have some fuck-me vibes going on, but you also have this dickhead attitude problem. Stop getting your panties in a wad when I speak. I've had enough of that in my lifetime." I leaned back again and crossed my arms.

"Noted," he said. No apology, no nothing.

Also noted. Prick.

"You beat *three* Dawsons in my bar"—his gaze finally left me, diverting to look at Taylor on the floor—"and throat-fucked one of them with my pool cue, apparently."

I wiggled my eyebrows. "Well, he lost a bet."

"What kind of bet did he make with you?"

"I don't think you really want to know the answer."

"Try me," he said, the muscle in his jaw tense.

"Fine," I said, tilting my head to the side. "Just a friendly wager on the game. If he won, I'd give him head—" Roman's sudden anger was palpable. Something vibrated off him in waves, penetrating my pores and crushing me. "And if I won, he'd give one of them head," I said, gesturing to the knocked-out shifters on the floor. "He was a pretty sore loser, though, so . . . I think you're up to speed."

"Were you going to give him head?" he demanded.

"Not that it's any of your fucking business, *wolf*, but I wasn't going to lose," I snapped.

The table rumbled, and a crack resounded through the quiet bar. A piece of wood came off in his hand.

"Hey!" Roxanne shouted as she reappeared carrying two plates. "What the shit, Roman? Stop breaking my tables."

He whipped his head to look at her. "They aren't your tables."

She set the plates in front of us. "They most certainly are. I run this place for you. All of it. Watch me walk and see what happens."

Now, I was no shifter, but I knew enough. Alphas didn't take that shit from anyone, sister or not. I couldn't figure out the dynamics, or why he didn't lose his temper right then and there.

But for whatever reason, he dipped his chin, ceding the argument as he gave her a non-verbal acknowledgement that she was right.

"Roxanne, do you mind getting me another gin?" I asked. "It'll be nice to have something to wash down these . . ." Boat-looking things. Folded sandwich? What the hell are these?

"Tacos," she said, giving me a weird look. "Jesus, you

really are from up north. Don't even know what a taco is," she mumbled as she went back to the bar.

I shrugged and picked one up, taking a bite. It was good. There was a spice to it I'd never experienced before . . .

Fire.

I'd swallowed fire.

It consumed my mouth, my tongue, my throat.

I felt it in my nose.

I coughed, and my eyes watered as I pounded my own chest.

Roman stood up in a flash, bellowing to Roxanne. "What the hell did you give her?"

Roxanne came over, putting my drink on the table, and beside it, what looked like a glass of milk. "Oh, calm down. They're chicken tacos."

"Chicken and what?" he asked while I coughed.

"Drink the milk. It'll help," she said, nudging it to me. She looked at her brother. "And mango habanero salsa."

I gulped the milk down, feeling a cool and soothing sensation.

"What the fuck?" I croaked. "It's like swallowing a fire poker . . . that still has flavor, somehow. I can't even explain it. It's like sorcery."

"Taco sorceress," Roxanne snickered. "I am using that."

"That's enough," Roman said. She rolled her eyes at him, pulled up a chair, turned it backwards, and straddled it. She crossed her arms over the top.

"Look, Fury," she started, "my brother isn't exactly used to entertaining company, so I can see how he comes across as a dick who doesn't know how to actually talk to a woman, but he says you're his mate. That's not a thing we shifters take very lightly."

Roman bristled at her words but stayed quiet.

"Right," I said, finally feeling like I could drink some gin. I wasn't touching the devil food anymore, even if it did smell divine. I took a sip and held the glass up in a cheers to her mixing skills. "I appreciate the pep talk and the attempted murder by tacos, but I'm spent for the day. I'd love to chat more, so maybe I can drop by tom—"

"You're not leaving," Roman said.

I sighed. Really?

This was supposed to be more meet and greet style, not down and heavy. Ugh. I needed to prep for the deep shit. Being a hundred and twenty-six, I just didn't have the angst of these young people to do this all willy-nilly.

"I am, actually," I replied as I stood up.

Roman moved his body, blocking mine. Our proximity was too much to bear. I could smell him. Rugged and earthy and dripping in sex appeal.

My mind and body were at war. My mind shouted warnings and memories of my past. My body ached in places it shouldn't. Not over him. A deeper part of me whispered a reminder that he may be blocking my way, but he wasn't using force. He hadn't touched me yet.

"You aren't leaving my side," he growled. "Not until I know more."

"Move aside, Old Yeller. I'm not going home with you," I said, sidestepping him just to find him in my way again.

He grabbed my arm, and I inhaled sharply, tensing, and ready to rip his arm off his body.

I wasn't here to kill him. That was not the job. I also wasn't supposed to reveal my powers. But anger coursed through me at his audacity, and I didn't know that I could hold back.

"Buddy, I don't care how hot you are or who you think I am. Grab me without my permission one more time and you're going to get very well acquainted with my foot up your ass. So unless you wanna be tasting shit for the next week, I suggest you take your hand off me and step the fuck back."

His expression shuttered, and I sensed that wolf of his peeking out. It wanted to play. Too bad for both of them I wouldn't fuck targets.

There's a saying about mixing business with pleasure. Don't. It makes things messy. Complicated.

I wouldn't let that happen here. Not with retirement at stake.

Even if I was his mate, which was hard to believe given he had a mate already.

She'd died, and she sure as fuck wasn't me.

"Roman," Roxanne said in a curt voice. He didn't lower his hand, but he looked away for a fleeting second and narrowed his eyes. A predatory response. He obviously wasn't one hundred percent in charge of that wolf of his right now. I tilted my head to the side, studying him. "Can I have a word with you?" she asked.

Clearly debating, his gaze flicked between me and her.

The woman who'd come in with him stepped up. "I'll keep, uh . . ."

"Fury," I supplied.

She beamed at me like I was helpful for offering my name instead of being called 'uh.' "I'll keep Fury company."

Roman seemed to debate it for a moment. Meanwhile, his touch against my skin was doing wicked things to my mind. It was always fifty-fifty with me and men. Half the time, their touch disgusted me. The other half, I found myself enjoying it. In this case, it was a little more than that, and had he not been my target, I would've been all on board to explore how deep that savageness went.

Unfortunately for both of us, he was.

I lifted three fingers, and his eyebrows drew together.

"Three," I said, ignoring the rush of heat that had coursed through me at his first touch.

"Two," I continued, lowering one finger. A giddy sort of excitement fueled an adrenaline spike I hadn't felt in a few decades.

"One," I whispered, lowering one more finger. I half hoped he'd hold on, but that was crazy, right? Maybe it was some aftereffect of being alive again.

Roman made the right choice and dropped his hand. "Stay here. I'll be right back."

"Mhmm," I hummed. His piercing blue gaze swept over me once more, both drinking me in and assessing me—for what, I wasn't sure. He stepped to the side and followed Roxanne behind the bar and into the back, giving me a nice view of his ass as he went.

"He's a stubborn one, isn't he?" I mused to the woman who'd said she'd watch me.

"You'll need to forgive his aggressiveness," she said after a moment. I turned to her and arched an eyebrow, listening. "He lost his first mate."

"Lost?" I repeated, knowing full well what she meant.

"She died," the woman added. "Killed by another supernatural. We never found the murderer, and it's eaten at him ever since. For fate to give him a second one . . ." She trailed off. "You're either a blessing or a curse."

Her earnest eyes held depth as she stared at me, as if weighing my worth. I was immediately intrigued, because out of everyone I'd met since coming back, she was the first who seemed to see something past my fake smile and blasé attitude.

"Which do you think it is?" I asked, out of curiosity more than anything.

She smiled faintly. "If what I've seen is anything to go by, probably a bit of both."

I smiled back, slightly amused. She was wrong.

I was a dead girl walking.

A demon sent straight from Hell to be his worst nightmare.

Being his mate wasn't a blessing because I was his curse.

He just didn't know it yet.

CHAPTER 8
ROMAN

My blood soared.

My pulse thundered.

My wolf was raging with a need to be near his mate.

But instead, I was in the back room with my older sister and resident pain in the ass.

"You need to chill," Roxanne said, turning on her heel and crossing her arms. "I can sense your wolf. It's been a long time since he's been this close to the surface. I understand that he wants his mate—"

"No offense, Roxanne, but you don't understand shit right now." A flash of hurt crossed her face, but she pushed it back and replaced it with a hard glower. I scrubbed a hand down my face, then sighed. My body was angled toward the now-closed door that led to my mate. I was mostly one foot out the door, ready to leave, even as I looked at my sister. "Maya died. My wolf lost his damn mind and . . . killed so many people after that. Now I have a second chance. A new mate . . . I don't know if I even wanted one, but I sure as shit can't leave her alone now that she's here. He won't have any of it."

"And you, Roman? What does the man want?" she asked, playing the part of older sister and life coach to a grown-ass alpha. I didn't need it, per se. But it helped. We'd lost our parents young, and all I had was Rox. She might not be alpha of the Western Riders, but she was still owed more for all that she had done for me.

"I . . ." I opened, then closed my mouth, and my gaze gravitated toward the door once more. My wolf let out a growl. An itch had settled under my skin from the very first look. One I couldn't deny for long. "I don't know what I want, but I can't let her go. I have to keep her close, Rox. Keep her safe."

Safe.

Like Maya should've been.

Pain lanced through me at the reminder of Maya, and while my wolf felt it, the current bond was pulling at him too hard for him to lose himself in the loss and grief.

When he looked at Fury, he saw redemption and companionship. He saw his future. His whole fucking world.

But I was worried she would be our end.

And what about Maya? My first mate. The love of my life. She was supposed to be it for me. That was how it was supposed to go. But it didn't.

Could I really *replace* her?

The very idea made me recoil.

"Look, Roman, you're clearly fucked in the head right now," she said with a sigh. "I get it. I do. But that woman out there, baby bro, she isn't going to be Maya. She won't sit by and let you trample your way in. I've known her all of twenty fucking minutes and I can see that."

I clenched my jaw because she was right. Hell, I'd talked

to her for five minutes and that was becoming painfully obvious.

"My wolf—"

"Will ruin this if you let him have control," she said. "After the San Jose massacre, you locked him out. I'd bet it's been a hot second since he tried for control. You've gotten used to his complacency, but right now he's riding you hard. I can see it on your face. Your eyes have been blue since you stepped into the bar."

Shit.

"I still don't know what she is," I said. "And it's driving me crazy."

"Yeah, well, it looks like it'll keep driving you crazy. You need to lock him down and find another solution to control your urges until you figure out what you wanna do with her," she said, making entirely too much sense and yet none at all.

My attention gravitated toward the door once more.

The scent of coming storms, fall leaves, and chaos calling to me like a siren.

Crack.

The echo sounded first, before the realization that Roxanne had slapped me.

I turned to her, glowering. "What the fuck, Rox?"

She shrugged. "Call it bar preservation. You looked like you were going to start pissing all over it. Your wolf in check now?"

Yes. Yes, he was. Albeit more than a little agitated.

I nodded once.

"Good. Now, what are we going to do about your mate out there? You know next to nothing about her, so you can't just take over her life. Maybe start slow. Ask her to dinner?" she suggested, trying to read me at the same time. The lilt in her voice told me she already knew I wouldn't be able to put the brakes on this that much.

And part of me didn't want to.

A dark, wicked side wanted to see that red hair wrapped around my fist and my cock pulsing between those cherry red lips. Physically, I couldn't deny that. I was rock hard now, tenting my pants like a fucking adolescent. In front of my sister, no less.

Thankfully, she took enough pity on me not to make a snide comment about it.

"Not good enough," I said. "I need her close. Beyond getting to know her, I need to know she's safe. At all times. The only way I can guarantee that is if she's with me."

"Roman." She sighed. Whatever else she was going to say didn't come out.

Footsteps started toward us, moving too fast. The door opened.

Caitlin burst in and came to a grinding halt. The guilty expression told me everything. "She's gone," my beta said. "She—"

"Where?" I asked, going hyper-alert as I started out the door with a single-minded purpose.

"The bathroom," she said. "She said she needed to take a piss. I let her go, not thinking . . ."

My feet were already moving, tracking my mate's scent.

Behind me, Roxanne groaned. "Damn it."

"I'm sorry, Roman," Caitlin stammered as I came to a full stop in the bathroom door.

I knew immediately what had happened. The tiny window, hardly bigger than an air vent at the top of the wall. The screen popped out. Written in lipstick on the mirror: *Sorry, not sorry. See ya later.*

I didn't realize I was growling under my breath until Caitlin stepped back.

"Roman," Roxanne said in warning. She sensed the shift. She knew what was coming.

My mate had run from me, and the last thing you should ever do with an alpha predator is run.

We give chase.

CHAPTER 9

I stared at the keycard in my hand and then squinted up at the matching sign on the building. It reminded me a bit of the demon dorms in its blocky gray atmosphere. Houston was hotter than Hell, though, and I couldn't figure out how to operate the damn sliding door. There was no place to insert the card. No sliding keypad. I'd observed two people entering about five minutes apart, and they'd just walked up, angled their hip toward a black box next to the sliding door, and it had simply opened.

After standing there bumping it with my hip—and no success—I was confused, exhausted, and about ready to put my fist through the glass just to get inside.

Then I felt eyes on me. The hairs on the back of my neck lifted. I whirled around and stopped straight in my tracks.

Blond hair. Blue eyes. Chiseled features. His lips were parted, taking me in. For a moment, I did the same, his similarities reminding me of another face from another time. A time where pale hands had beaten me black and blue. Where pouty lips had turned snide and cruel.

But there were differences too. His cheekbones were

higher. Eyes a shade darker, more lapis lazuli than powder blue. His hair was lighter, closer to white-blond than honey.

I blinked, then remembered my senses.

"Do you need something?" I asked, pointing my thumb at the black box beside the door I was certain was my way in.

"No—I . . . well, this is going to sound crazy, but you look just like someone I used to know," he said.

"Oh?" I asked, twisting my lips. His easy smile made me settle. "Someone good, I hope."

He chuckled, a deep, earthy sound. "I wish. Old girlfriend," he said. "Things didn't end so well between us."

"Ah," I drawled. "I see. Your fault or hers?" I couldn't help myself. I was nosy by nature, and over a hundred years of digging into people's psyche just to tear them apart had made it worse. I half expected him to frown and walk away, but he surprised me when he laughed.

"Bit of both, I think. It takes two to tango," he said with a shrug. "I didn't love her enough. Took for granted what I had. Didn't realize that somewhere along the way she'd stopped loving me too."

"You don't sound too torn up about it," I said, blowing a sticky strand of red hair out of my face.

"It's been a while. Had a lot of time to think about it. I'd try to get her back if I knew how, but she won't give me the time of day . . ." He trailed off and then smiled again, offering another shrug.

"Hmm." It sounded like they probably weren't good together to begin with, not that most people liked hearing that, in my experience. "Well, good luck with that." I turned back toward the door and debated kicking the damn thing open just to get out of the blasted heat.

"Use the keycard," he said.

"What?"

"The keycard." He came around to my side and lifted the hand holding it to the black box. The light at the corner buzzed from red to green. The doors slid open, and a rush of cool air-conditioning hit me.

"Oh," I said, not-so-subtly pulling my hand away when he didn't let go.

I side-eyed him, wondering if we were going to have an issue, but he backed up and smiled.

"Have a good one," he said with a wink.

"Thanks, you too . . ." I turned from him to the door and back, but he was already gone.

Huh. Weird. I was still shaking my head when I walked into the reception area. A younger guy with dimples and light brown hair looked me up and down, appraising.

"Can I help you?" he asked in a way that made his intention clear.

What the hell was it with dudes today?

I looked down at my high-waisted pants and crop top. My guild brand marking me as a demon was displayed openly on my shoulder, looking like a strange tribal tattoo when really it was the language of the dead.

Sure, I was fit and had nice tits. My legs were shapely. I was a redhead, but man. This aura shit the angels talked about was no joke.

"You could have helped me when I was struggling with the door," I deadpanned, tilting my head.

He looked taken aback then cleared his throat. "We have a policy not to allow anyone in—"

"Whatever," I said, bringing the small backpack around and taking out another keycard with a note saying 621. "Where are the elevators?"

"Down the hall and to the right," he said slowly. "Do you have proof of identification? I haven't seen you before, and—"

I whipped out my ID and tossed it on his table. The plastic *tink*ed as it landed. The guy pursed his lips, clearly not liking the way I didn't have time to flirt. Or maybe he didn't like that I was irritable and coming off like an asshole. Who knew? I wasn't going to bother asking.

He turned to the tablet and started typing my name. It only took three letters for it to pop up, and there in the picture was my unsmiling mugshot from the last time Jake and Duke had made me get my guild registration updated. I looked about as done with it as I felt right now.

His gaze flipped from my picture to me as I placed both hands on the edge of his desk and leaned forward. "We good here?"

His pupils dilated with fear and arousal. "Y-yes."

I smirked to myself as I took my ID and backed away. He was adjusting himself when I turned the corner, and I rolled my eyes.

Earth was different than it had been in my time, and somehow still the same.

The roaring twenties, as they later became known, weren't half as thrilling or freeing as today. But some of that probably had to do with me already being dead. My time here was temporary. A mere stepping-stone to the next place.

Life was fleeting and exhilarating because of the unknown, but I preferred the devil I knew—and in this case, that was me.

It took me a moment to operate the elevator. Apparently, the fancy keycard was needed to open and close every door in the building. Soft, jazzy music meant to soothe surrounded me as I rode up. I side-eyed the speakers because it was a shitty knockoff of actual jazz, and it annoyed me more than anything. As the elevator came to a stop, the doors dinged before opening. I followed the signs down the hall to the door that read 621.

Given how unimpressive Houston seemed so far, I wasn't expecting much in terms of accommodations. I turned the knob, leaning into it with my shoulder as I pushed the panel open.

The sprawling apartment with high ceilings, marble counters, and a wall of glass overlooking the concrete jungle was a surprise to say the least. I stepped inside, a grin working its way up my face as I kicked the door shut behind me.

"Now, this. *This* is what I'm talking about," I breathed. A record player in the corner played King Oliver, a favorite from my time.

I listened to "Dippermouth Blues," bopping my head along as I gave myself a tour of the spacious one-bedroom apartment. I walked into a room with a king-sized bed overflowing with fluffy pillows. A door led to a bathroom with a big soaking tub, and a mini fridge full of gin. I knew without a doubt that was Duke's doing. He'd arranged a lot of the go-between from the Afterlife to the living realm, and that included more than just the portal. He would have been the one to set me up here if Jake didn't, but Jake wouldn't have been so thoughtful as to include booze. And he sure as shit wouldn't be playing my favorite music. We were cool with each other, but not on that level.

I was admiring a massive flatscreen and considering parking my ass in front of it for the evening when there were two taps against the window. I looked up, and my dream of being alone and catching up on *Grey's Anatomy* was shot.

I sighed when I realized who my 'visitor' was.

Walking over to the window, Hades tapped again.

Impatient bag of feathers.

I slid it open, and he flew right in in a flap of black feathers.

"Your next target is located in the south side of the city . . ." I let him ramble on while I grabbed a gin out of the mini fridge and started running a bath. I lifted some bath salts from the side of the tub and sniffed them.

Mmm. Lilac. I dumped half of it in the water and grinned when it turned a deep shade of purple. I put my hair up and started to strip.

"Are you listening to me?" he asked after a long pause.

"Mhmm."

"Then why are you getting undressed? You need to be working on introducing yourself to your next target—"

"Listen, birdbrain, I don't want to be here any longer than necessary either. However, I've got a real body now that has real needs. One of which is a bath, and it's calling my name. Come back to me during work hours. Wait—I don't get up at nine. Let's say eleven to seven, Monday through Friday, shall we?"

I dropped my pants, and he groaned. The bird actually groaned.

"It's five o'clock on Tuesday," he said.

I rolled my eyes. "Fine, work hours starting tomorrow. I need a short day today." Which I did. In all honesty, finding out I was Roman's mate was going to put a kink in things. I needed to process that and work through how I wanted to handle him, and the best place to do that was a hot bath.

"Fury, this isn't a vacation. You're on the clock the entire time you're here—"

"Don't you have french fries to steal from someone?" I said lightly.

He hovered, and I could've sworn he was plotting something behind those beady little eyes. Given he was just a bird, forgive me for not being all that worried when he said "fine" in a way that would've made Karen the Dreadful proud, then left me in a flap of wings.

Padding across the tile floors barefoot, I swayed to the music. My tub was steaming hot and half-full by the time I returned. I dipped one foot in and sighed blissfully, then stepped in with the other. It only took a second for me to lower myself into the water and then settle back against the cold tub. The first bite against my skin made me stiffen, and then the porcelain warmed. I found myself relaxing again.

I basked in the tub for a few minutes before my thoughts inevitably turned to Roman.

Much like the birdy, I was a workaholic. I just worked in different ways. Namely, alone. Like everything else I did that was unorthodox for a demon, I liked to mull over my cases. Each of them was a bottle of wine, and I had to figure out the best way to age it.

Normally, it wasn't too difficult. But when I thought of Roman, it wasn't the cool, professional detachment I usually felt. It was replaced by heat. Lust. His file said he was the alpha of the Western Riders. It was the largest pack in North America and ran the west from Houston to Alaska. There had been mentions of an older sister, though Roxanne wasn't named. His parents had died young. Another alpha had challenged his dad to power, and his father lost. The new alpha killed Roman's mom to set a precedent, and really just ended up setting off a twelve-year-old Roman.

He killed a man three times his senior and then took control of the Western Riders.

Despite his dark beginnings, nothing I read led me to think he was evil. He'd been a good, if somewhat inattentive, mate before his was killed. He ruled his pack fairly. All things considered, out of the three, he was the one I'd most wondered about because he didn't have the track record to make me think he'd want to end the world.

The more I considered it, the more I thought there was something I was missing. While I definitely saw he had a dangerous edge to him during the brief time we interacted, there were no alarms going off in my mind. No signs of cruelty or true apathy to humanity. None of the detachment or sociopathic tics it seemed the other two had.

He was all alpha, the most powerful known to have existed at that.

But he was still just a man.

So what would bring him to the decision to end it all? What was his trigger? His weakness?

His first mate had died, so that couldn't be it.

His parents had died, and that was so long ago it couldn't be the catalyst that would set him on that path.

And while he seemed close to his sister, something told me she wasn't it either.

Hm. I needed to get to the bottom of it and figure out what made Roman Mikaelson tick.

He did seem very sore about the mate concept, and that wolf of his wanted me something fierce. I saw his arousal the moment our eyes met. Maybe I could use that. Get beneath the skin. Who better to open him up than his mate?

I frowned. Clenching my hand into a fist.

That was cold, even for me.

But I was a demon. It was my job to dig deep and poke and prod until I found something. If I weren't his mate and he was simply attracted to me, that wouldn't be so bad. But supes took this mate shit to a new level. I knew that much, even if I only felt an inkling of what he currently was dealing with.

He had to be pissed after I left him a message in lipstick and crawled out the bathroom window. When he found me again . . . I grinned, my hand opening and skimming across my bare stomach. My fingers dipped lower into the plum-colored water as I slid them through my wet folds. I lightly pressed against my clit, thinking about that big, bad beast of a man and what he'd do when that time came.

There was going to be hell to pay.

CHAPTER 10
ROMAN

Her scent called to me as I combed the streets, tracking her and following her path. It was faint, sometimes erratic, like she'd been trying to evade me. Turning corner after corner then back again before going in another direction.

Roxanne was right. I needed to push the wolf down. Keep him under control. But neither of us wanted to be without her. She needed to be with me. Safe. It would be hard to keep him in check when we essentially wanted the same thing. I could feel him beneath the surface now, irritable that she wasn't close.

A gust of hot wind pushed between the buildings, dragging the smell of her further away. I growled in frustration, trying to find her trail again.

It was gone.

Anger rose and my chest heaved as I took deep, ragged breaths. I wanted to shred something.

The pounding of my blood throbbed in my head.

"She gets under your skin, doesn't she?" an unfamiliar voice said.

I furrowed my brows, looking around. A crow was nestled on a stair railing that led into a building. I turned my head, looking up and down the sidewalks, but no one else was nearby.

"You can keep looking around, but it's just us here," the crow said.

I could still feel my wolf bubbling beneath the surface, but I was taken aback with the situation unfolding before me. It was a momentary distraction.

"You're a crow," I said. "And you're talking . . ."

"And you shift into a wolf," he retorted. "This is a world of supernaturals. Don't act so surprised there, alpha. It makes you look stupid."

I sniffed the air and narrowed my eyes. "You aren't a shifter, crow." A predatory growl erupted from my chest. "Where is Fury?"

"Calm down, Roman. We're on the same side, you and me. Mostly."

"And what side is that?"

"Take a walk with me," he said, flying down to the ground. "We'll talk on our way there."

"I'm not following a bird walking around downtown." Confusion and distrust warred with the desire to find my mate.

"Good point. Thanks for offering the ride." He flew up and landed on my shoulder. I tensed, every muscle in my body going rigid, telling me to rip the bird into pieces. "Head north," he said. When I didn't move, he threw his wing out, nodding his little head. "That way, alpha. I thought wolves had a sense of direction."

"Look, crow, start talking before I rip your feathers off," I said through clenched teeth.

"Start walking, *dog,* and I'll explain."

I closed my eyes, tightening my fists at my sides. I sniffed the air again but didn't find her scent. I nodded and started walking.

"Oh, grab that little doohickey right there," he said, dipping his head toward the stoop he'd been perched on. It was a keycard of some sort. I reached down, picking it up.

"Now what?" I asked.

"Now put it in your pocket," he said. "Thought that one was obvious."

Smart-ass. This damn bird was a smart-ass.

"I'm Hades."

"What?" I snapped.

"My name," he said. "I assume you'd rather I call you Roman instead of dog, so . . ."

"Fine. *Hades.*"

He held out a wing again. "That way."

I huffed, but headed north, waiting for him to say something. I felt his claws prick my skin. I wasn't exactly comfortable with a fucking talking bird—crow—Hades—balancing on my shoulder.

My wolf was momentarily quiet, assessing the situation with me.

"Take a left up here," he said finally, breaking the silence.

I huffed, my nostrils flaring. I didn't tolerate anyone giving me orders. "I thought you were going to explain something," I said, my irritation coming through loud and clear.

Hades ruffled his feathers, lifting a leg to scratch his neck. "I did say that, didn't I?" He put his leg back down, resetting his balance on my shoulder. "What do you want to know?"

"I want to know where Fury is," I growled.

"Calm yourself. That's where I'm taking you," he said.

I had to admit, there was a lot about this situation that was taking me by surprise. I hadn't been expecting help. I'd been expecting riddles. Tricks. Deceptions.

"Did she send you to find me?" I asked. I found myself hoping the answer was yes. I turned, taking the left he'd indicated.

He squawked in something vaguely like laughter. "No, decidedly not," he said. "Fury is . . . well, she's a pain in my ass. But you know how sometimes people need help even when they don't realize it?"

My heart skipped a beat, and I stopped. "Is she in trouble?"

"What? No. Take a breath, alpha. I mean, like, mentally. Emotionally. She's stupid—did I mention she's irritating?" He looked forward. "Three blocks, take another left."

I continued down the sidewalk. "And?"

"And I knew you were looking for her. I just happen to know where she lives."

"Are you her . . . pet?"

"Something like that," he said, then snapped his beak.

Suddenly, my wolf rippled beneath my skin and the hair on the back of my neck stood up. I smelled her; catching her scent on the wind just as I came to the corner. I picked up my pace, the crow pushing off my shoulder and taking flight. I ran, following him until he came to stop before a residential building. Her scent was strong. She'd been here, not long ago.

I tried to pry the sliding door at the seam, but it was locked. I shook the door, rattling it violently against its lock, but it didn't budge. I peered inside, seeing a male sitting at the counter. He made eye contact, then looked down. Daring to ignore me. No one would stand between me and protecting my mate. I would break the door, and then I would break his skinny neck for hiding her from me—

"Yo, Roman."

"What?" I yelled, spinning to look at Hades. He'd perched on a bench next to the entrance.

He nodded toward my pocket. "The thingy I told you to pick up? Use it. It's a lot easier than dealing with the cops for breaking and entering and—"

I reached into my trousers, pulling out the keycard, realizing what it was meant for. "Thanks," I muttered, swiping it, and entering the building.

"Six twenty-one," Hades called out. "Meet you there," he mumbled as the door shut.

I looked at the boy at the counter as he cowered. I sniffed the air. She'd been here. Right in this very spot. I leaned over the counter. I'd better not smell her *on him*.

"C-can I help you, s-sir?" the boy said.

"Elevators."

"I need to see some identification—"

I slammed my fist down. "Elevators, boy. Don't make me ask again."

His gaze shifted, and I looked in that direction, seeing the sign telling me where they were located. I turned and walked away.

"Sir, wait, I need to check you in—"

I ignored him, walked into an open lift, pushed six, and waited for the doors to close. She was here. In this building. I could feel her nearby. Everything inside me was on the verge of exploding but finding her would calm some of the rage. It would do nothing for the desire, but it would put the wolf to rest. For the moment.

I walked onto the sixth floor, finding apartment six twenty-one. I swiped the keycard and entered.

Her smell was overpowering. It was everywhere. I stiffened at the arousal permeating in the air. She was alone, but the scent was potent.

I stood in the entry with my eyes closed, breathing it in deeply, feeling it flood my veins. Then I heard a moan coming from down the hall. I snapped my head in the direction of the sound, rushing to the door.

I was not prepared.

Her body was draped in a bathtub filled with light purple water. Her legs spread wide, one hanging over the side of the tub. Her eyes were squeezed shut as she fingered herself, breathy moans escaping her lips.

I watched as she plunged her fingers in and out of herself. Her other hand gripped the edge of the tub, holding on as she writhed against her own ministrations.

My cock throbbed, heated and hard and ready. I wanted more than anything to rip her from that water and finish her off myself. Lick every last drop from her body. Fuck her until she came undone. I grabbed the doorframe in restraint, indecision warring within me. The wolf clawed to the surface, demanding we claim our mate. I pushed him down, the prospect of betraying Maya and what she meant to me was ever-present.

Her breathing became ragged, and her jaw clenched. I stared at her as her leg twitched, her mouth fell open, and the speed of her hand increased.

I watched her on the verge of release. I watched it climb. I watched her explode. Her eyes flew open and met mine. Staring at me, she let out a final moan and then screamed as she came. The sight of her getting off was too much for me to handle. My grip on the frame tightened, and it broke off in my hand.

"What the fuck are you doing here?" she growled when her tremors died down.

Reality slammed into me. Why I was here?

She looked down at my groin, at the straining bulge, and she lifted an eyebrow.

I cleared my throat. "You ran from me."

"Well, this is unfortunately burned into my memory now," Hades said, flying in and landing on the bathroom counter.

CHAPTER 11

"Are you kidding me?" I snapped, standing up in the bathtub, looking between that goddamned crow and Roman. "Running from you isn't a reason for you to break into my apartment."

"I didn't break in," he said. I watched his chest rise and fall as he struggled to maintain some sort of control over himself. This was so not good.

Roman's eyes were ice blue and heated. The dichotomy was striking. It also told me he was having difficulty beyond what I felt like dealing with. I reached for a towel, stepping over the edge and onto a bathmat. I wrapped it around myself. I wasn't shy in the slightest, but wolfman was clearly having to restrain himself.

His body was tense, and he was packing something impressive beneath his trousers. There was no doubt my fantasy assumptions only moments before weren't far off.

I'd known he was there from the moment he entered the apartment. At the time, though, I was close to the edge. Knowing he was there, then seeing him as I pushed myself over . . . well, torturing him a little made my orgasm ten times better.

Now that the lust had cooled, and I was thinking straight again, I realized that tempting him like that after taunting him may not have been a great idea.

I looked at the gaping hole in my doorframe. "Oh yeah? Well, you're holding a piece of my door, so tell me again how you didn't break into my home?"

He didn't speak as he held up a hand. He kept his eyes on mine, but I looked to see what he was holding. My damned keycard.

I shot my eyes over to Hades. He nodded his little head side to side, clearly pleased with himself. "You're an asshole," I said to him, lowering my voice.

"And you're a pain in the ass. Get to work," he whispered in return, jumping off the counter and taking flight out of the bathroom.

I looked back up at Roman.

Shit.

He looked like he was going to explode any moment. I couldn't figure out if he wanted to fuck me or fight me. I'd be lying if I said a little bit of both wouldn't be fun.

But this wasn't the time.

This mate thing complicated a lot, and I hadn't had enough time to process it.

"What do you want, Roman?" I asked, trying to exit the bathroom, but he blocked me.

"You ran," he answered, unmoving.

"Yeah. And?"

"What do you mean *and*? You ran," he repeated. When I stared at him, he added, "You're not supposed to run from me."

I sighed. "Well, I'm not running anywhere naked, and

now that you've come here, I have nowhere to run to. Thanks for that. So fucking move." I stepped forward, glaring at him. I would stand my ground.

"Lead the way," he grunted, barely moving enough for me to get by.

"Whatever," I mumbled, squeezing by him.

Our bodies brushed against each other as I slipped between him and the doorframe. The contact left a trail of goosebumps that had me clenching my teeth.

That was enough of that.

I pushed by quickly, padding down the hallway and into my bedroom. He was on my heels the entire way but stopped at the doorway and didn't follow me in. He stood at an angle, his back to my room as he averted his eyes and stared into the hallway.

I rummaged through a drawer, turning my head to glance at him over my shoulder. "Not worried that I might jump out the window and run from you again?" I asked, taking a tank top, shorts, and bra, and setting them on top of the dresser.

He exhaled roughly, still keeping his back turned.

"I mean, you already surveyed the goods, so I'm not sure why you're trying to be a gentleman now."

He said nothing, only clearing his throat in response.

But a quick look at his hands showed white-knuckled fists.

I'd known there would be hell to pay when I wrote the message in lipstick but seeing him in person so soon after was a little too much. His eyes were glowing blue, and the subtle growling hadn't stopped since he showed up. Whether or not he knew he was doing it, I still heard it. Roman Mikaelson's wolf wanted to mark me and never let me go. Completing my mission would be near impossible if I let him. Mates were complicated. Messy.

I dropped my towel and grabbed the clothes I'd laid out.

"What are you doing here, anyway?" I asked, slipping my underwear up and around my hips.

"You r—"

"Oh my god, yes, I ran from you. We've established that." I grabbed the spandex running shorts, putting them on. "But *why* are you following me here?"

A moment of silence spanned between us. It couldn't be that simple. He looked like he had so much more to him than a caveman mentality. So help me, if he said 'you ran' one more time, I'd club him over the head.

He risked a glance over his shoulder, his eyes raking my body before he turned away again. "I was going to say you *really* don't get it, do you? I'm here because you are my mate." He took a deep breath. "Yes, you ran, and I can't . . . I can't let you go unprotected."

It was hard to hold back my laughter. Walking dead girl, demon extraordinaire, did not worry about protection. I'd already been hit by a bus, and the day wasn't even over yet.

I sighed. "I don't need you to protect me. I'm fine on my own."

"It's not that simple. My wolf . . . our desire to protect you overrides what you think you need. I have to keep you near me. Keep you safe."

I pulled my sports bra over my head, adjusting my tits until they were comfortable. I slipped a loose tank top over it.

"That's a nice sentiment and all, but you can't stay here," I said. "You can turn around now," I added.

He turned slowly, taking in my form. He nodded. "I wasn't going to stay here."

Finally, we were in agreement—

"You're coming with me," he said.

I put my hand up, palm facing out. "Hold up. Rewind. Also? No. That's not going to happen."

I heard a rumbling in his chest as he furrowed his brows.

"Did you just growl *at* me?" I asked. "Let me explain something to you. I'm not leaving. This is my bed, I'm sleeping in it, and you can fuck right off thinking you can haul me to wherever you and your wolf want me to go."

"Am I interrupting something?" a female voice said.

I looked over, seeing Roxanne standing in my bedroom doorway. Roman practically snorted at her in response.

I threw my head back and groaned. "What are *you* doing here?" I asked. "Please don't tell me it's because 'I ran'," I said, using air quotes in what I hoped conveyed my extreme annoyance.

She cocked her head to the side and scrunched her nose, pulling her cheeks up in a face that said 'yeah, kinda.' "But I did bring drinks," she offered, holding up some bottles. "Thinking maybe the three of us can sit and chat. Again." She threw a glare over at Roman.

"I can't with you two," I said, walking to the door so I could go to the kitchen.

But Roman blocked me again, unmoving.

I pinched the bridge of my nose and squeezed my eyes shut. Taking a moment to think. "Kitchen, Roman. Glasses for drinks. Chairs for sitting," I grumbled.

He moved aside.

"Working on your people skills, I see," Roxanne muttered to him as they followed me to the other side of the apartment.

I grabbed some glasses and ice, bringing them to the living room and sitting as far away from them as possible.

Roxanne filled my glass with straight gin. I took a sip and let it roll on my tongue, pleased with how smooth it was. I looked at a ship on the bottle's label, unfamiliar with the brand. I had to admit, she had good taste.

I sighed. "The pigeon tell you how to get here too?" I asked Roxanne.

Her face scrunched up in confusion. "Huh?"

"Never mind. How did you find me?" I asked, taking another drink, and leaning back in my armchair.

She gave me an incredulous look and pointed to her nose.

Wolf. Right.

"I followed Roman's scent. You r—" My eyes went wide, and I glared daggers at her. She snickered, but instead she said, "wrote—you wrote on the bathroom mirror before leaving. He followed you, I handled a thing, then I followed him."

"And here we are," he said, finally joining in the conversation.

I looked over at him. His eyes were still blue, but he seemed to be breathing normally at least. "And here we are," I repeated.

Silence. Uncomfortable silence.

"Okeydokey," I said, breaking the tension. "So, I'm not good at entertaining, or whatever this is. I'm also not big on staying up super late. I may not look it, but I'm old and tired, and just grouchy in general. I also like my personal space, so . . ."

"I already told you, you aren't leaving my side," Roman said.

"And I already told you, I don't need protecting, and you aren't staying here," I said, anger starting to fill me again.

"Hey, hey, do you mind if I translate here?" Roxanne interjected.

"Translate what?" I asked.

She looked at Roman, and his jaw clenched. She widened her eyes at him, and he nodded.

"You know, just help the lines of communication between mates," she said.

I pressed my lips together and flared my nostrils as I exhaled. These two wolves . . .

She put her hands up in surrender. "I'm just trying to help. Sorta seems like maybe you're going in circles." She looked at her brother. "Am I on the right track?"

We both nodded.

"Okay," she said. "Now we're getting somewhere." She rubbed her hands together, scooting herself to sit on the edge of the couch. Roman sat in an armchair across from me on the other side of the coffee table.

I took a drink of my gin and set it down on a table next to me. I looked at her, motioning with my hand to continue.

"I think you've gathered by now that Roman isn't going to just give up. He says you're his mate. We don't take mates lightly. He can't just let it go, walk away, and leave you here," she said. "But I also understand that you don't exactly want to be caged, so to speak."

"You are correct," I said, crossing my arms over my chest. "So what do you suggest?"

"Well, I think I have a compromise. Neither of you will like it, exactly, but it's better than what you've achieved so far, which is a whole lot of nothing." She looked between us and waited for some sort of pushback. When neither of us said anything, she continued, "Roman, you don't want her left unprotected." He dipped his head in agreement. "But Fury doesn't want you up in her shit. She barely knows you." She looked at me, and I acquiesced with a single nod. "Then maybe you can stay with me."

"What the hell—" I started.

"Absolutely not—" Roman said at the same time.

She stood up and pointed at Roman. "When have I *ever* let you down, hmm? I get that she's your mate but get your shit in check. Under control. If you want to do this right, then fucking listen to me."

I waited for her to finish her rant before I cleared my throat and said, "I want to do this right as well, and that way is my way. That's where both of you leave, and I go to bed. Here. By myself."

Roman began to protest, but Roxanne spoke over him. "It's a fair offer, Fury."

"Horseshit, it's fair," I argued. "Why do I have to leave?"

She shrugged at me, crossed her arms, and asked, "Did you have a solution you wanted to present?"

"If I can't get rid of either of you, it seems like *fair* would be you staying here since you're both imposing on me one way or another. The least you could do is go out of your way instead of making me go out of mine."

Roxanne made a show of looking around, twisting her head in opposite directions, then turning her body in a circular motion. "Here?"

I nodded.

"Where?"

"I just said here."

"Right, but I thought maybe you were hiding a guest bedroom somewhere, so I wanted to check. Unless you were suggesting we share a bed, but I'm fairly certain you weren't heading in that direction."

I pursed my lips. She had a point. I nodded my head in the direction of the couch. "You can sleep there."

She barked a laugh. "Oh no, that's not gonna happen either. I'm inviting you to my home. With your own room, your own bed. And frankly, the city grates on my nerves."

I couldn't disagree with her there. "Well, it's hotter than Hell here, so I can see that."

"It's also the sound. It's non-stop." She pointed to her ears. "I need a break from it. I'm just south of the Beltway. Nothing fancy, but it's quieter."

"I don't know what that means, but I'll take your word for it." I huffed out a sigh. These fucking wolves. "Well, the city doesn't bother me, so it sounds more like a *you* problem. I think the couch is more than acceptable when I'm not the one who wants to leave here. So . . . are we done?"

Subtle rumbles came from Roman.

I rolled my eyes.

She pinched the bridge of her nose and took a deep breath. "Look, I am trying to help you. Him, of course, but also *you*. I'm not saying let's stay up and braid each other's hair. And if you want to smoke, go outside and keep it away from me. You have a cute setup here, really. Nice place. But the options are me, or him. You wanna stay in the city? Cool. I'm for it. Let's shack up here. He lives in the city," she said, pointing at Roman, "so if we stay here, he's not far from you. Ever. We're wolves. You're his mate. Do the fucking math and quit being a pain in the ass, for the love of god. I'm tired, I'm hangry, so you can either go with my plan, or fuck him and get it over with. Take your pick."

She plopped back down on the couch and reached for the bottle of gin. She brought it to her lips, tilting her head back and taking an impressive drink. She slammed it down and looked at us, waiting for an answer.

Roman's knuckles were turning white as he gripped the arms of the chair. He closed his eyes, exhaling through his nose loudly. Then he nodded.

I raised my eyebrows in surprise. Their dynamics were something else.

Roxanne gave me a questioning look, waiting for me to answer.

I narrowed my eyes. "I—ugh. Fine. I just want to go to sleep. If this will shut both of you up for now, then so be it." I pushed myself up to stand, and Roman did the same. "Calm down, Lassie. I'm going to get my bag."

I stormed into my room then started tossing things into my backpack. I wanted to pluck Hades' feathers out and throw him in front of a bus. See how he liked dropping into a heaping pile in front of Duke's desk before he came back. At least I thought he'd come back . . . surely, he would. We were from the same world. That was how it worked. Either way, this was his fault. Showing Roman where I lived. Ugh. I'd grab his skinny little bird neck and strangle him.

I heard faint footsteps down the hall. They came to a stop at my door. I looked up to find Roxanne leaning against the frame. "Knock," she said.

"Wants eyes on me packing my bag, does he?" I asked. She winked at me, smiling. "This shit is going to get old."

She nodded. "I know. This is just so we can get to a better place and talk this through. Compromise and all." She took a couple of steps forward, picking up my boots and handing them to me.

I grabbed them, stuffing them into the bag.

"It won't be that bad," she said, trying to make amends. "I have booze, and I make killer tacos." She chuckled, clearly thinking about my reaction to her tacos earlier.

"Do you have any pets?" I asked, zipping up the bag.

She looked at me, confused. "No," she finally answered. "I work a lot. And I'm a shifter. Territorial by nature. Pets aren't my thing. I suppose I could have a goldfish if I really wanted something."

"Well, I hope you like birds," I said.

"Yeah, sure. They're okay, I guess," she responded as I slung my bag over my shoulder.

"Not this fucker," I muttered as I turned and walked past her, heading for the door.

When I got to the living room, Roman stood up, and a rush of heat flooded me. *Down, girl.*

He opened his mouth to say something, but his phone buzzed in his shirt pocket. He pulled it out reluctantly, and pressed the button, then held it to his ear. "Caitlin. What is it?"

I had a heightened sense of hearing too, despite what the wolves may have thought of me. His beta needed him.

"I'm in the middle of something. I can't leave right now—"

A look from Roxanne cut him off. "Go, Roman. I've got this. She's with me."

He didn't answer her. Instead, he just looked back and forth between us, his eyes flashing between brown and blue.

"Goooo," she said, the annoyance in her voice matching my general mood.

His shoulders tensed more, if that were even possible, but he finally exhaled and grunted into the phone, "Be there in ten."

I looked at his sister. "You said I get my own room, right?"

"Mhm." She turned to the door so we could head out.

"Does it have a window?" I snorted to myself when Roman's nostrils flared.

He took three long strides, coming to stand in front of me. His body invaded my personal space, and a very bad part of me wanted to keep pushing his buttons. "You will not run from me again. I will find you," he said, his chest rising and falling with his heavy breathing. His eyes flashed with hunger and anger.

"Calm down, Roman. I'm just yanking your chain." I looked down at his groin, then back to his face. I winked at him and turned to follow Roxanne.

I couldn't resist a bit of fun, and tempting the wolf certainly fit that description, but it was playing with fire.

Good thing I was familiar with the burn.

CHAPTER 12

Roxanne pulled her car up in front of her house. I flung the door open and slid out, landing on the ground. My head was spinning, and I was pretty sure my stomach was in my throat.

"Oh my god, I thought you said it wasn't far. Just a little bit south," I managed, swallowing bile.

She closed her door and came to stand by me. "Sorry. It takes about an hour to get from Houston to Houston."

I looked at her in confusion. "What?"

"Traffic. I mean, it's a big city. Like, fourth largest, I think? Something like that. Either way, driving takes a while," she said, leaning against the car and crossing her arms. "You didn't say you got car sick, otherwise I would've warned you."

Well, that was because I hadn't known either. One, cars weren't much of a thing when I was alive. Two, Duke failed to mention my human-ish body would come with those perks. I couldn't even die. But I could feel nauseated? What kind of sick joke was this?

"It's a new development," I mumbled. "Guess we know

now, don't we?" Now that I was on solid ground, the waves of dizziness subsided, so I stood up slowly, dusting off my knees. "Well, lead the way. As pleasant as this day has been, I'm pretty much over it now."

I looked up at her home. It was cute. A little bigger than I'd thought, and it sat on a nice piece of open land. I hadn't expected that. Roxanne walked up the front path to the door, and I followed. She punched some numbers into a keypad on the handle and walked in. This new world was weird. It was one thing to watch some of these advancements on television shows acquired by the Department of Current Affairs. But now I was in it.

In the foyer, she pointed up the stairs. "Your room is up there. Go right, first door on the left. You have a bathroom attached too."

I nodded, taking in the tile floors and high ceilings. "Not a bad place you've got here. Is it just you, or should I expect you to have a friendly, furry visitor?"

She shot me a look. "It's just me."

Noted.

I started up the stairs. "Well, I'm—"

"I'm pouring myself another drink and ordering some takeout."

I spun myself around, stepping back down to the ground floor. "I'll be joining you for that drink."

"Are you hungry?"

Thinking about her fire tacos, I narrowed my eyes. "I'm not sure."

She laughed, knowing where my mind had gone. "C'mon. I'll get you something less spicy."

I walked into a large, open kitchen. It was so cozy. A little rustic. Open shelves lined the walls, but everything was organized and had its place. The wood block countertops and farmhouse sink were modernized, but they felt familiar. Like home. An odd feeling of nostalgia washed over me before a bitter memory ended it.

Roxanne grabbed a bottle from the counter and took two glasses from a shelf. She poured two fingers of whiskey in each, then pushed one over to me.

I saluted her with it. "Cheers." I took a sip, savoring the burn. "About that food . . ."

"Ah, right." She pulled out her phone and tapped on it for a minute. She looked up. "How about a chicken burger?"

I stared at her. "I thought burgers were made of cow."

She stared at me in return. "Chicken burgers it is." Then she went back to her phone. When she looked up, she pocketed it and then pointed to a living room with comfortable leather sofas. "Go. Sit. Food is on the way. You'll like it."

She was ballsy in an annoying, yet somehow endearing kind of way. Or maybe it was just because she was feeding me. But with that kind of bossy attitude, one might think she was the alpha instead of her brother.

With the bottle on the table, we sat across from each other, waiting for the other to speak.

"So. Didn't you say something about a pet bird? You didn't bring a cage or anything, and I didn't see him . . ."

I groaned. Hades. He had to have followed me.

"Um, yeah. So don't be shocked when he just happens to show up here. He's irritating like that."

"I thought . . . he just flies out on his own?" she asked.

I rolled my eyes and nodded.

"What the hell kind of bird is he?"

"Crow."

"You have a *crow*?"

As if the feather duster had been listening to us, there was a rapping on the glass.

Tap. Tap. Tap. Tap. Annoying-fucking-*tap*.

"Speak of the devil . . ." I said, getting up to let him in.

Roxanne watched me with confusion and intrigue as I opened the window. "How did it find you? I've never seen a pet crow, much less one that tracked its owner." She took a sip of whiskey.

"*He*, not it," Hades said, landing on top of a wingback chair. "And she doesn't own me."

That did it. Roxanne's whiskey got caught in her throat and she coughed, spewing liquid all over her marble coffee table.

I sighed, getting up and smacking her back while she tried to get air. "Roxanne, Hades. Hades, this is Roxanne. Don't be a douchebag, pigeon."

"I'm sorry, he fucking *talks*?" She coughed.

"Yeah, it gets old real fast," I said, glaring at him and sitting back down. I jerked my head, gesturing to tell him to go away. "Go somewhere and nap, will ya? Or do whatever it is that birds do."

"Tick tock," Hades said, pushing off the chair and taking flight.

I narrowed my eyes at him, watching him disappear. By this time, Roxanne had managed to catch her breath.

"He's an asshole. I'd apologize, but it's not my fault," I said, raising my glass.

"Care to explain that one?" she asked me.

"What? Why he's an asshole, or why it's not my fault? Because I honestly figured both were pretty obvious."

She shook her head. "Not that. Explain how you have a talking crow. He's yours, so I assume the asshole just comes with the territory," she quipped.

"Point to you," I said, acknowledging the quality of her jab. "Got him from a witch, actually. Lost a bet."

Her eyebrows knitted together in confusion. "You . . . *lost* a bet? I don't understand."

"What's not to understand? I lost and got stuck with him. Like a bloody curse."

She started laughing. "Well, that's just fucking mean."

Didn't I know it.

The doorbell rang, and Roxanne got up. I listened to her open the door, tell someone thanks, and come back in. She set some bags down on the counter and gestured for me to get up and come to the kitchen.

I walked over and grabbed the box she handed me.

We ate silently while we stood, leaning against the counter. I finished off my fries first, loving the taste of salt and grease. It tasted better in a human body, even with the whole being dead thing.

I took a bite of the chicken burger, feeling some heat as I swallowed. "This is spicy."

"This is Texas," she said in response.

"It's good," I commented. "I wasn't complaining."

She nodded, finishing her burger and wiping her hands on a napkin. "So, what's your story, Fury?"

I wiped my hands off too, then used the napkins to clean the corners of my mouth. "I already told you at the bar. There's not much to tell."

"Sure you did," she said, her tone indicating she didn't believe a word I'd said. "You're young, pretty, but you don't appear to be stupid."

"Why, thank you," I said, bowing my head. I walked over to the couch again, taking my seat next to the whiskey, and she followed me. "What about you? You're young enough. Pretty. There's no Mr. or Mrs. Roxanne?"

She smirked at me. "I like my privacy."

"That makes two of us, and yet here we are," I said. I

thought about where to go with the conversation. If I was going to be stuck with a babysitter, at least I could take advantage of the situation and get the information I needed to move forward. "So I figure, as my captor, you owe me a little bit of background, am I right?"

She threw her head back and laughed at me, pointing to the door with the hand holding her glass. "Door's right there, doll. Feel free to leave, but I will have to call Roman. The choice was him or me, remember?"

Well, she had me there.

When I didn't move, she took a sip, and said, "What do you want to know?"

I smiled. "I'm so glad you asked." I leaned back into the cushions and crossed my legs. I draped one arm over the back of the couch, and I held my whiskey on my lap. "So he says I'm his mate—"

"Do you deny it?"

I pursed my lips. "So with that . . . declaration, I figure it's probably good for me to know what the hell this family is all about. I mean, he's the alpha of the pack. I'm no shifter, but I understand the importance of what that title means."

She nodded. "Fair enough, but I don't hear a question."

"Tell me about your family. About the pack."

She cocked an eyebrow at me. "Our father was the alpha of the Western Riders. He formed the pack in his youth, and it grew in numbers and strength. Our family bloodline was strong . . . some said it was too strong." She traced her finger over the rim of her glass as she spoke. I didn't interrupt, even though I knew all of this. "There was always this stupid rumor of ancient magic, but that's how jealous people talk. My father was a good leader. He had a firm, commanding presence, but he was also fair. He had a stubborn streak in him, one that Roman inherited." She smirked as she said it, clearly thinking fondly of something he'd done to gain that same label.

"I think that may have passed on to both of you, but what do I know?" I smiled a little.

She huffed a short laugh. "At any rate, every story has a villain, right? A wolf named Marlon challenged my father to gain status as alpha. None of us really know how my father lost, but he did. And for Marlon, it wasn't enough to kill my father. He wanted to set an example. His great show of power. Marlon killed our mother in front of hundreds of Western Riders. He put us up front to watch, no doubt planning to kill us too. Everything changed that day. Roman was just twelve at the time. Not yet a man. The wolves holding Roman back never saw it coming. The pure unbridled rage that exploded from him the moment our mother was killed was unlike anything we'd ever seen before. He killed Marlon first. Then he slaughtered his followers—every single one of them—in seconds." She stared at her glass, not making a sound.

I uncrossed my legs, leaning forward and putting my elbows on my knees. "He killed everyone when he was twelve?"

She nodded, her eyes unfocused, reliving the past in her mind. It was a look I was all too familiar with, having worn it many times myself. She shook her head, as though it would remove the thoughts, then looked at me. "He's been alpha ever since." She slammed the rest of her whiskey back.

I whistled low. "You're telling me a twelve-year-old took over as alpha and no one tried to challenge that?"

She snorted. "If you would have seen what he did that day, you wouldn't have challenged it either."

I tilted my head to the side. "No, I suppose I wouldn't."

That was probably a bit of a lie. That kind of strength was intriguing. Not that I wanted to challenge him, but I wouldn't be opposed to seeing that side of him. I got to deal with dead, boring shithead people who were as awful as they came. They didn't have any spunk to them. Not really. That was reserved for the living.

"So after that—"

"My turn," Roxanne said, taking the opportunity to change the subject. "Normally, I'd play the big sister role and ask what your intentions are with my brother. But this is different."

"Have this conversation often, do you?"

She shrugged. "He's rich, and he's powerful. A lot of women want him."

"And what about him? Does he want a lot of these women?"

She leaned forward, pouring more in her glass, and then laughed. "Roman used to be quite the ladies' man. I've had that talk more times than I care to admit, but not since . . ." The look on her face changed, and a dark shadow came over her features. I knew instantly what would have caused this shift, and why it would affect even her.

"Caitlin mentioned his mate died," I said softly.

Roxanne nodded, taking a deep breath. "She was killed. Murdered, actually, by an unknown supernatural. We never could figure out what kind of supe they were, or what the motive was. No faction came forward. No one challenged Roman or tried to gain power or the allegiance of the Western Riders. No one came for me. No one came for the rest of the pack. Just Maya and the baby . . ."

What?

The baby?

Those two words hit me, though I tried to hide it. Parts of my own past writhed from the memories, making me nauseated again. "The baby?" I whispered.

"She was eight months pregnant with their child. My niece . . ." She shook her head.

I could hear the insurmountable pain that was coursing through her. A feeling I wasn't familiar with crept through my veins, even as I tried to tamp it down.

"What did he do?" I asked, taking another swig to rid myself of the emotion I felt like I was absorbing from her. I couldn't help but wonder if this was what I was missing. That thing that just felt off . . . ?

"Christ, what didn't he do? He lost it. He lost himself in his wolf. Killed more people in his blind rage than I care to think about. He was at war with himself, and he almost lost the pack because of it. He's pushed his wolf down ever since." She stopped to take a drink, holding the glass at her lips for a moment as though she were seeing something in her memories. "That is until you came along."

My gaze flew up to meet her stare. "I didn't actually *see* his wolf," I said. I wasn't sure why I thought I was being blamed for something, but it did sound that way.

"You saw those icy blue eyes, yeah?"

I nodded.

"Meet the wolf. You can see why he's hesitant to let you out of his sight."

Interesting. It certainly explained the difference between the real Roman and the picture I had in my file. It wasn't simply a trait, and it provided information that helped me understand a few things.

I wasn't sure how to feel about any of it. He claimed I was his mate, and there was some heated thing inside me that acknowledged a connection between us, but I couldn't let it happen. It fucked with entirely too much. Besides, I was dead. A demon. Pretty sure some wires had gotten crossed somewhere because demons and shifters weren't mates.

"You're right. I can see it." I stood up, ready for this weird day to end. I had my work cut out for me. "I'm going to go to bed. That's a lot of information to process, and I was tired hours ago when he busted into my bathroom, so—"

"Fury?" she said, interrupting my attempt to get out of the room.

"Yeah?"

"Please don't run again. Don't fuck with my brother. He's all I have left. Like it or not, he says you're his mate. A second chance at having a mate is rare. So rare it's more like legend. So do me a solid and don't piss off the wolf, okay?"

I gave her a non-committal hum because it was the best I could do.

"Good night, Roxanne," I said, walking out of the room. I paused, holding the doorframe. I turned and looked at her. It wasn't often someone did something nice for me. "Thank you for . . . well, for everything tonight. I appreciate it."

"Rox," she said. "My friends call me Rox. And you're welcome."

I pressed my lips together in a tight smile as I left the room.

First, I had a mate. Now, I had a friend.

This shit just kept getting harder and harder.

CHAPTER 13
EZRA

I pistoned in and out of her ass. That tight hole clenched around me. My cock throbbed as she moaned, "Yesss."

"Yes, what?" I purred, nearing the edge. She might be a quick fuck, but that didn't mean I wouldn't make it good.

Footsteps approached the couch where I had her bent over. My second-in-command, Kendrick, coughed twice under his breath. Whatever he had to say, he wanted her gone.

I groaned, picking up my pace. "Yes, what?" I repeated, a hint of irritation coloring my tone.

"Yes, Daddy!" she cried.

I went limp.

My eyebrows drew together, and my lips parted as I stared at the twenty-something vampire with complete and utter disgust. She had been hoping to gain my favor. Behind me, Kendrick chuckled, knowing exactly what had gone wrong here.

I pulled out, and she looked over her shoulder, dazed and heated with desire.

"We're done here," I said, dismissing her.

The colored lights of my club, Bite Me, danced over her skin as she frowned in confusion and hurt. I took a step back, not liking the emotion on her face.

"But—you said—"

"I have many kinks, girly, but that isn't one of them. Now go on, I'm busy." With that, I turned my back on her, tucked in my cock, and zipped my slacks.

Kendrick waited for her to walk away before speaking, but the mirth in his expression annoyed me.

"You needed something," I said, pouring myself a drink. All around me, blood and other body fluids were being exchanged. Bite Me was the most exclusive sex club in the city. Partially out of human curiosity since it catered to very specific tastes, namely the supernatural.

"One of our scouts discovered something very . . . intriguing this afternoon," Kendrick said. I took a sip of the rye whiskey and lifted an eyebrow, waiting for him to go on. "Roman Mikaelson has a second-chance mate."

I paused, then set the glass back down on the polished end table.

"That *is* intriguing," I purred, my sour mood waning at the possibilities that development presented. "How did the scout come to learn this?"

"He was at the elder Mikaelson's bar when a fight broke out. Supposedly, the girl was the reason. Roman showed up, and our guy watched the mate bond snap into place."

I stroked my jaw, running my thumb over my chin in contemplation. "A new mate," I mused. "Fascinating. Especially so close to the summit. Tell me about the girl. Who is she?"

"No one knows," Kendrick said. "She seems to have come out of nowhere, but news of her is spreading quickly.

Apparently, she handed the Dawsons their asses shortly before Mikaelson showed up."

"All of them?" I murmured. There was an itch inside me. A thread that needed to be pulled. After all my years, things had started to fade. Pleasures merely brought contentment. Sex and blood and other frivolities helped keep me here in the moment instead of drifting.

But for the first time in decades, I found myself curious.

It was a dangerous thing.

"Taylor and his three goons. Get this, shortly after Roman made everyone leave, she came out of a window alone. No one's seen her with him since, but she was seen with the elder Mikaelson heading out of the city."

"You've done well, Kendrick," I murmured. That itch burrowed deeper. I needed to scratch it. A second-chance mate that ran? Now that . . . that was just too good to pass up. "Send the twins to pick her up. I want to meet this girl."

Kendrick nodded. "Consider it done."

As he turned away, another thing occurred to me. "Do you know her name, at least?"

"Fury," he said after a pregnant pause.

"First or last?"

"Both, it would seem."

Hm. Very curious, indeed.

CHAPTER 14

I rolled over once more, cursing internally when sunlight peeked through the windows.

My first day back on Earth had been an utter shitshow, and the second wasn't shaping up any better after a night of endless tossing and turning. A thin sheen of sweat covered my skin. My dark red hair lay in messy strands across my pillow and eyes. My muscles were sore, and my throat was dry.

I felt hungover. Or maybe it was withdrawal, given I'd barely had anything to drink since coming back. It was hard to tell.

I was debating the merits of a shot for breakfast when something tapped on the window. I rolled over again and groaned into my pillow. Maybe if I ignored him, he'd go away . . .

Tap. Tap. Tap.

Motherfucker.

I flung the sheets aside and dragged my ass out of bed. The cute little clock on the nightstand read six thirty. In the morning.

At this rate, I might as well call it a double.

"You better have a damn good reason for getting me up this early," I grumbled as I undid the latches on the window. Hades flew past me in a flurry of black feathers and settled himself on the twining metal bed frame.

"Your next target—"

"Oh, for fuck's sake," I snapped, dragging my fingers through my tangled hair in frustration. "Listen here, because I'm only going to say this once. Duke sent you here to help us communicate. Not hound me. Not help my targets—which in case you forgot are going to end the fucking world—and not to wake me up at six thirty in the fucking morning."

Hades blinked. "Well, *you're* clearly not a morning person."

I facepalmed and gritted my teeth. "I'm not an anything person, pigeon. I don't like people, and that includes talking crows. So unless you have a message from Duke, fuck off. Next time you piss me off, I'm going to go bird hunting and we'll see if you come back."

Hades stared at me, not saying anything. The silence dragged on, and he didn't move.

I cracked. "Are you going to say anything?"

"I was waiting to make sure you were finished," he replied.

I closed my eyes and tried to remember all those anger management classes I'd taken in the Afterlife. Remember what Vlad the Impaler, my sponsor, had said.

Count to ten.

Then stab.

In hindsight, I probably shouldn't have picked one of the most notorious demons as my mentor. In life, he'd been an angry man with more than a few screws loose. I really wasn't sure how he'd passed the forty percent mark given his track record, but Jake said times were shittier back then. Standards and the way they were measured were different. Either way, in death, he made a weird kind of sense and gave seemingly good advice.

He also didn't try to fix me or look at me with pity.

Hence why I'd picked him.

So, taking dear old Vlad's advice, I closed my eyes and counted to ten.

I made it to eight before Hades said, "What are you doing?"

"Counting."

"Why?"

"Because if I reach ten and you're still being a dick, I'm within my rights to stab."

Hades sighed. "Fury, that's not what I'm—"

Two knocks on the door made us both pause. The knob turned, and Roxanne peeked her head in.

"Everything good here?" she asked.

"Why are you up so early?"

"Heard noise," she replied, rubbing her eye with the back of her hand. "I'm a light sleeper. Since I'm up, you want breakfast?"

My stomach gurgled in response.

She laughed. "I'll go get us some coffee and donuts. There's a place a few miles down the road that's pretty good, and they don't judge when I show up in pajamas."

"You don't have anything here?" I asked.

She shook her head. "Apart from some protein bars and a jar of peanut butter—no. I spend most of my time at After Dark, and cooking is work."

A-fucking-men to that.

"I like cake donuts. If they don't have that, get me a maple bar," I said.

"Make that two," Hades chimed in.

I side-eyed the pigeon, and Roxanne lifted an eyebrow.

"Uh huh, we'll see what they have."

With that, she closed the door, and it was just me and Feathers again.

"Last I checked, donuts aren't part of a crow's diet."

"Coming from the girl who lives on alcohol," Hades scoffed.

I narrowed my eyes. "Doctors say a glass a day helps the heart."

Hades cocked his head mockingly. "A glass of wine, not a gallon of hard liquor."

Semantics.

"Are you ever going to get to the point? You woke me up and—" I paused when I heard a loud thump downstairs.

Hades groaned, a sound somewhere between a weird purr and a growl. "That's what I've been trying to—"

I held up a hand. "Roxanne," I called. Not a shout, but louder than I had been.

No answer. My skin prickled. I slowly turned to the door.

My footsteps were soft but not quite silent as I started toward it. Over a hundred years of practice had given me a grace I hadn't had in my twenties, but I still wasn't a born supernatural. I was just a dead one.

My fingers brushed over the cool metal. I turned the knob slowly, wincing when it squeaked. "Rox?" I called again, feeling like the dumb girl in a horror movie who goes to check only to become a victim herself.

Least I wouldn't stay dead, I thought on a sarcastic, cheery note. That would really suck for Roxanne, though.

Doubly so because supernaturals didn't get to go to the Afterlife. Their souls couldn't make the journey. Something about their magic extinguished them instantly, meaning if she died, she'd be dead-dead.

That sobered me instantly, and hangover or not, I pulled my shoulder back as I inched the door open.

"Hades, I need you to fly downstairs and tell me what you see," I said quietly.

"We're a little too late for that."

What?

I turned around only to find myself staring into a pair of orange eyes.

"Sorry about this," the man said. A needle jabbed into my arm.

I moved quickly, stomping on his foot then throwing my forehead into his nose. A wicked crack sounded that would've made me gleeful if not for the sluggishness quickly washing over me.

"What did you do to me?" I breathed as black spots formed in my vision.

A nap sounded really good right about now. Under different circumstances.

"Just a little drug to help you sleep," he said, catching my shoulders even as he bled all over me. His grip was strong, but not painful.

Well, at least my kidnapper was a gentleman.

That had to count for something.

CHAPTER 15
ROMAN

Crack.

My fist connected with Taylor Dawson's cheekbone. His head snapped back, and he groaned, taking his punishment as silently as he could.

"Really? You said that? Just . . . 'you ran'?" Caitlin asked as she leaned against a table, arms crossed.

Crack.

Taylor's nose exploded and he grunted, and I could sense his wolf begging to surface. But Taylor was smarter. At least in this. I'd watched the security footage. Heard him. I knew what he'd intended to do to Fury. What they'd all intended to do. Yes, she was my mate, but that aside, I didn't condone rape. Especially not in my establishments.

I took a handkerchief from my pocket, wiping the sweat off my forehead and dabbing at the blood on my hand.

I nodded, acknowledging Caitlin's question. "Yes. Three or four or ten times. I don't even know."

I sighed, and she snickered. "Roman, come on. You've got to do better than that."

I gave her a deadpan look. "I'm well aware, but when

she's around, I'm at odds with my wolf the whole time. I end up focused on tamping him down and then I can't even string a sentence together."

Caitlin sighed. "True as that may be, she's not going to give you the benefit of the doubt. She's not a shifter."

Crack.

My fist connected with the side of Taylor's head, knuckles to temple. His neck strained as his head whipped around like a bobble before smashing into the back of the chair. A low groan of pain left his lips before he went silent. Still conscious but starting to waver. I needed to get on with the actual punishment for his crime, but I couldn't deny my wolf's need for blood. In truth, we both needed it. This male had meant harm to our mate. He was lucky I would let him leave here alive.

I needed him to send a message. Besides, death would be too easy.

"Shifters aren't the only ones who have mates," I pointed out to Caitlin. Turning my back on the alpha strapped to a metal chair, I walked over to the fireplace. Two fat logs glowed bright orange, flames leaping off them into the air. I picked up a silver branding iron.

Pain prickled in my palm, the silver agitating my skin just by touching it. I'd used this tool often enough in my first years as alpha that the skin on my right hand was completely calloused over and nearly as hard as the rocky fireplace.

I dipped the other end in the flames and waited for the metal to change color.

"We may not be the only ones, but something tells me she doesn't come from a kind that does. All of us that do have a natural inclination to form a pack and stick together. We don't do well alone." She glanced at Taylor. His head was bowed, and sweat-slicked hair hung forward in straggled pieces. "I get the feeling she's used to being alone."

"You're not wrong," I agreed reluctantly. "My mate . . ." I trailed off when the image of Fury was replaced by Maya in my mind. Her light blonde hair was already being eclipsed by Fury's red halo, and it wasn't just powder-blue eyes that haunted me in my sleep now, but the darkest shade of brown I'd ever seen. "Fury is unlike anyone I've ever met. Will was right that there's an air about her that's familiar to what was left behind . . . to what we felt at Maya's death, but it's not the same. While I gravitate toward it, Fury's feels more honest."

"It's not as deceptively inviting," Caitlin agreed. "I don't feel like she's going to pull all of my secrets out of me by making me trust her. It's more like you know you can't, but you want to be near her anyway. She's a flame you want to run your hand over just to see if you can without getting burned."

I lifted my eyebrows at my second-in-command, and she averted her gaze.

"Put a lot of thought into her aura, have you?"

Caitlin lifted her shoulder in a half shrug, the apologetic look leaving her eyes. "Normally you have better judgement than anyone, but in this, it will be impossible for you to be impartial. Someone has to look out for you and the pack when you can't." She smiled to cover up the awkwardness of it.

"As long as I don't have to concern myself with my second vying for her attention," I replied smoothly, the rest of it forgotten. "Then again, Rava may skin us both alive if that happened."

Caitlin chuckled under her breath. "That was one time, Roman. One, and you'd already moved on to another she-wolf. I was just doing my job and picking up the pieces." She gave me a sly smile.

"It was only one time because you mated her."

She shrugged again. "You're just lucky you'd already moved on. I would've taken her from you in a heartbeat, and neither of us could've stopped it." Her carefree jest fell flat when my own predicament became an uncomfortable comparison. With one big difference: Rava had been head over heels in love with Caitlin from the first moment they saw each other, and Fury most definitely was not.

Something I both appreciated and was frustrated by.

"I have to see her again today," I said after a moment, my mood souring. "Can you call Rox and ask her what time she's coming in? I'll meet them at After Dark and pick Fury up there."

Instead of giving me shit like before, she dipped her chin in understanding and moved away from the table. "You got it," she said, before stepping out. Her footsteps faded, and then it was just me and Taylor.

I glanced down at the branding iron and lifted it when the metal glowed the same orange hue as the logs. I turned back around, and Taylor lifted his head.

Before, there'd been anger and pride and even acceptance on his face.

Now it was just fear.

He knew what was coming. I could tell by the way he thrashed against the silver cuffs that held his arms behind his back and legs to the chair.

"You don't have to do this," he said. "I learned my lesson. I promise. I'll never touch the girl again. I'll—"

"You'll never touch her again because I say you won't," my wolf said, speaking through me in a gravelly tone. The word of an alpha was law, but my word? It was unbreakable. "Taylor Dawson, alpha of the Dawson Pack, son of Cherise and Milo Dawson—you have been found guilty of plotting to rape and coerce a female, a behavior unfitting of any pack member. You were an alpha. What you do bleeds into your pack. You're meant to care for them. Lead them. It's unbecoming to abuse your power." As I spoke, his wolf started to surface. Blue flickered over his irises. The chains on the chair rattled.

"You can't do this," he started, voice rising in tandem with his panic. "You can't—"

"You're hereby sentenced to live as a rogue for the next two hundred years. You will be exiled from all pack lands and unable to shift. This is the punishment I give to you."

With the words spoken by my wolf and sealed with his magic, I grabbed a fistful of Taylor's hair and wrenched his head back. Then I pressed the silver emblem to his forehead.

The next part was more unpleasant than the first.

If not for the scent of burning flesh, then because his shrill screams grated my ears. My wolf wanted to shove the rod straight through him and be done with it, but I had to grit my teeth and keep my hold steady because that wasn't the way we did things here.

I waited as long as my wolf would allow before pulling the branding iron back.

A circle insignia now darkened the flesh on his forehead between the eyes. Even blistered and bleeding, the 'R' on top of my family's crest made it painfully clear who and what he was.

A rogue.

An outsider.

Someone who was no longer welcome, and barely a shifter in his own right. If he survived his two-hundred-year exile without any further issues, I'd reconsider. Until then, it was done.

I didn't hear Caitlin enter amidst his screaming, but she was standing at the door when I turned to place it back on the metal rack. I paused, noticing the carefully blank expression on her face. I'd only seen it a handful of times in my life, and none of them had been good.

Fear gripped my heart, the worst coming to mind immediately.

"What happened?" I said, in the same growly tone of my wolf. Normally, I made a point not to use it on her, but the heightened stress my wolf was under had left him impatient.

He wanted answers now.

Neither of us were prepared for what came next.

"Vampires took Fury."

CHAPTER 16

My body went airborne, slamming into something hard above me shortly after I came off the ground. I groaned.

Where the hell am I?

My eyelids cracked, and past the fogginess still weighing me down, I registered the compartment I was being kept in as the trunk of a car.

"Son of a—" My curse cut off as the wheels slowed then jerked to a stop.

My shoulders were painfully stiff from having my arms tugged harshly behind my back and secured at the wrists. I tugged lightly. The biting feel of the plastic told me they were zip ties.

I wasn't scared, really. Considering I was already dead, there wasn't much left for me to fear. It was mostly the situation of being drugged and kidnapped that I found off-putting. The ties were a bit tight for my liking, but I was familiar enough with the feeling that I could ignore it for the most part.

There were no footsteps. No sound of warning. One

moment I was on my side in a—thankfully clean—trunk, and the next the hatch lifted and two boys who couldn't have been older than eighteen or nineteen peered down at me. Their matching orange eyes and pale skin gave me a good idea of what I was up against.

"Oh, good," the one on the right said. "You're awake. Sorry about that. Had to make sure you wouldn't try anything funny while I was driving. Safety first and all that."

My eyebrows inched higher. "Right," I drawled. "Listen, I don't know who you two are, or why you want me, but—"

"Name's Tony, and that's Alphonzo. We call him Al for short," the other one said with a boyish grin. He was the one I headbutted. Blood smudged his pale skin around the neckline of his black shirt. He'd cleaned up hastily. "It's not us who wants you—nice on the eyes as you are. Our boss hired us to pick you up. He wants to meet you."

The first one leaned over and lifted me out of the trunk, taking care not to bang me against anything. With his thin frame and average height, the kid was definitely a vampire. There was no way he would've been able to lift me so easily otherwise.

"Why are you being so nice?" I asked skeptically. "I mean, I'm not complaining, but you did kidnap me, and I headbutted Tony over there."

"Boss didn't say he wanted you roughed up," Tony answered as Al put me down nicely, giving me a second to regain my footing as a wave of vertigo crashed over me. "We bring you in all scratched up and bruised, and it'll be our fault. No can do. The De Luca twins do the job right. Besides, you can be forgiven for trying to defend yourself. We *did* kidnap you, after all." He smirked. How had I ended up with the world's nicest kidnappers?

"You still haven't mentioned who your boss is," I pointed out as Al led me through a brightly lit parking garage. It was half empty, but the cars that were here were *nice*. Whoever he was, the guy was loaded.

"Isn't it obvious?" Tony said, as we approached an elevator that was manned on either side. Also vampires.

A creeping feeling was working its way over me as they pressed a button and the double metal doors slid open. We stepped inside with only a nod of acknowledgement from the guards. Al hit the button for the second floor, and my curiosity piqued.

"If it is who I'm starting to think it is, drugging me was kind of a dick move. I would've come voluntarily," I said, as we came to another stop.

Tony chuckled as the double doors slid open once more.

Music played softly in the background. Softer than I would've expected given the faint red glowing lights, scantily dressed people, and—oh yeah—fucking. Certainly one way to start the day.

Beside us, a group of five were getting it on. One female was sitting on a guy's face while sucking another's dick like it was an Olympic sport. Dude number one ate her out while a second chick sucked his cock on all fours as she got plowed from behind. Judging by the dark red smudges on their skin, there was a little more going on than my initial take.

This was *definitely* who I'd thought it was.

The De Luca twins escorted me through the sex club without pausing. Their professionalism was really something, because no matter what their flavor of kink was, this place had it. That was for damn sure. The Afterlife had similar places. I'd even been to a few, but too many demons frequented them, and I wasn't big on mixing business and pleasure. If I was going to fuck someone other than myself, I wanted to be sure I wouldn't have to see them semi-regularly. The same went for watching or being watched. The last thing I wanted was to be on the brink of getting off then catching sight of Karen the Horrible spreadeagled. Gag. No thank you.

We turned the corner and came to the end of our little tour. A wraparound set of lush black couches were pushed all the way back against the wall. Four men and one woman sat on them, but I barely noticed any of them.

Not when Ezra Xue peered up at me and sucked the breath from my lungs.

He was tall, but not large. The lean muscle apparent beneath his suit hinted at a different sort of predator than the wolf alpha. Where Roman was a wall of muscle with biceps the size of my thighs, Ezra was a lithe panther who would stalk me from the shadows. His shoulders were wide, his hips narrow. Dark hair that was so inky black stood apart from everything else. His skin was a shade more amber than the De Luca twins, but only by a touch. Despite all that, the thing I noticed most were his almond-shaped green eyes. They were the same color as polished emeralds, and they were currently narrowed on me.

I lifted an eyebrow in condemnation. "So this is the big, bad boss who sends a couple of kids to do his dirty work?"

Tony and Al's objections were white noise to me as a slow, sexy smirk spread across the alpha vampire's face.

"You must be Fury," he said, his lips caressing my name with an almost possessive lilt I hoped I'd imagined. "I must say, when I heard the wolf had another mate, I expected you to put up more of a fight—"

I pulled my wrists and the zip ties snapped. Tony's eyes widened a little in my peripheral vision, and Ezra chuckled.

Unbeknownst to all of them, demons outclassed every supe in the living world and the Afterlife when it came to strength. It was our greatest asset. One I enjoyed thoroughly abusing when it suited me.

"Call me curious. I wanted to see who went through the trouble of kidnapping me." I paused, a flush creeping across my skin. My heart was beating hard despite the lack of danger or anxiety surrounding my situation. "Now that I know this is a petty jab at Roman, I'm bored."

"You don't care for the wolf?" Ezra asked, leaning forward. His elbows rested on his knees, and he laced his fingers together in front of him.

"Did I say that?"

"You ran from him," Ezra mused, drawing a long eye roll from me. What was it with everyone focusing on that? "I want to know why."

"Mighty bold of you to expect I'll answer. Is that an alpha thing?" I asked, dangerously close to the edge of flirting. Where my body *wanted* Roman, his brutish demands grated on me. With Ezra, I could see some of the same brazenness, but it was more a request.

"Probably." He shrugged. "I'm used to getting my way." Ezra unlocked his fingers and stood, slowly walking toward me. "How about this? Answer my questions, and—" His smooth velvet tone came to an abrupt halt when we were only a few feet apart. He paused, nostrils flaring. A hungry look entered his eye.

"And?" I prompted impatiently.

A tense moment passed where it was unclear if he was planning to eat me or fuck me. It faded when his head dipped, and a dark chuckle slid from his lips. He must've been more unstable than the file let on. This guy had issues. Somehow, though, I still didn't see that kernel of dark that made me think he'd end the world. That bothered me. I considered myself a good judge of character with a sixth sense for sorting bad people from less bad. I'd met demons worse than these guys, which really affirmed I needed to find Hades and get him to send a message to Duke.

"Well, this is interesting. Unexpected." He nodded to himself. "But not unwelcome."

"What?" I squinted. His words only added to my theory that he was a few screws loose.

Ezra Xue stepped forward, eating the distance between us, and inclined his head. I blinked, waiting for the moment where he stopped and tried to use his closeness to intimidate me. It never came.

His lips crashed into mine. Cool, but firm. He licked the seam of my mouth, and when that didn't make me open up, *he bit me.*

Not hard enough to draw blood, but enough to make his intentions clear. He cradled my jaw with one hand, his thumb slightly too tight on my neck to be sweet. The other he threaded through my hair, pulling me closer.

I reached up to grab his hair, planning to wrench him away. Instead, my fingers wrapped around his silky black locks. He sucked on my bottom lip, making my mind falter. The attraction between us flared, heat coursing through my veins.

He was a target . . .

But it was just a kiss, *right*?

There was no harm in a little fun on the job, and when someone kissed like he did . . . My lips parted, and I felt his answering grin. His tongue met my own, making me wonder what else he could do with it. I groaned, settling into him, not minding the audience when I knew I'd never have to see them again after this job.

He slipped his hand from my hair to run it down the length of my back. He grabbed a handful of my ass and pulled me into him, making me feel his erection.

I bit him back. I needed to slow this down, but something inside me was screaming not to.

Then the music cut out. The club fell silent. An inhuman growl came from only ten feet behind me.

"Get your hands off my *mate*." Roman's voice sent a shiver through me, especially when Ezra did no such thing.

The vampire lifted his head, releasing my lips and giving me a saucy grin before turning his cheek to look at the werewolf.

"I think you mean *our mate*. Looks like you're not the only one who got a second chance."

CHAPTER 17
DORIAN

The familiar rhythm of measured footsteps echoed in the hallway, interrupting my thoughts. I didn't need to look at the clock to know what time it was. James's routine was as rigid and by the book as my own. I kept my arms crossed, staring out the library window at the manicured green lawn of my estate.

The door opened, and James entered silently.

"Morning, James." I took a deep breath, turning away from the window and walking to my reading chair.

"Good morning, sir," he said, placing a tray on the side table as I sat down. The *Wall Street Journal* lay folded next to a cup of Earl Grey tea. "Do you have any exciting plans for today?"

"You know I don't."

"Can't blame me for hoping, sir," he said, clasping his hands behind his back. "Breakfast will be up shortly. Is there anything else I can get you beforehand?"

"You mean beside the copy of How to Navigate Tinder that you left in my bedroom? No. Just the eggs Benedict," I said, raising an eyebrow in reference to his suggestive reading material.

There was the slightest twinkle in James's eyes as he nodded. "Very well, sir." He turned and walked out of my library, leaving me with my tea and my thoughts.

How to Navigate Tinder. It was an absurd suggestion, and a remarkable reminder of how the world had evolved. I'd watched humanity change for centuries. The wars, the famine, the death . . . the progress. Despite what that hopeful fae thought, I didn't need a date. Or to get laid, since I knew very well what that app was for. Of all the things I could possibly want in this world or the next, that was not it. Across the decades, across the world, sex was by far the easiest thing to find.

I picked up the cup, sipping the hot tea. I wasn't sure if I even enjoyed it anymore. It wasn't bad. It was just routine. I wished I could have said I looked forward to it every morning. I'd hear humans discuss their love affair with coffee, claiming it was their addiction. At times, I pitied their ignorance. Other times, I envied it. Nothing so trivial could've made me happy.

Few things in the world had ever brought me true joy, and the one who truly had died over a thousand years ago, taking all echoes of happiness with her.

The same footsteps sounded in the hallway, interrupting my thoughts again, but this time they had an urgency to them. I looked up at the door as James entered.

"Sir, you have a call from Roxanne. I believe you'll want to take it," he said, extending a phone to me.

I nodded as he exited the room. Putting the phone to my ear, I greeted one of those few that had brought me a semblance of joy. "It's before nine a.m., Rox. Are you ill?"

"God, I wish. Maybe then this would all be a fever

dream," she answered. Her voice wasn't its normal pitch. It was scratchy and dry, and not full of snark and life.

"I'm listening," I said.

"I'm sorry to bother you, Dorian, I really am. But I need your help. Favor for a friend," she said.

Roxanne never asked for help, unless it was picking out artwork, or an evening gown.

"What's wrong?" I asked.

"It would be much easier in person. Can you come down to Bite Me?" I could hear the hesitation in her voice.

"You can't be serious," I said. "You want me to come to Ezra's place? Ezra's. Why would I do that? And furthermore, what are you doing there?"

"I—" Shouting erupted in the background, cutting her off.

I pulled the phone from my ear in surprise, and a buzzing sensation crept across my skin.

"Will you all shut up for, like, three minutes, please? I'm on the phone trying to get some answers," she yelled.

"*Oh, is there a hotline for troubleshooting supernatural love connections? I must've missed that in my Houston Tourist Guide.*"

"Could you *not* be you for just a hot second?" I heard Roxanne say in response to an unfamiliar female voice.

"Rox," I interjected. "I need more information. What exactly do you need from me?"

She groaned. "We have a situation, Dorian. You've been around a long time, seen a lot. Have you ever heard of two alphas ending up with the same second-chance mate?"

Did she just say . . .? Ezra *and* Roman?

Silence spanned between us as my mind raced for the first time in hundreds of years. Shouting filled the background of whatever room they were in at the club. My curiosity was piqued. I wanted to know more. I wanted to see it for myself. If anything, it would be entertaining.

"D?" Roxanne said, derailing my train of thought.

"I'll be there in five minutes."

For the first time in a millennium, I didn't know what to expect.

CHAPTER 18

Who could tell which was worse: finding out some wires were crossed in the fabric of the universe and I had two mates on this assignment from . . . well, Hell, or being in the middle of a shouting match after a night of drinking and a morning of getting drugged? The only silver lining was that Roxanne somehow knew Dorian Radcliffe and had called him. I no longer had to orchestrate some happenstance meeting between us. Which was good. I'd been working out how to manipulate a secluded fae who was older than dirt and kept coming up short. The downside was, well, the rest of this situation.

I pinched the bridge of my nose while Roman and Ezra had a pissing contest over me. I needed a drink.

"It isn't possible," Roman repeated, sounding like a skipping record. He struggled to control himself, and his wolf. His muscles vibrated, taut and tense.

"What would you know about what's even possible for supernaturals, shifter? You're like, what, thirty-three? You haven't seen shit in your lifespan," Ezra said.

Roman rumbled as Roxanne interjected. "Oh, c'mon,

Ezra. You mean to tell me you've seen this? You know damn well you haven't heard of this either."

He shrugged, walking over to a small private bar in his office. 'Office.' It was a mini lounge, private and clearly off-limits to anyone at the club. I leaned against the edge of a green couch, wishing I could teleport out and sleep off this nightmare. Was retirement really worth this job?

Ezra picked a bottle of good gin and poured the clear liquid into a chilled rocks glass. He twisted a lemon into it and walked back over to me. At least he had good taste in liquor. Score one for things in common, I suppose. He leaned against the couch as well, surprising me when he handed me the glass.

"Looks like you needed a drink," he said with a wicked smile and flirtatious wink.

"Well, cheers to you for being perceptive," I said, holding up the glass in thanks before drinking some.

Roman seethed at Ezra's proximity to me, and Roxanne clearly judged me for my choices. Walking toward me, she said, "You do realize it's only a few after nine in the morning, right?"

"Liquid breakfast never hurt me before," I said. Which was, in fact, true. Demon perk.

"Mmm hmm. Given I was drugged about three hours ago and never got donuts—I'm starving," she said, looking up at Ezra with annoyance.

I held my drink out to her, and she pressed her lips together pointedly. Okay, then. I turned to Ezra, and asked, "You did drug my friend and deprived us of our donuts. You owe her. Do you have food here? A not-vampire menu?"

"Of course. It's early for the kitchen, but they can bring something," he said, pulling his phone from his pocket. He tapped out a message.

"If you bring her dog food—" Roman growled, his eyes shimmering an icy blue.

"Calm down, I wouldn't dream of it. My mate has asked me to bring her friend food, and that I will do," Ezra purred.

I sighed. Loudly. "Thanks for that."

He chuckled as he put his phone back in his pocket, then crossed his arms.

"You drugged her?" a voice said from the corner behind us.

I jumped a little at the unexpected intrusion. It would seem our fae had arrived, and he was stealthy. I tucked that piece of information away for later.

Dorian walked out of the shadows and I drank him in.

Oh. My. Upper Management.

His picture didn't come close to doing him justice either. My files were worthless. Supernaturals may have been an accident. A break in the human design. But that body and bone structure were not.

His steps were measured. His shoulders were broad and muscular, accentuating the V shape of his back and torso. The way he kept one hand in his pocket as he strode forward exuded confidence. Even in a dark charcoal gray suit, he radiated power and strength. His white-blond hair was almost a pale blue in the right light, and his amber eyes surveyed the room while I admired the sharp angles of his squared jawline.

I took another drink of my gin, electricity buzzing across my skin.

"Top o' the morning to you too, Dorian," Ezra said.

"I asked you a question. Don't make me ask again," he said.

Ezra rolled his eyes. "No, I didn't drug her."

Roman scoffed, and Dorian raised his eyebrows, looking at Roxanne. "He didn't. His little henchmen did," she said.

Ezra grinned and shrugged, pushing himself off the couch as he walked past everyone. "I answered the question you asked, your mighty lordship. I'd like you to remember you're in my club. The rules apply here."

"I was invited, and I understand the rules. They were written before you were made," Dorian said, staring the vampire down. His tone was so cold it filled the room with a chill.

"Of course they were." Ezra smirked, turning to me. "Fury, this is Dorian Radcliffe. An old friend of Roxanne's, apparently, and probably the oldest fae out there."

I drained my drink in two swallows and placed the glass on the dark mahogany desk with a clink. "Well, then, now that we've established that." Dorian snapped his head up to look at me. Glad I had his attention. "Can we move this little get-together along? It's been a peachy start to the day, what with waking up early and being kidnapped, but I'd like to figure a few things out, and Rox says you're the man —err, fae—to do it. So . . ."

"Impossible . . ." he whispered, narrowing his eyes. "You're . . ."

I paused, narrowing my eyes in return.

Did he know what I was? If he outed me, this job was over. His file had said nothing about being a mind reader. Or knowing how to identify supernaturals and demons. What had tipped him off? Or did that special ability come with being the oldest living fae in the world?

He took a step toward me.

I stopped leaning on the couch and squared my shoulders, taking a defensive stance. "What's impossible?" I asked him, trying to ignore the way my skin began to itch.

He stopped in front of me, his towering height not intimidating me in the slightest as he looked me up and down.

I stared at him, waiting for a response. "Let's do this. Say what you need to say, Dorian." The second his name left my mouth, that buzzing itch on my skin rippled across my entire body, setting my skin on fire in a cold flame unlike anything I'd ever felt.

He closed his eyes, angling his head upward, taking a slow, deep breath and exhaling, as though preparing himself. He opened them again and stared at me as he said, "You're my mate."

This could not be happening. A loud ringing in my ears drowned everything out.

As my mind tried to process the words he'd just said, I heard Ezra laughing. "Well, I have to admit. I didn't see *that* coming."

Roman shuddered as Roxanne grabbed him, whispering harsh words about control. She looked over at Dorian incredulously. "What the hell is going on?"

He kept his eyes on me, never so much as glancing toward her. "I'm not entirely sure. You both claim to have a mate bond with her. It would seem I do as well."

Roman managed to speak through his visible anger and frustration. "This doesn't make sense, Dorian. We can't all have the same second-chance mate. It's unheard of."

Ezra laughed again, and we all looked over at him.

"Something funny?" I asked him, seconds away from knocking that smug smile off his face.

"Surely you see the humor in this. It's as fucked up as it gets." He crossed his arms and looked down at his feet, his shoulders lightly shaking from his laugh. "None of us likes the other, and fate decides to throw us the same mate? What are the odds of that happening?"

What were the odds, indeed? And where was Hades? I needed to talk to Duke, and soon. This wasn't supposed to happen. Once was a problem, but three times was—as Roman kept pointing out—impossible.

"Dorian, have you ever heard of something like this happening?" Roxanne asked, sitting back down, and rubbing her temples. "I mean, *before* it was complicated. Now? I dunno. You're the most knowledgeable supe, and you've been around the longest. What do you know about this? You can see for yourself that it's real."

Dorian walked over to Ezra's bar. "Do you mind?" Ezra shook his head, gesturing for him to go on. He poured himself a club soda and took a sip before he began. "Second-chance mates do exist in the scrolls, but they're so rare they've essentially become legend."

His honeyed voice mimicked the words Roxanne had said to me the night before. I wondered if he had said them to her before.

"Roxanne said you lost your mate too," I said, interrupting them. I had some questions of my own.

Dorian glared at me. How someone could look at me with a heated intensity that felt ice cold was beyond me. "I did. Over a thousand years ago."

I looked over at Roman, feeling somewhat bad for bringing it up after my heart-to-heart with his sister. "I know what happened to Roman's. What happened to yours?"

"She was killed."

I sighed. "Who killed her?"

"Does it matter?"

"I suppose not." I took a deep breath. "Ezra, what about you?"

"She rejected me," he said without emotion.

"Okay, so that means this isn't a second-chance situation, right? I mean, if she rejected you, then you were never —" Roxanne cleared her throat, and I looked to her. She shook her head slightly, her eyes widened in a silent warning. Oh . . .

"It means that whatever controls mate bonds didn't break when she rejected me." Ezra shifted his weight and looked at the other guys. "It doesn't matter anyway. She was killed a year later."

"Okay. So, how many second-chance mates have you seen or read about in your lifetime?" I asked, looking over at Dorian.

"Until today? It's happened sixteen times in the past fifteen hundred years that I know of, so no, I haven't seen or heard of two alphas sharing one, and certainly not three. The timelines didn't overlap so it wasn't a possibility." Dorian sipped his drink, walking around the bar and sitting in a chair at a small table. "I'm surprised, and somewhat disappointed, really, that no one is going to ask the real question here."

"How is that not the real question?" Roman said.

Dorian tapped his finger on the table, then looked up at me. "Fury?" The way he said my name sounded strained. "Care to ask the question?"

I cocked an eyebrow. This hot fae was calling me out. I just didn't know if he knew the full extent of it or not. He was cold and calculated, and I couldn't quite read him. Out of all three alphas, he seemed to be the only one who could blow. But the others? Not so much. Either way, I knew what he wanted from me in that moment. "What happens when a fae, a werewolf, and a vampire walk into a bar?" I answered, purposefully walking around it, and buying myself time to think.

He huffed an unamused laugh, raising an eyebrow in my direction. I looked around the room. "We can play it that way if you want. Tell me, what does happen when a fae, a werewolf, and a vampire walk into a bar?"

"They apparently end up mated to me," I mumbled, avoiding what he wanted me to say.

Ezra laughed again while everyone else looked in my direction.

"Why is that, I wonder? Three different supernaturals find themselves mated to the same woman . . ." he mused.

"My charming personality and tight body? You have to admit, I have a great ass," I said.

Dorian looked at me, point-blank, tired of my games. "What are you?"

A knock at the door saved me from answering.

"It's just someone bringing food," Ezra said, then yelled for them to come in.

A vampire wearing a white kitchen coat brought in a large tray filled with assorted breakfast items. "Sorry for the wait. We had to send out for the additional pastries and fruit you requested, sir." He nodded to Ezra and exited the room.

"You had them get donuts?" I walked over, excited enough to see food that I momentarily forgot the tension in the room. Hangry was not going to be a good look on me.

Roxanne got up, and scooped scrambled eggs and bacon onto a plate before shoveling the food in. I reached for a donut and shoved half of it in my mouth, moaning around the sugary dough. I took the next bite and swallowed, then picked up another donut and bit into it.

"Answer the question, Fury," Dorian said, bringing us back to the impending conversation.

"I can't," I said around a mouthful of food. I swallowed and took another bite, knowing full well how rude I was being. I didn't want to exactly make myself attractive in the moment. I wanted to find a way out of this situation, but I didn't see that happening without a miracle. "I already had this conversation with Roman. I was born human, and something changed when I turned twenty-three."

"What changed?" he asked.

"I became not-human," I answered. "I thought you were the smart one."

Roxanne got up and headed back to the food tray, looking more like herself. "We had this conversation with her, Dorian." She picked up some fruit and a donut and put it on her plate. "We got the same answers."

The room swayed a little, and I started to lose my balance. Ezra caught my elbow and righted me.

"Fury?" Tingling prickles traveled over my skin. Dorian needed to stop saying my name. It was doing something to me, and it was making me lose my concentration.

Sound went fuzzy and my lips felt numb as a cramping sensation ripped through my stomach. I watched as Roxanne took her donut and sniffed it, then began yelling as she threw it to the ground.

Dorian, Roman, and Ezra grabbed my body as I fell, the world spinning at an impossible rate. I was fairly certain she said 'poison' in her shouting . . .

I'd thought I needed a miracle to end the conversation. Turns out I just needed to be poisoned. Good. I hope it killed me. I had a bone to pick with Duke, and I needed answers.

CHAPTER 19

My body slammed into the ground in Duke's empty office. The lights were off, but a nice evening light filtered in from his window. I decided to stay on the ground for a moment and groan. Maybe nap.

"Are you just going to lie there, or did you plan on being completely useless in the Afterlife too?"

I lifted and turned my head, looking at a perch in the corner. "Hades, you undersized turkey, where the hell have you been?"

"Well, after I tried to warn you about the vampires with syringes—"

I propped myself up on my elbows and glared at him. "You *knew*? Why the—" I groaned. "Why didn't you tell me?"

He turned his head to the side, looking at me for a moment before answering. I could've sworn he narrowed his beady little eyes at me. "I can't imagine why. Maybe I was trying, but someone was busy interrupting me and serving up idle threats? I wonder . . ." he mused, then reached a claw up to scratch his neck.

"Oh shut up. You could've saved me the headache of being drugged and stuffed in a trunk. I needed you before I died. Now I'm here, and man, do I have some questions for Duke."

"He'll be here in a minute."

I looked around the dark office. "How do you know that?"

"It's the Afterlife. He knows when someone's in his office," he scoffed. "Honestly, Fury. They told me you were the best when they assigned me to you, but you really do keep those stupid human qualities even in death, don't you?"

I scrambled to stand up, intending on strangling the crow. He couldn't die, but I thought it might make me feel better. "I am the best, you pigeon. I just didn't plan on being blindsided by three mates—" I said, stomping across the room before the lights came on and I walked right into Duke's chest.

"Ow, Duke! What the hell?"

"Nice to see you too, Fury," Duke said, rubbing his chest where my face had planted. He looked behind him then back at me. "Ah, it would seem I came before you were going to . . . what? Strangle Hades?"

"Yes, actually. Now, if you don't mind giving us a little privacy—"

"Leave him alone, Fury," he said, moving to sit at his desk. He clapped his hands, and the lights came on.

I laughed. "You have The Clapper installed in your office?" I asked, somewhat surprised he would use one.

"Sure, why not? Unfortunate name, though. The Clap. The Clapper. Someone kept their mouth shut in that marketing meeting, am I right?" he said, lifting his legs to rest them on the desk. "So what brings you here this time, kid?"

I gave Hades a dirty look. "I guess pigeon forgot to fly his feathered ass here and tell you that this mission isn't all it's cracked up to be."

The crow rolled his eyes.

"I read the files, Fury. You knew this wasn't going to be an easy one. If it were, the angels would have—"

"I'm their mate, Duke."

I watched his expression carefully. Much as it pained me to admit, I had to ask myself, *did he know?* Because someone had to. Dorian said himself that second-chance mates were rare. Legendary.

Yet, I was one to three of the most powerful beings in the living world.

"Fury, I . . ." He let out a tight breath, his eyes wide. "That's . . . I had no idea," he said softly after a moment.

I believed him. Plopping down in the chair across from him, I sighed deeply.

"How is that even possible?" he asked. "You're dead, and beyond that, shouldn't they each have had a mate already? I thought they did. I could've sworn I read that in the files—"

"Three mates," I said, holding up three fingers. "Each one of them was killed. I'm their second-chance . . . and I was sent there to punish them."

Duke cursed under his breath. I could've really gone for a stiff drink right about then, but he didn't keep alcohol in his office. While I'd gone one way after dying, drowning my anger in liquor, Duke had gone the other and stayed away from it. He said it wouldn't do his problems any good, only make them worse.

I knew there was logic in the old man's words, but I couldn't seem to stop myself.

"That's . . . that's a tough one, kiddo. I have to hope that Upper Management didn't know about this, because if so—"

"It's fucked up," I said, speaking plainly. "I'm a demon, and even I think it's fucked up. I also have a really hard time believing that no one knew. The risk witches saw these guys ending the world, yeah? Then they sent angels? All three of their mates were killed." *And Maya had a baby . . .* I didn't say it because I couldn't let that get to me now, but it sickened me to my stomach to think about. "They're powerful, Duke. Dorian alone . . . it's not adding up. Mates don't just die. Mates to powerful people aren't just killed. It's not that easy. They have guards. They have power of their own—"

"You think angels killed them?" he questioned incredulously. "That's a bold claim, Fury. Those mates were innocents."

"C'mon. You have to see that something isn't right," I said.

"Even so, it doesn't mean the risk witches saw this coming," he countered.

"Bullshit," I said, slamming my hands down on the edge of his desk in frustration. The surface split, long jagged fissures running up the wood grain from each of my hands. It groaned before toppling over in a plume of dust and debris.

"I'm sorry," I said, getting to my feet and tugging a hand through my hair. "I'll fix it—"

"Sit down, baby girl. It's fine." He motioned to the chair across from him like I hadn't just collapsed his desk. It wasn't exactly the first time my temper had gotten the better of me, but I'd worked on it. I'd put in the time with Vlad at anger management. It had been over three decades since I'd snapped, and that thought cooled the fire burning in me. I couldn't let my anger have this power over me, and giving in was doing just that. "You're angry, and rightfully so in this case. Whether they knew or didn't, they've put you in a bad situation. So what are you going to do about it?"

I sat back in the chair, drawing my legs up to cross them. I rested my elbows on my knees and propped my chin on my right hand. "I don't know. This job just keeps getting more complicated. It's not just the mate thing. They know I'm different. They just don't know how—and now I died right in front of them, so if I go back there, I'll show up in a new body. That means more questions. I'm not sure how I'm going to play that and turn the tables, especially when I now feel shitty about what I'm doing."

Duke nodded and ran a hand over his short, buzzed hair, down the back of his head. "Well, I can understand that, but they're also supposed to end the world. As shitty as it seems, think about all the people who would die if that happened—in their world and ours. The Afterlife and the living realm will cease to exist. You, me, Henrietta, and my girls would be extinguished. Jake. Demons and trapped souls awaiting punishment or recycling, for better or for worse. They succeed, and everything we know is gone. We got to live our lives, but what about the people on Earth? What about all the kids, the babies, the families? It may seem like you're in a bad place right now, but the risk witches saw them ending it *all*. What about *them*?"

My chest tightened uncomfortably.

"I wish they could find someone else to do this job," I said.

"You can still back out. Keep at it here and you'll get to retirement by putting in the work."

I laughed caustically under my breath. "No," I breathed. "I won't. That's the thing. The files—Jake said they've tried everyone. No one could do it. And meeting them . . . I kind of understand why. They're different. They don't even seem like bad guys, for the most part. I don't think they would've ended up in the bottom forty percent if they were human. Which means whatever brings it on is complicated, but it's there. Buried so deep even I can't see it yet." I dragged in a breath of air, trying to make my lungs expand despite the pain in my chest. "If I walk away now, I don't think they'll find someone who can get to the source of the issue and fix it. There's a reason they brought me in, mate or no mate. I *am* the best. I can find it and stop it, but if I walk away now, I don't think I'll get my chance to hit retirement. Even if I do, eventually they'll blow—and then what was it all for?" I shook my head. "I can't let my feelings be the reason the world ends."

Duke pressed his lips together in a sad, knowing smile. "It sounds like you've made up your mind."

I had, but I also wondered if there was ever a choice, really. Not even a selfish person would walk away now. It would still mean their end eventually.

"I have to go back," I said quietly. Neither of us moved.

Duke reached across the space where his desk had been and grasped my leg, giving it a comforting squeeze. "I'll be here when the job is done. No matter what. You'll have the time to heal and know that you saved other young women like yourself from dying too young."

My throat clogged with emotion, and I swallowed it down. Where were my blackout aviators when I needed them?

I took his hand in mine and held it, drawing strength for what I had to do.

Pigeon was remarkably quiet through the exchange. Thank fuck. I was grateful I was allowed to have a moment every now and then.

I got to my feet, and Duke followed me. Hades flew over and perched on his shoulder as we started down the hall. When we got to the portal room, I paused before stepping through. "How long has passed since I died?"

"A few seconds, but you really need to be more careful. It's not just the alphas who'll take notice when your bodies start to pile up."

I nodded to myself, making a mental note to be more careful. Maybe there was something to be said for Roman's overprotectiveness.

"I take it there's no way to send me back to the same body?"

Duke shook his head. "That vessel is gone. You have a soul, and the portal gives it back its flesh form, but we can't put you in a dead one."

I nodded. Yeah, the corpse was going to make this a bitch to explain. I might need to just play the mysterious card for a bit. Maybe that would make them keep me closer and I could start digging . . . The thought made my chest ache, but it wasn't as bad.

I started for the portal, and then paused again.

"Are you sure you got this?" he asked one more time.

I took a deep breath and lifted my arm. Hades flew over and settled on it, a begrudging respect in his beady eyes.

"I am," I said, feeling more grounded than I had since the night Jake pulled me into his office.

Then I stepped into the portal.

When I opened my eyes, it was total chaos.

CHAPTER 20
EZRA

Sometimes being a mind reader had its perks.

Like when your mate dropped dead less than an hour after you'd found her.

Roman was losing his mind, the shift taking over. Roxanne was giving the corpse chest compressions, and when that didn't work, she switched to jamming her fingers down her throat—as if throwing up would save a body that was already dead.

Even Dorian, the oldest fae in living memory, and probably oldest supernatural altogether, was tense. His pale hands were gripping my office desk hard enough it might have crumpled already if it weren't reinforced with steel, per my request after I'd broken it one too many times.

Alas, being supernaturally strong had its drawbacks on occasion.

I rose to my feet and walked out of my office. Kendrick was nearby.

"We've already narrowed down the suspects, but they ran. I have people out searching for them now. Do you need anything—"

"A pair of blacked-out sunglasses and a tablecloth or blanket of some sort. Maybe a tarp?" I mused.

Kendrick did a double take, then took a moment to stare blankly. "Ezra, I know that your way of handling grief—"

"You, there." I stopped a vampire girl walking by.

"Sir?" she replied in a high-pitched squeak.

I reached out and cupped her chin, turning it. "These will do," I murmured, then plucked off the sunglasses she'd pushed up above her forehead. The hair it held back fell forward, and her lips parted in surprise, but she didn't argue. She knew who I was. All of my species did. I made an example of those who broke my rules.

The kind no one could forget.

I turned back to Kendrick. "Get me the tarp and compensate her."

My attention turned back to my office, where things had gone silent. I had a feeling my mate had made her grand reappearance.

I walked back and slipped inside, releasing the tight breath I'd been holding since her body dropped.

She sat in my chair, boots kicked up on the desk and her red hair pulled back. I looked forward to the day I got to pull that hair and take her cherry mouth . . . but there would be time for that later.

I set the sunglasses down and pushed them across the desk, silently.

Her eyebrows quirked up. Then she narrowed her gaze. I—and every other alpha in the room, no doubt—heard her heart rate pick up, but she took the glasses with a muttered "thanks."

I inclined my head and gave her a confident smirk before moving away, toward the window.

"So," she drawled, filling the heavy silence. "You guys

going to do anything about that?" She jutted her chin out toward the dead body on the ground. Her dead body.

A knock at the door had the other alphas on edge. Roman stepped closer to her, Dorian toward the door. I sighed.

"Come in, Kendrick."

My second stepped inside, then froze in his tracks—the same thing everyone else had done. I suppose it would've been a jarring thing to experience. I may have had the same reaction had I not been reading her mind from the second she walked into my club.

Normally, I tuned out because I had no interest in hearing what others were thinking. Their thoughts bored me. Most things did. It was always the same. But not this delectable little . . . *demon*.

No, she was different in every way—down to her soul.

Because she wasn't a supe in the true sense, nor was she human.

She was dead, and she'd come back a demon.

One intent on punishing me—and her other mates.

I hadn't figured out why, not until she returned with a renewed sense of purpose. I couldn't really hold it against her, though. Not when she thought we were going to end the world.

On the contrary, it made me more intrigued. More curious. More . . . obsessive.

Fury wanted to play games with us. To tie us up in knots over her and figure out each and every little weakness.

Little did my mate know, I loved playing games just as much as she did.

And thankfully, I didn't have to play fair.

CHAPTER 21

The man Ezra had called Kendrick stood at the door, frozen, carrying what looked like a canvas tarp. No one moved. No one spoke. What was there to say? I'd died right in front of them. My body lay on the floor in the same room. And here I sat, legs kicked up and a smile on my face.

"C'mon, I wasn't gone that long. Say something." I wasn't entirely sure how to start it off either, if I were being honest. "Oh, and cover that," I added, gesturing to the expired version of myself. "No one wants to see it anymore."

That did it.

The room exploded in a frenzy of shouts and curses. All except Ezra. He didn't strike me as the silent type, yet here we were. Through all the shouting, aimed in my direction, he looked at his friend, and said, "Leave the tarp, and make sure no one comes in." Kendrick blinked a couple of times, then nodded, leaving it on a table and walking out the door.

I held up my hand to stop the onslaught of questions. "Can I get a drink?"

Roman looked at his sister, then back at me. "Are you

serious right now?" he said through clenched teeth. His muscles were still trembling with the need to shift. Clearly his wolf had almost taken over at my death. He had more control than he'd realized if that hadn't fully set him off. It was something for me to consider.

"Yeah, I'm serious. I just died. I think I can have a drink." I looked at Ezra since he seemed to be fine giving me hard liquor at early o'clock. "Gin?"

"Hold up," Roman said. "I have some questions that need to be answered first. You—" Roxanne grabbed his arm as though she was trying to calm him. "No, I'm fine. Stop." He looked back at me, twirling his hand in a circular motion around the scene before us. "Explain this. Now."

I looked him up and down, trying to figure out how he was managing to be calmer than he ever had before. "You first. Why are you fine? I can see you shaking. Part of your suit is ripped. You almost shifted. Why should I talk right now and risk you going wolf-man on us?"

I gazed around the room. Ezra inclined his head in agreement while Dorian seemed content to glare at me like a particularly tricky experiment he wanted to dissect. Roxanne's eyes were wide with unshed tears that she was trying to cover as the shock and adrenaline started to come down.

"I'm . . . I can see you're safe. So can my wolf." He looked away for a second, and I could tell that wasn't all, but neither Dorian nor Ezra would push it. "Now answer *us.* What the hell just happened?"

I pulled my legs off the desk and sat forward. "It would seem the alphas have spoken," I joked.

"Stop it," Roxanne said, almost shouting. "What the hell, Fury? You just *died.* Your body is right there, so *stop.*" She looked over at the dead version, then back at me. I felt a sudden pang of guilt. She'd been desperately trying to save my life. She didn't know. She thought she was going to lose a friend—her brother's mate—and she was the only one actively attempting to bring me back to life.

"Point taken." I nodded. "I'm sorry, Rox." I got up and crossed the room, picking up the thick tarp. Walking to my prone body on the floor, I shook and fanned the cloth sheet out, dropping it over dead-me. The slack-jawed face and wide-open eyes were really not helping anything here.

I sat on the couch, knowing this was only going to go one way. If I focused on that, I was still in the driver's seat. Or whatever the saying was.

Dorian came over and sat down across from me. I looked up, meeting his gaze.

"How did you do that?" he asked, probably thinking it was the best way to get me to answer.

"I didn't," I said. "I have no control over it."

"Bullshit."

"Okay," I responded. "Do you want me to lie? Make up some elaborate story about witchcraft and tarot cards, or that I made some deal with the devil to sell my soul and get three mates?"

Ezra snorted at my retort. Roman and Dorian stared me down before the former spoke.

"When I questioned you in Roxanne's bar, you said something happened to you when you were twenty-three that made you not-human. You said the same thing to Dorian. What was it?"

I pointed at the dead body. "That."

"What do you mean 'that'?" Dorian asked.

"I mean, my body died. And then it came back," I answered, motioning to myself. This was where it got tricky, but it was best if I tried to keep things as vague as possible. Feigning ignorance would help. They may not believe it, but right now it was the best I had.

Roxanne stood up, wiping her eyes with the back of her hand. "But how, Fury? How did this happen? What are you? What does this even—"

Dorian placed his hand on her arm and shook his head. There was something between them. Something deep. Solid. Similar to what I had with Duke, but not the same. Part of me was glad for it. Each of them would need someone when the job was done and I had disappeared for real. The thought caused a pang inside me, but I pushed it down, the conversation with Duke still fresh in my mind. I *had* to do this. It was the only way.

"I don't know what more I can tell you. You know what I know. Now you've all seen it for yourself."

"I don't accept that as your truth. There's something you aren't telling us," Dorian said.

I sighed, throwing my head back. "Okay, so it was witches and tarot cards, and I sold my soul to the devil for three mates. Happy?"

Roman stood with his arms crossed, looking down at the ground. As though he'd had a sudden and alarming thought, his head popped up. "Does anyone else know about you?"

"You mean does anyone know that this happens?" I motioned between me and the tarp. He nodded. "No. I'm not from around here, remember?"

"This has happened before, though. So someone could know about it," Roman surmised, looking at Dorian.

"I took care of it up north. No one there knows," I said. It was a lie, but also a truth. Not a single soul alive knew about me and my life up north. Nope. That miserable life was long gone, as were all the horrible people in it.

Ezra came over and handed me a gin with a twist of lemon again, right on cue. "Explains why you drink so much."

I snapped my head up. "What does?"

He looked over at the dead-me. "That. Because it won't kill you."

"Oh, yeah," I said, realizing what he meant. I raised my glass. "Cheers to that." It came out drier than I'd meant it to, but the eyes in the room were watching my every move.

Ezra sat next to Dorian, throwing his arm across the back of the couch, and crossing his legs, looking thoroughly bored. "We need to figure something out. She isn't going to answer questions to your liking right now, and we can't all just live here in my office."

Roxanne interjected, "Probably shouldn't forget the important detail that someone just tried to kill her."

"How do we for sure know they were trying to kill me?" I asked. I'd barely been there for a day. The thought was somewhat troubling. Dying clearly wasn't an issue, but someone was trying to cause problems, and that meant they were getting in the way of me doing my job. That just complicated things more.

All four of them glared at me with annoyed looks that said 'really?'.

Dorian leaned forward, propping his elbows on his knees, and clasping his hands. "Roxanne is right. She'll come home with me."

"Wait a minute," Roman said, his voice turning to gravel. His wolf was driving him hard. I wondered how much of the man also objected. "Why you?"

"Do you want me to list the reasons, shifter, because I figured they were blatantly obvious to everyone," Dorian said, looking at Roman's ripped suit from his almost-rage-shift.

"I'm fine with that," Ezra piped up. Everyone looked at him, and he shrugged. "Dorian has a point. Deny it all you want, Roman, but right now, she's probably safest with him."

I watched with curiosity as Roman's anger struggled to the surface, his eyes swirling between icy blue and a warm brown.

Dorian stood up, facing him. "We may not be friends, but I'm not your enemy. We are somehow mates with the same woman, and I can't explain why yet. She isn't human, but none of us knows or can feel what she is—and Fury isn't being forthcoming." He shot me a look I dismissed. Damn right I wasn't. The living weren't supposed to know about the dead. "This isn't a pissing contest. She was with Roxanne when she was kidnapped—"

"By him," Roxanne sniped, pointing at Ezra, who grinned his agreement, tilting his head to the side.

Dorian nodded. "But she was still kidnapped, and you were drugged in the process. She was poisoned here, in the vampire's club. Tell me why she's safer with any of you," he said, looking around. "I'm listening."

"Not that anyone seems to care, but I'm fine with this arrangement," I said, joining in the argument.

Four supernaturals stared at me, wearing a variation of shocked faces.

Dorian narrowed his gaze at me. "Why?"

"Does it matter?" I asked him. "It's what you wanted, anyway."

"Enlighten me," he said.

I rolled my eyes and sighed. "Do you really want me to go through a checklist, because I thought you just made the 'blatantly obvious' points to everyone?" I said, throwing his words back at him.

"My focus right now is finding out who poisoned her. Someone went after her, and they did it on my territory," Ezra said, his tone darkening. He cracked his knuckles, exuding confidence and complete assuredness when he looked at me. "My guys are already on it. We'll find them."

Roman grunted in frustration. "I want to be here when they're questioned."

"As do I," Dorian added.

Ezra dipped his head. "I'd expect nothing less. But until then, she can't be with me. Not when I can't trust my own people."

Roman looked at Roxanne, and she nodded in agreement. "I hate to say it, but Dorian and Ezra are right. Your wolf wants her safe. More than anything, I know that's your struggle. She will be." Dorian raised his eyebrows to her. "Oh, stop it. I've agreed with you before. We've been friends for a long time. I know when you're right, even when you piss me off. And right now, you're right. Keep her safe." She looked at me with a tight-lipped smile.

Probably not the time to mention that keeping me safe wasn't really a priority when I could come right back. Though, the dead bodies *were* becoming a problem.

Roman sighed. "Fine. I agree."

I clapped my hands, then rubbed them together. "Great. Now we have the custody agreement all set up—"

"Wait," Roman interjected. "You won't answer why you're in agreement. Is this a game to you? Part of some plan you have to run off and send us all on a chase? I can't deal with that right now, Fury. This is harder than you can imagine."

I held my hands up in mock surrender. "I'm not going to run off or plan some elaborate escape."

Dorian cocked an eyebrow at me. "Why should we believe you?"

"You can't, I suppose," I admitted. "Guess you'll just have to trust me."

Ezra snorted, and Roman let out a harsh breath.

Roxanne stood up, walking to me, and looking me straight in the eye. "I asked you once already, and I'll ask you again. Please don't run." Her eyes widened slightly, reminding me of the rest of our conversation. A vulnerable conversation she wouldn't share in front of three alphas.

Last night I wasn't as committed to my answer. I had loose plans, then. I was working on finding a way to bring Ezra and Dorian into my life. By some glitch in design, that had happened. Albeit in a monumentally screwed-up way. Now I had to stay, and I could at least give her that. "I'm not going anywhere, Rox." I nodded slightly and gave her a tight-lipped smile in return, keeping eye contact to let her know I understood exactly what she meant.

"How do we do this?" Roman asked, ending the moment between me and his sister. "Does she stay with you for a few days, then we trade? Keep her moving?"

Dorian ran a hand through his neatly styled hair. "Possibly. Ezra, do you think it will take long to catch who poisoned her?"

He laughed. "Probably no more than a few days."

"Good. We have the summit coming up, and that problem needs to be dealt with before then. If you need assistance, I'll send you some fae. We need to get this under control," Dorian said.

"I have shifters who can help too, if needed," Roman added reluctantly.

"So . . . I'll spend a few days with each of you until we make a new plan?" I asked, mentally calculating how long I would have to work around them. It would be easier if I had more than a day, so I wouldn't complain if that was what they gave me.

"I think it may be best," Dorian answered, looking at my other . . . mates. "Ezra, keep us updated with what you find. We stay in contact."

The guys shook hands in agreement, but Roxanne shocked me when she came up to me and wrapped her arms around my shoulders, pulling me close in a tight hug. For a moment, I stood there, unsure what to do. I hadn't been hugged in longer than I could remember. Not even Duke did that. And the fuck buddies I'd found in the Afterlife weren't really the hugging type either.

I hesitated, an unnamed emotion clawing at my insides, before I reached my arms around, hugging her in return.

"Thanks for trying to save me earlier," I told her. And I meant it.

Releasing her, I nodded to everyone. "All right, Dorian. What next?"

Dorian said nothing as he grabbed my hand and a whooshing feeling shot through my body. My stomach jumped into my throat, and my head spun in circles.

Teleporting on Earth caused motion sickness. Awesome.

It wasn't even noon yet.

I really needed to catch a break.

CHAPTER 22

We reappeared in a garden that could have rivaled Versailles.

The marble fountain of baby cupids and sirens shot water fifteen feet in the air to land in the crystal-clear pool that was easily twenty feet in diameter. Rose bushes and other flowered plants lined the walkways. I took it in as I bent at the waist, hands on my knees, breathing hard.

"Are you all right?"

"Dizzy," I grumbled, turning to look off to the right. The garden just went on and on, as far as I could see. And while my sight wasn't as impressive as my strength, I'd had 20/20 vision when I was alive—before my shithead ex punched me too hard and damaged the cornea. Thankfully, in death they'd reverted to pre-asshole quality.

"Interesting," Dorian murmured. "You can't sift?"

I could tell he was digging. That was obvious. I'd expected it, and fortunately he was unlikely to ever find the answer, even with me telling him the truth.

"No," I grunted. "I also get motion sick easily, so I'd prefer to stick to my own two feet as much as we can." I stood up, looking in the other directions. It was much of the same–winding paths in a garden of flowers—apart from the mansion.

It stood extravagant and proud. Colonial style, despite the clear updating on the outside to make it look less like, well, a plantation.

"Not what I expected."

Dorian lifted an eyebrow. "Oh? And what did you expect?"

Sweat was forming on my brow, and I swiped at it with the back of my hand and pinched the front of my shirt to fan myself. "Less Anne of Green Gables meets The Secret Garden set in Hell, and more—" I broke off, twisting my lips as I considered. "Castle on a cliff. Somewhere it's always gloomy. And cold. Like you."

His lips twitched as he lifted his eyebrows. I could tell he was amused, even though he hid it. I'd guessed right, of course. Then again, I did read in the file he lived on an island off the coast of Scotland. In a castle on a cliff. Very doom and gloom.

"Well, you're right about one thing," he said, then started walking. I had to jog to keep up, making the sweating issue worse. "This place is Hell." He got to the door first, but instead of entering like I expected, he pulled it open and sidestepped, waiting for me somewhat impatiently.

"Then why do you live here?" I asked, knowing he didn't but needing to play the game. I walked inside and sighed in bliss as the air conditioner hit me. I almost didn't hear his answer because I was so wrapped up in the cool feeling on my skin.

"I don't."

"This isn't your house?" I asked without looking.

"It's an estate I have to stay in during the summit. That's it. Texas wasn't my first choice for neutral ground. I wanted Quebec, but neither Ezra nor the wolf alpha at the time went for that. I was overruled."

"Overruled," I mused. "Does that happen often?"

"No."

Simple. Straightforward. Resounding.

I sensed a hint of something. "But it did this time?"

"When you get to be as old as I am, you pick your battles," Dorian replied. "The location of an event that's held once a decade is not one of them."

"Hmm," I hummed, a little put out. He was self-assured, and while that wasn't a bad thing, it wasn't the most workable. They tended to be harder to break. Not impossible— no one was. Just harder.

I perused the room. Old paintings scattered the white walls. Dark hardwood floors were hidden beneath a large Persian rug. A wing-backed armchair that looked old but well-maintained sat next to a hardwood end table that had been carved in the image of a stag. Its horns came up and wound together to form the tabletop.

"You have expensive tastes," I mentioned casually.

Dorian stood at the door, staring at me with unnerving amber eyes. "It's only worth something because the creators are dead."

"What is?"

"All of it. Worth is relative. I furnished my estates with things I found in my travels, but as time went on, the people who made these things died. Their death made the items they left behind valuable because they could no longer create." He shrugged.

"Our lives must seem so fleeting to you," I said softly,

taking a closer look at the pieces in the room. "You step through them and take your piece, then carry on."

"Some might say I'm bringing them meaning by carrying on these artists' legacies."

"By your argument, meaning is only found in death. If that were the case, living would be rather pointless."

When he didn't say anything, I slowly smiled.

I'd found a truth buried beneath his cold exterior.

"Perhaps it is," he said quietly.

The weight of the moment was lifted when a young man made his way toward us from down the hall behind Dorian. "Sir?" he said with barely contained excitement. "Might I ask who your lady friend is?"

"I'm—" I started.

"This is Fury. She'll be staying with us a few days," he replied.

I lifted my eyebrows. He hadn't called me his mate. Did I detect some hesitance there? My, my. This was shaping up better than I'd expected. It seemed I'd hit too close to the truth, and now he was running.

I smiled again, and it only served to agitate Dorian further.

His lips flatlined and those amber eyes turned hard. "Don't touch anything that looks expensive. Don't leave. Don't bother me. You think you can handle that?"

"Where are you going?"

"Work. The fae don't run themselves. I'll see you for dinner."

Then he was gone, and it was simply me and my babysitter.

The other fae smiled in apology, his bright purple eyes kind. "Dorian Radcliffe is . . . a hardworking man. Devoted to the responsibilities he's found himself committed to."

It was a poor justification for his even poorer manners, but it wasn't this guy's fault. "I can see that," I said. "How long have you known him?"

"Oh, a few hundred years or so," he answered happily. "My name is James. I'm his personal assistant and the keeper of his estates. I could give you a tour of the mansion if you'd like?"

I smiled like a wolf in sheepskin. This was exactly what I needed.

"I'd like that very much."

CHAPTER 23
DORIAN

I paused mid-sentence, the husky sound of her laughter echoing down my halls. My cock hardened. The point of the pen dug too deep into the report I was checking over and the middle snapped in half under my crushingly tight grip. Ink bled everywhere, and I cursed.

Eight hours.

This had been my life for *eight hours*.

I'd struggled to get into my work, thoughts of our conversation and everything I'd seen today nagging at me. Eventually I would find a way to concentrate, but it wasn't for long.

The sound of her voice called to me.

A siren I was fairly certain would drown me in her depths.

If it wasn't her voice, it was her scent, and when James came to deliver lunch, she'd followed him. She'd walked around my office in loose pants and a tank top. She'd stopped to touch something here or there. Commenting on it. Ever since that moment, I found my attention had gravitated to every object she took notice of. Asking myself what did she find interesting about it? Why? Could it somehow give me a clue to what she was, or why being in her vicinity was driving me *insane*?

I was an old supernatural. The oldest. If not untouched by time, then hardened by it. I did not grow fascinated easily. I did not obsess. My attention did not wander. And yet, it was.

I dropped the broken remains of the pen in the trash and glanced up at the clock. Dinner would be ready at any moment, and with it, a mental sparring match with my mate would be served.

That word silenced my other thoughts. Drawing mixed emotions. While I felt an innate pull toward her, a desire to protect her, an even greater one to fuck her, it didn't instantly create feelings.

It simply created possibility.

Last time, I was a young fae and fell head over heels in love. Morvain had been a kind woman. Soft. Easy to love and hard to lose. Her death tore me apart. My life had been boiled down to two distinct phases.

Before . . . and after.

The after was cold and lonely and desolate. There was no possibility.

But now . . .

I shook my head. My jaw clenched hard.

I needed to get to know the girl. To learn who she was. *What* she was. My instincts would drive me to protect her whether she needed it or not, and perhaps, I may even fuck her. Anything more was out of the question.

I left my office with a purpose. Agitation still gnawed at me. I hadn't felt that emotion—or much of any, really—in so long that it was harder to grapple with than I'd anticipated. But if fifteen hundred years had given me anything, it was the ability to play a part.

I trailed down the hall, following the sound of her voice. When I walked by the dining room and found it empty, uncertainty filled me. James was never late. Dinner was always at seven thirty, sharp. So where . . .

I didn't have the chance to finish the thought. I rounded the corner into a sitting room with a large television. I often forgot it existed since I never had the desire to use it.

"*Previously on* Grey's Anatomy."

Sitting on the oversized sectional, James was passed out. I frowned. Clear bottles littered the floor in a path from his side to Fury's. She sat at the opposite end with her knee propped up and a half-empty bottle of gin in hand. Her eyes were surprisingly clear, though dilated.

I let out a harsh breath. "What happened to James?"

She ignored me, but I could tell she heard by the slight twitch of her lips.

I stepped in front of the TV and repeated myself, something I almost never had to do. "What happened to James, Fury?"

"He's a lightweight. Who knew? Anyway, can you be a window instead of a wall and step two feet to the left?"

I gritted my teeth. She truly was nothing like Morvain. Where my mate had been sweet, Fury was prickly. Morvain was selfless, Fury inconsiderate. I stepped forward, blocking the screen entirely, and it was only then that I remembered their greatest difference.

Morvain had been innocent.

The devilish glint in Fury's dark eyes showed she was anything but, and she knew exactly what she was doing.

I snatched the remote off the couch and squinted at it.

"Big red button on the top right," she said.

I stilled, realizing that she knew why I'd paused. I'd only used a television a handful of times in the last few decades. I hadn't known which button, and she'd read that on my face as easily as if I'd said it out loud.

I cut the power, and the sound stopped, leaving us in the quiet with James's tiny snores and the crickets for company. "How'd you know?"

"Seen the look before," she muttered. "Ex-lover had the same expression on his face when going down on me."

I blinked, and she snorted then stood. "You must really know how to choose them."

Our bodies were only a few inches apart when she looked up. This close, I could tell that her eyes weren't actually dark brown like I'd thought. They were black. Truly black.

"I did say *ex*, didn't I?" She smirked before stepping around me.

I looked at James, debating the merits of waking him up.

"Leave him," she said from the doorway. I looked over my shoulder. "I'm pretty sure this is his first break from making you dinner in a century. Let the guy sleep. If you're hungry, we can order," she paused, as if looking for the word, "takeout. I think that's what Roxanne called it. The food that comes to your door? Anyway, unless you want a liquid dinner, I wouldn't recommend me cooking."

Without turning back, I followed her out into the hall, my curiosity driving me forward. "Where did you say you were from again?"

"Up north."

I sensed the truth, even if she was evading. This girl was skilled at twisting her words. I'd figured that out quickly but relearned the lesson several times over on each occasion we spoke. "They have takeout up north," I replied, calling her on it.

She smiled like she found something funny. "Not when I was there. It's a pretty remote area."

As strange as it was, again, she was telling the truth.

And for the first time, I thought I'd learned something valuable.

Fury wasn't as young as she looked. Nor was she apathetic enough to be truly old. She hadn't questioned how James had been with me for a century, and for a born-human-turned supernatural, she didn't seem at all surprised by our ages. The question was: exactly how old was she?

She continued down the hall before turning into the kitchen. I trailed after her. The scent of coming storms and fall leaves pulled at me, demanding I follow her.

"Tell me, Fury-from-up-north, what kind of food do you eat?"

"No tacos. I'm not feeling like a masochist tonight." She scrunched her nose and took another sip straight out of the gin bottle. By sip, I mean drained another quarter of it in one go.

"Have you ever died from alcohol poisoning?" I asked mildly. She really did drink a lot. In the nine or so hours I'd known her, the only thing she'd consumed was alcohol and poisoned donuts.

"Nope," she said. "But I'm not afraid to try."

I narrowed my eyes. While I wasn't truly worried about it—knowing she'd come back—I wasn't in the mood to test it. Walking over, I reached out to pluck the bottle from her hand. When it didn't move an inch, I stopped pulling.

"You're strong," I noted.

"How observant," she said dryly.

"Yet you die."

"Oh boy, here we go again. Why don't you order that food we were talking about before you try to jump down the rabbit hole?"

"You understand modern slang and like television, yet the word takeout is foreign to you," I continued, ignoring her. "So contradictory," I said, more to myself than her.

She lifted an unamused eyebrow. "Are we still on this?"

"You could tell me what you are and save us both the trouble."

She narrowed her eyes, then yanked the bottle away from me and drained the rest. When it was empty, she set it on the counter and said, "Are you going to be a gentleman and buy me dinner, or not?"

I chuckled under my breath.

"What?"

"I'll get you dinner, Fury," I said, leaning in close. "But you came to the wrong place if you wanted a gentleman."

My eyes dipped to her lips. She licked them, her tiny pink tongue darting out.

The urge to bite her surged, but I stepped away.

My desire to fuck her was strong.

But my need to break her open and learn every little secret—that was stronger.

CHAPTER 24

EZRA

"I'm heading out. What's the status on our poisoners?" I asked, still staring out the window. Kendrick had just stepped into my office; his reflection met my eyes in the glass.

"They've fled Houston. It seems they had help, though we don't know who from, or if they're headed to the source."

I nodded once. "How long until they're apprehended?"

Kendrick sighed. I wasn't going to like the answer. "Likely a day. Maybe two. They initially took a bus, but they think they're clever, hopping around from one mode of transportation to the next. We're currently tracking the latest. Getting them without causing collateral damage takes time."

I dipped my chin. "Keep me updated. I want to know when they're caught. Have you finished combing through the rest of our staff and security?"

"Yes," he said, sounding a bit surer, if not tired. It had been a long ten hours since Dorian took my mate and sifted out of my club. "Three of them had doctored stories with false records. They've been let go and told to leave the city before the summit. None of them had anything indicating involvement, however. It seems to be just the two who fled."

Hm. "I suppose we'll see once they're brought in for questioning."

Kendrick didn't say anything. This was usually when he nodded and stepped out. Back to work. Always work. After so long, even play had become work in a sense. I wondered if he felt it as much as I did. Perhaps even more, given he was twenty years my senior.

Kendrick was my second-in-command, but he was also my maker and my friend.

"We'll find them," he promised quietly. "I won't rest until they're captured and we know *why* they came after her to begin with."

"I know." He wasn't lying. He was good like that. When Kendrick said he would do something, he did it. That was why he was my second. "Speaking of my mate, I need to check in with her. See how Dorian has been. He's got a cruel streak in him. Runs deep."

"You think he'd use it on her?"

"No," I said, shaking my head. The city lights made my own green eyes more impossibly bright in my reflection. "I wouldn't have relinquished her so easily if I thought other-wise. She may not be able to die, but that doesn't mean she can't be hurt. I'm hoping some time with him wears her down before she comes to me."

"So, you plan to pursue the bond?" Kendrick mused, stepping further into my office.

"Yes, but not immediately. There's work to be done before I can bond with her fully."

My old friend lifted his eyebrows, his lips twisting

together. "By work, I'm assuming you mean there are games to play?"

"It's all the same," I answered with a grin. "Fury is different. She's not like Lenora."

"Because she hasn't rejected you?" Kendrick replied. To some, it might've seemed a little callous, but there was no love lost between me and the woman who'd been my mate.

"Because she won't," I said. "Not when I'm done. I don't care if she accepts the other two. That's her business with them. But between us . . ." I said. "I'll be her confidant. Her friend. Her lover. She won't turn me away by the time I'm done."

"Mhmm," Kendrick replied uneasily. I could understand his hesitance, in a way. He cared for me. He didn't want to see me get hurt again.

Despite my and Lenora's lack of feelings, the severing of our bond when she rejected me—and then died—was the catalyst for a very long stretch in that dark place we all knew deep down. Normally, we could forget it was there. Let the music drown it out. Let sex and blood fill the void.

Not then. When she died, nothing could fill the hollowness that consumed me. I was truly empty for the first time in what would become my hundred-and-seventy-year-long existence.

The things I'd done as a result were truly . . . horrifying.

While the world didn't know how much some of those events troubled me still, Kendrick did. I'd lost control of myself so thoroughly that it had taken fifty years to find myself again. I wouldn't have been able to without him by my side. Of course he wouldn't want to see me in that place again.

I turned my back on the glass wall overlooking the concrete jungle below.

"This time will be different," I told him, putting my hand on his shoulder.

I was out the door when he quietly replied, "For both our sakes, I hope you're right."

The sounds of orgasms and soft, sultry music followed as I walked out of Bite Me. I took the elevator down and nodded to the club guards when they lowered their eyes and dipped their heads in respect. A quick, fleeting look at their minds told me they were both loyal. The one on the left had joined my clan with his mate for protection. The one on the right was ambitious and hoping to gain power by moving through the ranks. Both were standard reasons for joining and neither were worth a deeper look nor would be considered a cause for concern.

The parking garage was uncharacteristically half empty. Word had gotten around about what had happened to Fury in front of me and the other alphas. It made us look weak. Incompetent. Some people were staying away because they were scared to get caught in the crossfire. Others wanted to sit in the shadows and see how this played out. Either way, Bite Me had dropped in business considerably over the last ten hours, and the walk to my Audi R8 was uneventful. I unlocked my car and opened the door, the scent of leather and chrome enveloping me. I started it up and pulled out onto the road before turning my thoughts to Fury.

The image of her eating steak au poivre with that pompous asshole Dorian filled my mind. I narrowed my eyes and put my foot on the gas, listening to their conversation play out.

"*What do you do for work?*"

"*I work in a prison,*" she said in response. "*Out of state. I'm afraid I can't disclose any details.*"

I chuckled.

"What do you do there?"

"Rehabilitate."

That earned a snort.

While technically, yes, she rehabilitated, her means were certainly unconventional. Humans would never approve of her methods. She would make a fine clan enforcer, however. I mulled that over as I got onto the highway, listening to their conversation in the back of my mind.

Dorian asked her where she came from, what she did, what she liked and what she didn't. For the most part, she gave him half-answers. Bullshit truths that weren't outright lies but they might as well have been.

By the time I got to my apartment on the west side of town, their little dinner had come to a close and he was escorting her to her room. After a few awkward moments and a dismissive goodbye on Fury's part, she was finally alone, and so was I.

I took the elevator up to my penthouse suite after parking. Without turning the lights on, I unbuttoned my shirt and stripped out of it—tossing it over the back of an armchair. My black tattoos reflected in the glass door that led out to the balcony as I padded across the living room and into the kitchen to pour myself a glass of O negative.

At the same time, my mate was stripping out of her clothes for a little *me time.*

Intrigued and already hard at the thought, I took a seat in the armchair and closed my eyes.

Pale, creamy skin filled my vision. She brought the water in the bathtub to a near boil before stepping in. Fury lowered herself into the water and moaned softly, making my cock twitch.

Unable to help myself, I purred, *Need some help?*

CHAPTER 25

I lost my grip on the side of the tub, gasping to scream, and going under the water all at once. I flailed around like a cat tossed in, trying to regain my composure and find my bearings.

Finally, I sat up, wiping the suds and water off my face, and all I could hear was laughter echoing in my head.

"What is going on?" I said out loud, looking around the bathroom.

There was just one problem. No one was there.

I just wanted to offer my assistance to finish what we started earlier.

Ezra. The voice in my head was the vampire.

"I wasn't aware you could read minds."

Not many are. That said, I would've thought something as powerful as Upper Management would do a better job at collecting information for you.

Oh fuck.

He knew about Upper Management . . . which meant . . .

I know everything, or most of it. I've been listening in since you entered my club earlier. Who would've thought that there really is an Afterlife—

"Shut up," I snapped. "I need you to stop talking for, like, ten seconds."

He laughed again, a deep chuckle that reverberated in my skull.

I wanted to scream and claw at my head, but instinct told me that was pointless.

I took deep breaths, sitting in the water of my once relaxing bath. Any attempts I might have made for an orgasm were long gone, scared off by a voice in my head. Literally.

It doesn't have to be that way, he purred in my mind. *You like to be watched. I like to watch. Touch yourself for me. I'll make you see stars.*

My core tightened at his insinuation, and while my body was curiously on board with that suggestion, the part of my brain that recognized I was in *deep* shit said now wasn't the time.

"It doesn't work that way," I said, trying to formulate something meaningful. The only thing that truly came to mind was the obvious...

My mission was a complete and utter failure.

Everything I'd learned about them. Every inch I'd gained with these boys ... men ... was for nothing. Ezra knew my secret. He knew who I was, and why I was here.

How could I fix them now?

It was hard to break someone who knew that was what you were doing.

You've never let that stop you before, the voice in my head taunted. *Every soul you've been assigned, you've told them the truth. That they'd died and gone to Hell. You still broke them.*

"I'm confused," I said into the quiet. "Whose side are you even on?"

Yours. His answer was immediate. Unshakable.

"Why?" I asked. "Is this because of the mate bond? You barely know me. Why not reject me and be done with it if you know why I'm really here?"

Because I don't want to. What you are and why you were sent here don't matter to me.

"I don't understand," I breathed harshly. "It should matter to you. If I break you, it's going to hurt. If I fix you, I'll still have to leave in the end. There's no happy ending for this—"

I don't care.

I rested my forehead against my knees. The water was cooling, but I didn't have it in me to move.

"Then you're a masochist who's signing yourself up for pain."

Maybe I am, his mental voice mused. *You could use that.*

I wanted to bash my head into the tub. His reaction to this wasn't sane.

I wouldn't recommend self-harm . . . unless you're in the mood to talk to Dorian.

"Does Dorian know about this?" I asked aloud into the empty bathroom.

No. Neither does Roman. I've gone to great lengths to keep this particular gift of mine a secret.

"Clearly it's worked since my file didn't say anything about it either. Fucking poltergeists. They have *one* job, and they can't even do that," I grumbled under my breath. I could blame them. That part was easy. And in truth—this wasn't my fault. I didn't fuck up. They did.

Unfortunately, there were no do-overs like when I died. I couldn't go back and restart my mission. In both worlds, time moved linear progression, and the only way I could go was forward.

"Are you going to tell the others?"

Roman and Dorian? No. I enjoy watching you fuck with them too much. Not much rattles that old fae bastard. It'll do him good to have something to focus on.

Well, I suppose as far as mind-reading vampires went, that was about the best I could hope for. I narrowed my eyes, another thought occurring to me.

"What do you want in return?"

Tell me about the Afterlife and Jake from AR. I want to know what it's like being a demon and part of a guild. You spent the last hundred years in an entirely different world. A world no one even knows exists. Tell me about it, and I won't breathe a word of this to anyone.

All things considered that wasn't a bad deal. How many times had I already wanted to talk to Duke about things? Sending the crow wasn't enough, and I couldn't just keep dying. I had to be careful, or too many people would take notice. Having someone who knew—*really knew*—who and what I was could come in handy.

"And if I don't tell you about those things?"

I felt his mental shrug, as if it ran through me. *You think a lot. It's only a matter of time before I'd hear it all, anyway.*

I glowered at the tile wall, feeling obstinate when I knew this was only an illusion of choice. "I could train myself to not think of it. I'll think about Dorian's abs instead."

A feather-soft touch ran down my thigh. I could've sworn it was actually there.

Will you? his taunting, teasing voice whispered through me—followed by the feeling of fingers trailing down my back then over my breast.

I sucked in a sharp breath. "You didn't say you could do this." I gasped as his mental hands ran down my abdomen and over my legs. He touched me everywhere . . . and yet not where I wanted him.

I prefer show versus tell.

I felt his smirk right before a psychic tongue flicked over my nipple. It pebbled instantly, and my legs stiffened.

"Stop," I hissed between my teeth as a moan built in my throat.

The torturous touching stopped, and part of me wished it hadn't.

"You've made your point, and I'll accept the terms of the deal if you're honest with me. I want to know what you can do—and what you know about Roman and Dorian. If you know everything, then you know why I'm here."

We end the world, he said in a far more serious tone. At least he understood the gravity of that.

"Yes, and I have to find a way to prevent that, or everyone dies."

I stood up in the tub, flipping the knob to drain the water. Wrapping a fluffy towel around me, I walked from the bathroom into my room and sat on the bed to dry off.

I'll help you, Fury. Contrary to what the angels in your Afterlife have said, I might be a monster, but I'm not evil. There are shades of gray in everything, but not in this. Whatever happens, I will help you and won't get in the way.

I sighed again, unwrapping myself then squeezing the water from my hair into the cotton towel. I ran a comb through my tangles slowly. "And there are no ulterior motives?"

I didn't say that.

I huffed a laugh and tossed the towel onto the floor. Reaching over, I clicked the light off and pulled my legs up and under the soft covers. "I suppose I should've expected that. You like to play games, and I didn't need the file to know that bit of information."

His deep laugh filled my mind, and sleep washed over me, begging to pull me under. My thoughts slowed as I started to drift.

Sleep tight, kitten. You and I are going to get to know each other. And lucky for me, you can't lie.

No. No, I couldn't.

CHAPTER 26

Banging jarred me awake, and for a brief second, I thought I was back in the demon dorms where Barb the Bitter and her ex were at it again, fucking in the early hours loud enough to wake the dead.

I blinked twice and rubbed the sleep from my eyes.

The silk sheets that pooled around my waist and the billowy white curtains reminded me this was most definitely *not* the dorm.

"Sir, the lady is sleeping—"

"She's been asleep for eighteen hours. Either she drank herself into a coma, she's dead again, or she fled. I'm going in."

I lifted my head at the sound of Dorian's voice. The door opened, slamming into the wall, and cracking the plaster. The big, broody fae stepped in, mouth open to yell at me when he caught sight of my naked body and pert breasts. The ladies were standing to attention this morning under his watchful gaze.

"I—you—"

"At a loss for words?" I mused, reaching up to stretch

my arms. His amber gaze turned hard. "Color me surprised. When was the last time that happened? Hundred years ago? Two?"

"At least a hundred and fifty," came James' weak reply from the door. To his credit, he kept his eyeballs off my tits, instead focusing on the patterned ceiling fifteen feet above us.

"A hundred and fifty," I repeated. "Well, that's gotta be a new record."

"Fury," Dorian said through clenched teeth. "Why are you naked?"

"Because I bathed and then realized I didn't have any clothes." I shrugged. "Besides, I sleep naked most of the time. I've lived alone for—" My words fell short, and my jaw snapped shut. Nope. I was not starting off the morning accidentally giving away my age. He'd undoubtedly figure it out eventually, but I needed to keep him guessing. Especially when I had Ezra to deal with.

Dorian sighed. Instead of pressing for what I'd been about to say, he asked, "Why didn't you open the door when I knocked?"

"You call that knocking?" I replied with a lifted eyebrow.

James let out a choked sound, making Dorian press his lips together.

Hmm. Angry fae. Do I poke or do I let it lie?

"Answer the question."

"If you must know, I was asleep until about two seconds before you opened the door. In case you'd forgotten, I was kidnapped and drugged at the ass crack of dawn yesterday, and I didn't get to sleep until late."

"Why not?" A pucker formed between his brows in confusion as he stared at me unhappily. His chiseled jawline was doing bad things to my already wound-up body.

"I had to take care of some things."

"What things?"

James tried to come to the rescue, reading between the lines where his dense-as-fuck master could not. "I think the lady—"

"Can tell me herself," Dorian said in a hard tone. "What things?"

I looked between the two of them. James' cheeks were beet red. He glanced down from the ceiling momentarily to flash me a look of apology. Meanwhile, Dorian stared coldly, my tits forgotten.

I grabbed the end of the sheet and tossed it aside, slipping my bare legs down the bed. My feet touched the cool floor, and a chill spread over me—though that might've been Dorian's gaze.

"I was talking to the voices in my head, and then they offered to give me an orgasm," I replied before walking into the bathroom and closing the door firmly behind me.

I heard Dorian's muffled complaints through the crack but tuned it out for the most part.

I recall you turning me down, Ezra chimed in. Figured he'd been listening in.

"He doesn't know that," I said under my breath as I rummaged through the cabinets to find an unopened toothbrush and toothpaste.

"What was that?" Dorian called, and I knew damn well he could hear me crystal clear at this range.

"Just talking to the voices," I called back, before flipping the water on.

Ezra's dark chuckle in my mind drowned out the sound of the faucet.

Just think it. You don't have to speak. I'll know. Dorian's old, and I have no doubt he's seen mind readers before. He'll grow suspicious if you keep speaking aloud.

I swished a mouthful of water and then spat. *Don't you have a job to be doing? Poisoners to catch?* I thought in his general direction. Least I felt like it was. I wasn't the mind reader here.

I'm multitasking. It's one of my many admirable qualities.

I rolled my eyes but got no response. I guess he took the hint and stepped out. Or he just made me think he did. There was no telling until he made his presence known, and I didn't have it in me to keep worrying over it. I wiped my mouth with the back of my hand and walked over to the door.

I turned the knob and cracked it open. "While I'm not modest, I'm pretty sure James doesn't feel like seeing my naked ass all day. Care to find me some clothes?"

Dorian turned to glare at me, and clothes appeared on my body.

I blinked, staring down at myself.

Damn. Those files really didn't say shit, did they?

I opened the door slowly. "Thank you," I said, still a bit wary. He'd dressed me in pants, a long-sleeved shirt, and a white puffy vest. The only problem was that it was summer. In Houston.

"We going somewhere?"

"Yes, I have urgent business to attend to, and you're coming with me."

"Oh? I am?" I questioned. "Where?"

He grabbed my elbow in a tight but not painful grip. The fabric between us was a stiff barrier, but my skin still warmed beneath his touch. "My home. My *real* home."

Then the ground disappeared, and my heart started to

hammer. I felt hot and cold. My vision turned black. Solid ground couldn't rise up soon enough, but when it did, I collapsed onto my knees. My hands fell with me as Dorian released me upon landing.

I registered the cold first. It was bone deep, a chill that wouldn't lift. The stone beneath me was frigid to the touch, like ice, but harder. Colder.

The next thing I registered?

The cliff I was kneeling on that overlooked the ocean. A salty spray whipped my face as the waves crashed against the unyielding base.

"Welcome to the Isle of Glass. You might know it as Avalon."

CHAPTER 27

Dorian burst through the double doors at the front of his castle, and I followed in his shadow, taking in the scenery. I held my hands behind my back, looking around at the opulent rugs and decor. Above us, grand iron chandeliers hung from the ceilings, their candles giving off a magically enhanced light.

Fae bustled about, left and right, obviously in a rush. I knew fae weren't all as grouchy as Dorian, so it was clear they were upset about something. Maybe it was that his sudden return had ruined their short vacation from him. I could see that.

"Tristan," he yelled into the foyer before moving swiftly down the hall.

Artwork and ancient tapestries lined the walls, and I wanted to get a better look at them when we weren't in a hurry to go . . . wherever we were going.

A beautiful fae man appeared next to us, walking in step with Dorian. A navy uniform hugged his lean frame. Olive skin accentuated the contours of his high cheekbones, and his purposeful blue eyes never once gazed in my direction.

"Sir, Elaine and the guards are in your study awaiting your instruction," he said.

"Which wards were tripped?" Dorian asked.

"The northwest corner of the island, sir," Tristan replied. He waited a moment before adding, "They found tracks as well, sir. Footsteps."

Dorian's pace slowed a fraction, clearly affected by that new piece of information.

I pursed and twisted my lips, not understanding much of what was happening.

We crossed into what was apparently Dorian's study when he stopped suddenly, turning around.

"What?" I asked, looking behind me to see what he was looking at.

"Tristan, take her upstairs to the green sitting room."

"Wait a minute, you're the one who said I was coming here with you," I argued, crossing my arms, and jutting out my hip. "Can you make up your mind?"

He stepped toward me, and said, "Not now." Looking to who I assumed was his second, or a really handsome butler, he added, "I'll call for you when I'm done. Keep her company." He stepped back into his office where I saw a tall, beautiful woman in armor and six male guards standing at attention.

Then he shut the door in my face.

I spun on my heel, taking in my surroundings and my new comrade. "Okay, hot stuff. Looks like you're my new babysitter. Show me around."

A look of shock crossed Tristan's face before a laugh escaped him. "You are most certainly *not* what I was expecting," he said, as he began walking down the hallway.

"Don't sift out of here. I can't follow," I told him,

making sure he didn't just disappear and leave me lost in a castle.

"I know." He held his hands behind his back, turning a corner and going up a set of stairs.

Since my files were absolute garbage, I needed to know what I was dealing with, and I had to do it casually without being obvious.

"Reading my mind, or can you just read my powers?" I teased, playfully elbowing him.

He scrunched his eyebrows together. "Fae can't read minds."

Well, thank the stars for that. A bit of tension I was holding in my shoulders relaxed. If he'd said otherwise, I would've had to consider the option of jumping off the impressive cliff outside and just calling the whole thing off.

"Ah, so you're saying my lack of powers are really just that obvious," I said, taking a turn down the hallway and following his lead. The place was a maze.

He stopped. "Ms. Fury—"

"Just Fury."

He hummed. "Fury . . ." I nodded, and he continued. "Dorian has told me about you. I know you're an unknown supernatural, that you are his mate, and that you're quite smart, and dare I say, cunning. As his second, he has filled me in."

I cocked an eyebrow and tilted my head. "Point taken, Tristan."

He smiled slightly, dipping his head, and turned to continue walking.

"So, where are we going, or did you plan on walking me around until he's done with the knights of the round table in there?"

He huffed a laugh. "I was taking you to a sitting room where you would feel comfortable waiting."

I started to respond but stopped short when I saw some of the tapestries lining the walls. Tristan took notice and returned to me. Standing still, I stared up at the grand and detailed needlework. I looked left to see that I'd passed two others, then I moved down to look at them.

"They're quite beautiful, aren't they?" he asked me, breaking the silence as he stood next to me.

"They are," I said, drawn in for reasons I couldn't explain. Something about them called to me. "Who made them?"

"Many different fae. They tell the story of our people. War, peace, love, triumph, loss. The stories you know in the human world are nothing compared to the truth of Avalon, or the fae." Tristan looked at the tapestries with reverence and respect.

I was itching to touch it, and that made me want to know more about it.

"Somehow, I can't picture Dorian doing needlework in his downtime," I mumbled, as my fae babysitter coughed to cover the barest hint of a laugh at his sour leader's expense. I pointed at the one in front of us. "Will you tell me about this one?"

Tristan turned his attention to me and smiled. Pointing at the intricate border, he said, "Here. If you follow this pattern, the knotwork used tells us this story was from the seventh century." His finger trailed the symbols in the corners and my eyes followed. "Those symbols are—"

"Pictish."

He looked over at me with his eyebrows raised in surprise.

I shrugged. "I'm not much of a people person, so I read a lot."

"Well, you're right. They're Pictish. This one tells the story of a hunter's family. See the animals?" he asked, pointing to various figures.

I nodded, moving slowly to the next one. "And this?"

"Ah, I've always loved this one. This is the Wild Hunt," he said, his own eyes roaming over the tapestry in admiration.

Never before had any kind of art spoken to me or kept me enthralled to this degree. I couldn't explain it. I stopped in front of another as we crept down the hallway to the sitting room.

An embroidered fae with glowing amber eyes stood out in the middle. The golden thread used matched the color exactly, and I felt like I was looking at Dorian, just without the chill he managed to elicit all the time.

The scene on the tapestry pulled my gaze away from the center fae, and what I saw was . . . curious.

Pain and . . . destruction.

"Tristan?" I nodded to the one I was in front of. "What happened here?"

I hoped he'd give me some insight into the story being told. Did it tell me something about his powers? Was it something far more sinister? Was it representative of Dorian just being a moody prick?

Any of those things were possible, especially the latter. Without words, it was up for interpretation. That was what pissed me off about art sometimes. Sometimes a flower was just a flower. Why did it have to also be a vagina? The tapestry said something about Dorian. I needed to know what.

Tristan hesitated. "I'm not sure I'm the one who should

explain this particular piece. I believe you'll need to ask Dorian that yourself."

"Oh, c'mon. It's just a story, right?" I flung my hand out toward the wall. "I'm not asking for the password to the secret vaults."

He shook his head.

"What's she asking for?" Dorian asked, appearing next to me.

"Nice of you to join us," I said. "Tristan was just telling me about some of these tapestries, but he got cold feet when I asked him about this one." I jutted my thumb at the wall next to me.

Dorian's eyes darkened when he saw the one in question. "Tristan, will you ask a steward to bring us the order I requested from the kitchen? Have it sent to the sitting room, please."

"Yes, sir." He inclined his head. Meeting my eyes, he dipped his head again. "Fury. It was a pleasure." And then he disappeared.

"You really know how to run 'em off, don't you?"

Dorian's cold stare gave away nothing.

I sighed. "Cool, if you don't feel like talking to me, maybe you could take me back to Houston and ignore me there? It's about the same."

"I'm not ignoring you. I'm thinking."

I raised my eyebrows. "This is thinking? Well, hot damn. What does it look like when you're dragging someone halfway across the world to not speak to them? Asking for a friend."

He put his hands in his pockets and cleared his throat. "Will you join me in the sitting room now?"

I walked past him, waving my hand. "It was supposed to be green, right?" I asked, seeing a set of open double doors that led to a large room I assumed had been prepared for me.

I whistled softly when I entered. The fireplace was huge. So big I could've walked into it. Its heat filled the room, warming the air and ripping away the cold that seemed to follow me. Green and cream oriental rugs covered the stone floors. Artwork with ornate gold framing adorned the walls, and oak bookcases held what had to be a thousand books.

A table near two wingback chairs had a silver tray sitting on top. On it were plates covered with silver domes, and what looked like a wine decanter and two glasses.

Dorian came up behind me and gestured for me to sit.

I twisted my lips, thinking about him telling me he wasn't a gentleman. If it quacks like a duck . . .

"Thanks." I reached for the decanter, then hesitated. I really didn't like wine all that much. I wanted something less fruity and more . . . hard liquor.

"It's fae wine," Dorian said, sensing my dilemma. When he saw the question in my eye, he added, "It's much better than the swill humans drink. And far more potent, so please don't guzzle it like you're trying to impress the rest of the frat house."

I glared at him and poured a large serving. I raised my glass in a toast and took a drink.

Damn. He wasn't kidding. Potent was an under-statement.

He sat next to me, pouring his own glass, though it was a much smaller serving.

From our seats, on the opposite side of the wall, was a painting. It was placed as the focal point of the room, as though one would sit in these very chairs simply to look at it. She was a stunningly beautiful fae with white hair and soulful blue eyes.

"Who's that?" I asked, raising my eyebrows in the direction of the painting while I took another sip of wine.

Dorian sighed and raised the goblet to his lips, sipping his wine, taking his time to savor it before swallowing. He traced the tip of his glass with his finger, drawing out the silence between us. He inhaled deeply before he said, "My daughter."

CHAPTER 28

I choked on my wine. That happened. Probably hadn't ever happened before, but if anything could cause me to choke on alcohol, it was hearing that Dorian had a daughter.

The poltergeists were fired. Not that I *could* fire them. But *if* I could . . .

"Where is she?" I asked, looking around.

Part of my mind imagined a little girl with a white dress and pink ribbons running around the corner and jumping into her father's arms. But the picture before me wasn't a little girl. She was a young adult. Who knew how old, really, but she didn't look as old as the other fae did when they stopped aging.

"She's here, but she won't be coming to join us," Dorian answered, staring into the fireplace. "She's in stasis."

What the hell was that?

"In stasis?" I asked. "Care to explain a little bit more there? I'm not exactly up to date on fae culture." Apparently.

He took a drink. "Stasis is an in-between for fae. An

undisturbed, dreamless sleep where we skip generations of time—centuries—in peace. It's rejuvenating, and it gives us time to . . . take a break from the living world. We live a long time . . ." He trailed off, staring at nothing in particular.

I waited to see if he was going to continue, and I shifted my weight in the chair so I could face him. When he didn't speak again, I nudged his arm gently. "Dorian?"

"Hmm?" He looked up, meeting my gaze.

"You didn't finish. You said, 'we live a long time' and then you stopped." I could tell by the look on his face there was more to say.

"We do. We live a long time, and it can become monotonous. Exhausting. Joyless. At a certain point, it's just . . ." He took a moment, closing his eyes and inhaling a deep breath. "Existing. So we enter stasis to rest, and then we can return to the world refreshed."

The weight of his words were heavy, and our conversation at dinner the night before echoed in my mind. I hadn't understood why he seemed so cold until that moment. To live so long and just feel like you were taking up space in the world and nothing more . . .

I'd only been dead for a hundred and three years. It was a drop in the bucket for him. But I had to wonder, was that what my afterlife would look like? The ancients I knew didn't seem to act this way. Vlad was pretty content, which said a lot for a guy who'd lived during the Middle Ages. I wasn't sure about my own future, and I didn't like that I was suddenly thinking about it.

I chewed on the inside of my cheek while I thought, my eyes roaming, then coming to rest on the portrait again. "You said your daughter is in stasis?"

He nodded. "Yes." Something shimmered in his eyes. A memory. A longing. It was clear as day.

"You miss her, don't you?"

His voice was quiet when he answered, "Every day that goes by." He took a small sip of his wine, then rubbed his thumb up and down the side of his glass. "That's why we're here."

Was she coming out of stasis? I immediately questioned if this was about to become a weird situation where I met the daughter of a fae I'd planned to break. That wouldn't be awkward or anything.

Dorian read the look on my face and shook his head. "You misunderstand. Tristan came to inform me that wards on the island were triggered. Someone came here, and they were looking for something."

"Here? On . . . in Avalon? I didn't think humans knew it existed. Surely, you have it concealed. If whatever enchantments you have didn't work, I'm sure the weather would turn them right off. I thought Avalon was supposed to be green and pretty. Not so cold and bitter that nomads in Siberia would vacation here for the warmth. If someone ended up here, it was an accident, and they were looking for a phone to call for help."

He glared at me, and I shrugged.

"You might be right. It has happened over the years a time or two. However, this time is different. Elaine and her guards found footsteps. Whoever they belonged to, they had purpose, and they were entirely too close for comfort."

He gave me a disapproving look as I poured more wine. I returned it. I didn't need him judging me. "What were they too close to?"

"Where we keep those in stasis," he said, his tone turning somber.

"I don't understand. If they accidentally woke people up, couldn't they just go back to sleep?" Unless someone was there to kill the sleeping fae . . . but that sounded insane. Who even knew where to look for them? Or that they went into stasis?

"It doesn't work that way. It's more complicated than that." His expression looked simultaneously pained and angry. I couldn't get a read on him.

"Uncomplicate it for me," I suggested.

He chose instead to look at me, contemplating something. I'd counted to thirty-seven in my head before he finally spoke again. "I believe you'll think less of me if I do."

That statement shocked me more than I would've expected. Warring parts of my mind said I wouldn't—and another part said this was information I needed.

"Do you care if I do?" I asked, skirting around his statement. "You may claim I'm your mate, Dorian, but I'm not sure you care one way or another what I think."

The tiniest hint of a smile peeked on one side of his lips. "I do find you fascinating, Fury. Know that."

Skirting around my statement as well. Interesting.

"Why don't you try me?"

He sighed. "Lyra, my daughter, can't wake from stasis. She didn't go into it willingly."

I sat back in my chair, waiting for the ball to drop. What had he done?

As though he'd heard my question, he said, "I had to."

His icy exterior broke for a fraction of a second. The tiniest crack in his voice and slip in his tone. It was barely noticeable, and a human never would've caught it. But I did. He was . . . heartbroken. Somehow, I felt it. This ache in my chest I couldn't explain. I knew what emotional pain felt like, and I knew this pain wasn't my own.

"She was mentally unstable. I had to put her in stasis for her safety, and for the safety of others," he finished.

Was this what the risk witches had seen? Dorian, leader of the fae, would help end the world . . . because he'd forced his daughter into stasis? Would he do it to others? It was certainly unorthodox. Then again, so was I. Feeling torn between how to view that revelation, I sat quietly. To compel someone to stop living their life, forcing them into what was essentially a coma against their will . . . it was monstrous on a grand scale. And yet, I saw what it did to him. His mate had died, and he was alone, left with a mentally unstable child he had to protect. And what does a parent do? I wouldn't know. Some deeper part of me that I never spoke to anymore knew that I would have done anything to keep my child safe. Maybe that was what he had done . . . and that didn't seem so monstrous.

Dorian broke my train of thought when he spoke again. "Change how you see me?"

I huffed a humorless laugh. "I honestly don't know what to think. I can't imagine having to make that choice. I'm, um . . . I'm sorry you had to."

His head tilted to the side in surprise as though he was searching for a lie in my words and coming up short. It was probably the most honest I'd been with him. No false truths or twisted words. His lips were tight, and then he slightly dipped his head in thanks before he stood up and walked across the room, coming to a stop in front of the fireplace.

I took a deep drink and then another. I felt dizzy, then remembered how strong fae wine was. I probably should've eaten something. I'd been asleep for the entire night and most of the day before he'd decided to drag me to the Arctic Circle. I reached over and took the silver dome off a plate in front of us to find a spicy chicken burger with fries.

I looked up. "You made this for me?"

He turned. "Well, no, I didn't. I had the kitchen make it for you. You said you enjoyed it at Roxanne's."

His random thoughtfulness surprised me. I smiled at him and dug in. I downed the entire thing in six bites. After stuffing my face with fries, I dipped a couple in the wine. It wasn't the best taste. Better to drink the wine instead. The decanter was empty, so I looked around to see if there was any more.

Dorian caught my eye and realized what I was looking for. "I can have them bring some hot tea, if you'd like."

I frowned. "Not exactly what I was looking for."

The look of disapproval came again. "You drink too much."

Whatever moment we'd shared earlier was gone, and the icy wall that Dorian surrounded himself with was back up.

"It's not as bad as it sounds. You should try it sometime," I said, eating another fry.

He glanced at her portrait, then went back to looking at the fire. "I have." A few moments passed before he drank the rest of his wine then threw the glass into the fire, the delicate crystal splintering as it collided with the stone. The sound of it shattering echoed in my ears.

I opened my mouth when his phone rang, and he answered it.

At the same time, Ezra whispered in my mind, *See you soon.*

"They have them," Dorian said, putting his phone in his jacket pocket. "Time to go."

CHAPTER 29

Fae wine and sifting did not go together.

We landed on the bank of a river outside an unmarked warehouse where I doubled at the waist and emptied my stomach.

"I told you not to drink so much," Dorian said, completely unsympathetic.

I wiped my mouth with the back of my hand and glared up at him. "It's not my drinking that's the problem," I growled. It wasn't completely accurate, but blaming it on the wine would just highlight my crutch . . . one I'd found myself leaning on more and more since returning to Earth. Also, Dorian would be right, and I couldn't have that.

"Hm, could've fooled me," he answered dryly.

I hauled myself up and rubbed at my tender stomach while he strode away. "What about my clothes?" I called out, motioning to the long sleeves and puffy vest. I already had boob sweat, and I was pretty sure the tiny hairs around my face had started to curl.

Dorian glanced at me over his shoulder and the clothes disappeared, replaced by a loose tank top and linen shorts. I eyed the strappy new wedges, noting that he'd put me in heels.

I lifted an eyebrow at him in question.

A subtle, almost non-existent smirk was all I got in reply before he continued.

Fucker.

At least he had good taste in shoes. The clothes weren't exactly my style, but they were light and airy, letting my skin breathe in the humidity instead of dying from it.

I followed him, picking up the pace when he reached the door. Two guards stood outside once again. They were different vampires, but still seemed to be on the up-and-up and didn't question my presence, instead just nodding at me in respect.

We entered the darkened warehouse. The sounds of screaming and bones cracking were the first thing to greet my ears.

Dorian glowered in the low light, following the noise down two rows of unmarked crates.

Our two poisoners sat back-to-back in plastic chairs. In front of one of them, Roman stood with bleeding knuckles and a grim expression. Ezra was off to the side, leaning against a wall of crates. His sharp eyes caught sight of me first.

I opened my mouth to say something when a shadow moved. I turned my head to catch the flapping of wings. Hades landed on my right shoulder; his beady eyes narrowed on me.

I groaned.

"Don't act so surprised to see me," the crow muttered in annoyance.

"This isn't my surprised face," I replied. "I was hoping you'd be roadkill by now, pigeon."

"I'm a bird. I don't walk across the street. I would have to be supremely stupid to get hit by a car—" He broke off sharply at the look on my face. Yup. The insult had finally hit.

Hades let out an irritated squawk in my ear. "Keep it up. I'll shit in your liquor."

"Do it and we'll find out how many lives you have, birdie. I'm not afraid of going hunting. You'd look nice mounted on Dorian's wall."

With that, Hades took off, flapping his wings and knocking me in the head as he went to oversee us from the safety of the crates.

It was only then that I noticed all eyes on me. My mates and my killers.

How sweet.

"You have a talking crow?" Dorian asked.

"Lost a bet with a witch. Got stuck with the pigeon," I muttered, repeating the lie I'd told Roxanne and hoping Dorian wouldn't call me out for it. It may as well have been true. I would not have picked an asshole crow for a go-between. He was useless at his actual job. Like the poltergeists. God, when I was done here, I was going to put in a complaint with Jake about giving the Afterlife an overhaul because there were way too many slackers not doing their damn jobs.

Ezra chuckled, only a second too late to be laughing at my comment. Must've been listening in.

I'm always listening, kitten. Your thoughts . . . they're refreshing.

"Shouldn't we be interrogating these guys?" I asked, clapping my hands to bring us all back to the important thing: the people trying to kill me.

"It looks like the wolf got started without us," Dorian said, a chill entering his voice.

Ezra shrugged. "I gave Roman a heads-up before calling you. I knew you'd sift in and do whatever you wanted. Besides, the dog needed to get out his aggression."

Roman bristled at Ezra's jab.

I rolled my eyes, ignoring the shifter's comeback insult. While the one he'd been working on looked pretty roughed up, the other did not. His eyes were sharp. Keen. He watched me, his lips pulled back in a snide expression.

"Did you get anything out of him?" I asked Roman, jutting my chin toward Pulpface, as he would hereby be dubbed until his inevitable death. It was healing quickly because he was a vampire, but still resembled a misshapen lump of bloodied meat more than a face.

"No," Ezra replied before Roman could. "He won't talk."

Their minds are also being blocked somehow. Spells can do that, which implies they're working with a witch, he added in my mind.

Do they know you can read minds? I asked.

Unclear, but also highly unlikely.

Hm. Looked like this wasn't a cut-and-dried hit-and-run. No one would've bothered with that sort of protection if it were.

I moved toward them, walking around them both, hands behind my back. They usually started to sweat when I didn't dive right into questioning.

"We'll see about that," Dorian said, tugging the sleeves of his shirt up his forearms. "Fury, you may want to step out—"

"Not a chance," I said before he could finish. "Besides, I have a feeling you'll need me."

"Doubtful," the fae replied with complete and utter arrogance.

I stepped back and motioned for him to come forward. Dorian knelt in front of the non-pummeled vampire. His amber eyes glowed brighter for a moment. "Why did you try to kill Fury?"

Our vampire glared back with a hatred in his eyes I recognized all too well. It was almost like being back in the Afterlife.

Vampire Number Two reared back to slam his head into Dorian's nose but the fae saw it coming and caught him by the throat.

I tilted my head, curious about his method.

"I said, *why did you try to kill Fury*?" His eyes burned brighter this time.

Still no response.

I shot Ezra a questioning look.

He can make those weaker than him do what he wants by commanding it. They should have no choice but to answer.

That was terrifying . . . and intriguing.

He could've tried to use that power to make me spill my secrets.

He hadn't.

I'm not the only one who likes games. Dorian's just forgotten the thrill. He's finding it again, with you.

Goosebumps formed on the exposed skin of my arms, and Roman saw them, his eyebrows drawing together in concern. "If you need to step out, no one will judge you—"

"Oh, for fuck's sake," I grumbled. "Roman, I'm fine. Dorian, get on with it or step aside." I motioned with my hand and then crossed my arms.

Dorian narrowed his eyes at me.

"You think you can make him talk?" he asked, not questioning my abilities, but instead inciting a challenge.

A part of me knew I shouldn't rise to the occasion. He was only doing this because he wanted to learn more about me, after all. But, well, the thing was—I was a demon. This was what I did. While I didn't *love* the Afterlife, I truly didn't mind my job. There was a sort of comfort in it.

After so long *rehabilitating* souls, my fingers itched to be back at it.

I couldn't handle the guys that way, but these schmucks? They were getting in the way of my actual job. They were no one. Just a means to an end, whether I got the answers I needed or not.

Nameless, faceless vampires meant to do the dirty work and take the fall.

They didn't seem particularly confident, which made me think they knew there was no getting out.

The real mastermind wasn't going to save them.

And yet, they didn't seem overly fearful either.

A curious combination.

Instead of answering him, I strode forward. He backed away, giving me space.

"Pain will not work on us," Pulpface said, his jaw finally healed enough to speak. "Neither will fear. We have nothing to lose. You can break us, bind us, but you will not win."

"I know." I nodded slowly. "You're not hired help. This is personal. You'll see this through to the end," I said quietly.

Vampire Number Two blinked, evidently a little surprised by my fast deductions.

"I admire that, in a way. The ability to carry out orders

and do what you say you will. It's hard to find good lackeys these days." And, man, did I know it.

"Who said we were taking orders?" Vampire Two chimed in.

I smiled but kept my face devoid of any true emotion. He paled. "You're here. Whoever orchestrated this, it wasn't you two. Someone smart enough to cover their tracks doesn't get caught. Not easily, anyhow. If I had to guess, I'd say you're just the beginning of a problem for me. But to what end?" I mused aloud, watching their reactions closely.

"We have seen the truth," Pulpface said. "We know what you are. We know what you will do." He recited the rhetoric smoothly, like a true zealot. For a fleeting moment, I wondered if he knew.

"Oh?" I questioned. "What am I?"

"A devil," Vampire Two spat. "Straight from Hell."

If I hadn't already considered the possibility that he knew what I was, my heart might've skipped a beat. But instead of giving myself away, I smiled. "That's a new one. I like it. So I'm a devil from Hell, and that's why you want me dead? Seems a bit hypocritical for vampires."

"He told us you'd do this," Pulpface said.

He. Now that drew my interest.

"Do what?" I asked, instead of poking at the more obvious question. People tended to reveal more when you didn't do exactly as they expected. Unpredictability threw them off.

"Gaslight us," he grunted.

"Gaslight?" I repeated, unable to help the chuckle. "I haven't said you're crazy yet, but could you truly blame me after you tried to kill me?"

"We know the truth," Vampire Two said again. There

was some sort of resolution on his face. As if he were ready for something.

"You keep saying that. Do you mind enlightening me?"

While I'd prepared myself for the slight possibility that they somehow knew I was a demon, I hadn't considered what would happen next. Nothing could've prepared me for the words that came out of his mouth.

"You're going to end the world," Pulpface whispered cruelly.

I froze. Shock filled me, though I quickly hid it.

"But we are not the ones to stop you. We're only the messengers."

"What's the message?" Dorian said, finally choosing to speak at the very moment it seemed I'd lost my voice.

I'd barely recovered when they both turned to look at me.

Whatever they had to say, it had to be good.

Or in this case, so very bad.

They spoke in unison. "Welcome back, Sunny."

My face blanked. My heart dropped. I stepped forward, wrenching Vamp Two from his seat—despite the fact that he'd been chained there. I grasped him by his front and pulled hard enough the metal bent and squealed.

"What did you say?" I whispered low, my control hinging on non-existent for the first time in a very long time.

Instead of an answer, I got a bloody smile and a rasping laugh.

Then blood started pouring from every orifice of his body.

It stained his eyes and ran down his cheeks.

It leaked from his ears, dripping onto his black T-shirt.

It gushed from his nose as if something were forcibly emptying him of it.

He was dead in the time it took for me to drop him. So was his buddy, by the looks of it.

My hands fell to my sides, clenched into fists. I bit the inside of my cheek, tasting blood. Those words replayed in my mind even though the messengers were dead.

"What the—" Roman started.

"Spell." Ezra sighed. "They must've just been waiting to trigger it."

Mentally, I was fading. Receding. The desire to fight or flee was surfacing.

Bile climbed back up my throat . . .

"Who's Sunny?" Dorian asked.

I wanted to tell him now wasn't the time. Not to push this. In the same way his daughter was off-limits, so was this. But I couldn't even say that. "No one."

"Bullshit," he said, calling me out. Little did he know, it was the wrong time to make a stand. "Is your real name Sunny?"

My breathing grew thin. Not frantic but panicked all the same.

I strode up to him and tilted my head back.

"I'm only going to tell you this once, so listen closely." I closed what little gap was still between us until we were only inches apart. "My name is Fury. You can call me that or any number of things, honestly, I don't particularly care. But if you ever call me Sunny, it'll be the last word you say."

With that, I stepped around him and started down the aisle of crates. I only paused when I reached the end, looking up to see Hades staring down at me, unmoving. The crow had heard, and I could see he was unsettled by the revelation. He angled his head, and I nodded once in confirmation, jerking my head to the side toward the exit. Hades had a job to do. As he took flight, I turned, peering at the guys over my shoulder. "It's time to switch. I'm going with Ezra today."

If my words hurt him, he didn't let it show. Dorian's face turned as cold as I felt. "Very well."

I walked out of the warehouse without another word, and I didn't look back.

CHAPTER 30
EZRA

Fury's mind was racing a million miles an hour. Images clashed. Memories attempted to surface. She battled them, trying to stuff them all down.

I sighed heavily.

"I see her time with you hasn't done much to soften either of your demeanors," I quipped to Dorian.

The fae bastard looked torn between chasing after her and leaving it be. I needed to divert his attention. "She's hiding something," he replied, ignoring my comment entirely.

"And which of us isn't hiding things from her?" I said quietly. That did the trick.

He turned away from staring at the spot where she'd rounded the corner and disappeared from sight.

"That's—" Roman started. I already knew what he would say without needing to read his mind.

"It's not different. Neither of you like it. *That* is the only difference."

"People are trying to kill her for it," Dorian said.

"People try to kill us all the time. At least my people do."

I shrugged, feigning disinterest in them. "There will always be a threat, but something tells me our little kitten has claws. Push her too much, and I suspect she might actually use them on you."

Something I wasn't opposed to watching, though I'd much rather she used them on me—preferably while I was balls deep inside her.

"Some people need pushing," Dorian replied in a dark voice.

"And how well did that work out for you? Last I checked, she's opting to stay with me—but what do I know?" I nodded once in their direction. "Now if you'll excuse me—"

"Do you think they were telling the truth?" the wolf said.

I froze mid-stride. "You think she's a devil sent from Hell?" I said mockingly. "Or that she's come to end the world?"

"I didn't say—" Roman blustered, though Dorian was notably silent. Knowing that asshole, he was waiting for me to slip. While Roman was young and still prone to displays of emotion, Dorian was a more cunning sort.

"No, you didn't *think*," I sneered. "Really, look at the two of you. Dorian's being a demanding prick when something happened here that clearly triggered her. Meanwhile, you're over there listening to the words of two very obviously brainwashed puppets." I shook my head, completely unremorseful for gaslighting them both. "It's no wonder she chose me, given the options."

I skimmed the surface thoughts in his mind. Unlike Dorian, who either had a natural resistance to my talents or had a block put on himself before I met him, Roman was an open book. Anger and guilt swirled inside him as he warred with the wolf.

"Whether she chose you or not, you'll still need to trade with Mikaelson before the summit," Dorian said. "I expect to be taking her back during that time. Try to make sure she doesn't die or run off before then."

The bastard sifted out before either Roman or I could reply.

"I'll be in touch when she's ready," I said over my shoulder, walking to the exit with my car keys in hand. "Oh, and you may want to work on shit with your wolf before then. If you keep trying to protect her, you'll be the one who gets hurt."

CHAPTER 31

Welcome back, Sunny.

Those words played on repeat in my mind. A never-ending loop of anxiety and confusion. For the first time in a very long time, I felt incredibly lost and more than a little angry.

Because someone—somewhere out there—knew about me.

Who I used to be.

The victim of domestic abuse.

The housewife from the roaring twenties who was depressed and browbeaten, living her shitty life in a shitty world where women's only roles were to cook and clean and please their husbands. Nothing more than a prize to be won. A trophy to show off. I got married, and he carted me off, locking me inside a little yellow house with a white picket fence. A façade. A cage. My prison . . . with nothing but liquor to ease the physical and mental pain and suffering. It may have been my husband who abused me, but it was society that allowed it. The outlook that women were property and meant to be loyal as dogs wasn't new or specific to him.

It was a mentality as old as time.

But then I'd died. I'd stepped outside time, pushing that past as far away from me as I could. Stuffing it down so deep that I would never have to see it again. I broke the glass ceiling and became the best damn demon in the After-life. I was so good even Upper Management wanted me. They'd sent me here to do a job . . . one I was now fairly certain I was failing.

I threaded my hands through my hair and pulled.

When had things gotten so complicated?

Was it truly during the interrogation? Or before that?

When Dorian told me I drank too much, I felt called out and seen for the first time.

When Ezra spoke to me until I fell asleep, I felt less alone.

When Roman spoke of protecting me, I felt guilt about what I was doing to him when all he cared about was my safety. When had anyone besides Duke ever cared about my safety?

Fuck me, this mission was doomed from the very beginning.

Kitten, Ezra's mental voice prodded me lightly, but not gently.

"Go away," I grumbled, lying down in the giant white bed. The ceiling fan hummed as it blasted cool air at my face, pushing loose hairs over my face and around my eyes.

No can do. I've given you time to brood, but you're spiraling.

Spiraling? I narrowed my eyes at the door that led to the rest of his penthouse.

Would you rather I say you're being overly dramatic? Don't get me wrong, I love a good moping session, but you're beating yourself up for shit that isn't your fault.

"Go away," I huffed, throwing a pillow at the door. It exploded in a shower of feathers.

Oops.

That wasn't nice.

"You're not nice. You're invading my privacy by being in my head, and I can't even get away from it. Now's really not the time to test me, Fangs."

Fangs? He mentally scoffed.

"I should be calling you stalker right now. Don't push your luck."

Look. Ezra sighed. *In most cases, I can simply tune it all out. Even if I try to ignore your thoughts, though, I find it incredibly difficult the closer we are. It's a side effect of you being my mate.*

I rolled my eyes. "Well, it's not like *I* can control it, nor do I have a witch on hand to help me like those fuckers who poisoned me did."

Silence wrapped around me for a suspended moment. I thought Ezra might've gotten the hint. Then he asked, *Do you want to talk about it?*

"Fuck no," I groaned. "I don't want to talk or think about anything. I just want to be left alone."

I heard the latch turn and then I was being picked up. Strong arms wrapped around me, cool to the touch. If I hadn't already known it was him, the scent of blood, leather, and whiskey would've given it away.

"Ezra, so help me god—"

"There isn't a god. You've said so in your thoughts. Makes that threat a bit weak, don't you think?"

I gritted my teeth. "Put me down."

"Or?"

"Or I'm not responsible for what happens if you don't," I answered tartly.

His full lips twisted into a smirk. "Well, when you put it that way . . ."

I didn't register that we were moving at first, and when I did, it was already over. Black dots appeared in my vision as vertigo made my head swim.

They cleared just in time for me to look up into the night sky. The dark abyss opened over me. The air was thick with tension and heavy clouds sat over Houston.

"Where are—" I started to ask.

Then he dropped me.

My fall was short and broken by the crash of water enveloping my body. Being mid-sentence, I sucked a mouthful of it in before I realized my mistake.

My eyes flew open. I was disoriented for only a moment, before the blue lights of the pool registered. My butt hit the bottom, and I righted myself, pushing off the glass floor with my bare feet.

Pressure built in my lungs, the air expelling outward when my head broke the water. Cool droplets fell down my face, curving around my neck, straight toward the plunging V of my now soaked and see-through white shirt. I ran a hand over my eyes, pushing the stray hairs away from my face.

Ezra stood on the side of the pool. His suit jacket was gone, as were his shoes and socks. He was pulling off his button-down shirt when I said, "What are you doing?"

"You know what I'm doing. Don't be dense."

My glare sharpened. I strode toward the edge of the pool, moving only a little slower since I had to wade through water to get there.

His shirt was off, and his pants unbuttoned by the time I reached the edge.

My fingers curled around the siding and I hauled myself up with ease, a torrent of water pouring off of me while I did so.

Ezra dropped his slacks, kicking them away.

"Why are you being such an ass?" I demanded, lifting my hands in the universal sign of 'what the hell?'

Ezra turned his chiseled jaw without fully circling around, giving me an angled display of his fully inked back. A dragon wrapped around his torso; with Chinese characters I couldn't read filling up almost all the space it didn't.

I took an unconscious step forward, tilting my chin to get a better look.

"Because it's what you need right now. You don't want to talk? Fine. I'm not going to make you. If you wanted someone to push you over that edge, you would've gone back with Dorian. I'm also not going to treat you like you're made of glass because we both know you're not. The silent treatment won't work on me like it does with Roman, and you already know that."

I frowned, taking a step back. He moved faster than I expected, turning, and grabbing me. His hard forearm looped around my waist, pressing my front to his. The ink that traveled up his sculpted chest to his neck had me swallowing. I really was a sucker for a nice body with tattoos.

"I don't do relationships with targets, Ezra. For someone who seems to know so much about me, you'd think you'd know that." The words were acidic. Biting. I wanted to get him away, to create space, give myself room to breathe—and remember why I'd come down here to begin with.

"This isn't a relationship. It's a solution," he said in a

deep voice. He inclined his head forward, those emerald eyes piercing straight through me. "You said you don't want to think, remember? I can't help listening, and you can't help thinking. So I'm giving us both something else to do. Now are you going to get in the fucking pool, or do I have to throw you in again?"

My breathing went shallow.

I felt hot and cold, but it had very little to do with the winds whipping around us.

"Okay," I said, taking a step back.

He released me easily and motioned for me to get back in the water.

I padded over to the edge, careful not to slip and crack my head open on the side of the deck. I may be dead, but I didn't heal like the rest of them, and a dead body was honestly the last thing I needed right now.

I squatted next to the water and then slid back onto my butt. I kicked my legs over the side and made the snap decision to pull my shirt off. Given I could see the outline of the lacy white bra under it, the material wasn't doing much to hide things, anyway. I opted to keep the shorts on since Dorian had put me in a thong when he changed my clothes earlier.

Behind me, a breath hissed between Ezra's teeth. One that made me realize he was listening once again.

I slid over the side and into the crystal-clear water.

It had been a long time since I'd been in a pool. Over fifty years.

A serial killer who liked to lure away and drown little kids who didn't listen to their parents. He'd killed twelve before he was caught.

It had been difficult keeping myself in check on that job.

Too many times I'd come close to breaking him, and not in a productive way.

After that, Jake had stopped assigning me assholes who killed or hurt kids. I had a harder time remaining indifferent enough to keep the game going and rehabilitate while punishing. In that particular case, it hadn't helped that Vlad was encouraging me to impale him on a pike. He'd insisted it was good for the soul. I was pretty sure he meant his own, but still . . .

"Punishing souls truly doesn't bother you, does it?" Ezra asked quietly, standing right behind me.

"No," I said. "If anything, I find redemption in it." I shrugged softly. "I'm good at what I do."

"What makes you so good?" he asked.

"I turn people's vices on them and make them empathize with their victims. You never truly understand someone until you've lived through it, so I make them do that. Again and again. It's a ritual of sorts. The repetition . . . it works. I pick apart their lives then break them down to those pieces—so that when they're rebuilt to go back to Earth, they turn out all right." I lifted my chin to stare up at the clouds. A misting of warm rain started to fall. "I don't think I'm making any Gandhis, but over half the people I send back make it over the forty percent mark the next time around. Of the ones who don't, half of them I'd asked for their sentences to be extended. They weren't ready to return yet, but Upper Management overruled me."

"Why?" he asked, moving around me to stand a few feet away.

I watched him with my peripheral vision. "There's a system in place. Every action gets points given or taken away. If someone comes in below the forty percent, then those points are converted into time. Every bad thing makes it longer, but the good things shorten it. The problem with the system is it doesn't account for individuals." I'd had this argument with Jake many, many times. It came up annually for us at the very least, and every time Jake said he'd take my notes to the ones upstairs—but that's the thing with bureaucracy. It doesn't change. By the time it gets through the chain of people, assuming it even does, the last thing anyone wants to do is rock the boat. What we have works, right? Why fix what's not broken? I never understood that logic when playing with morality. It seemed . . . lazy. "It's made to make all things equal, even if one person needs more years than another to truly reform, they do the same time regardless of where they're actually at by the end."

"And the souls who fall below the forty percent, but aren't ones you requested more time for?"

"Irredeemable," I answered simply. "Some souls truly lack the ability to feel empathy or remorse. Without that, the odds of actually doing better are less than one percent. I usually recommend those souls be exterminated. Extinguished permanently. Sometimes they listen. Sometimes they don't."

Such as the case of my child serial killer.

Despite how hard it was for me, I did everything right. But he wouldn't break properly. The pieces he was made of didn't possess the ability to. The fabric that made up his soul was completely incapable of feeling remorse.

When they sent him back to Earth, despite my strong urging to exterminate, I tried to wash my hands of it. Then the reports came in of who he'd become in his next life.

Jeffrey Dahmer.

After that, Jake tended to back me up when I was certain there was no coming back for a soul.

"It's truly that easy for you to make the call? Knowing that's the true end to someone's existence?" he asked, not judging but curious.

"It is," I said, weaving my hands through the water. "When a soul twists, there's nothing to be done about it. In the same way it can happen and create a supernatural, it can also create a psychopath. I don't make the call lightly, but when I know, I know."

"Where do supernaturals go in the Afterlife?"

I didn't answer immediately, but as usual with him, he heard it in my mind.

"Ahh," he said. "I see."

"Your magic is different from that of the Afterlife. They don't run on the same wavelength. There's this giant system, but supernaturals are a glitch in the coding, essentially. You all get to live preternaturally long lives and have these bomb-ass powers on Earth—but this is it for you. No do-overs, I'm afraid." I offered him a half smile, but he didn't return it.

"You're wrong there."

I blinked. "About?"

"The no do-overs part. In that, we're a lot alike." I drifted closer to him. A shiver worked its way over my arms. While the heat was unbearable, the gusts of wind this high up could make it feel chilly.

"You die and come back?" I asked, lifting an eyebrow.

"I can't die. Period."

My lips parted.

Because that, well, it certainly wasn't in my fucking file. That was for damn sure.

Ezra let out a deep chuckle, clearly having heard my thoughts.

"What is actually in your files?"

"Clearly not the important shit," I griped. "One would think knowing that one of my targets can't die . . ." I trailed off at the expression on his face.

Then it clicked.

"None of you can," I whispered. "That's why nothing they sent worked. I wondered why they were bothering with me instead of just having you all taken out . . ." The pained smile he gave me said it all. "They tried, didn't they?"

"If it was 'them', I didn't know it. But yes, I should've died hundreds of times over my lifetime. Dorian, probably thousands. Same for the wolf pup. He was ripped apart at twelve. Did you know that? They tore him to pieces, and that motherfucker healed and then *slaughtered* them. I wasn't there when it happened, but I was involved in the cleanup." Ezra wore a faraway expression, like he was seeing something that wasn't there. "After that, I've had no doubts he's the same as me and the old bastard. Clearly, I'm right since your Upper Management sent you down here to fix us."

I felt horrified and yet relieved at once, but I wasn't entirely sure what type of response I was supposed to have. It was a strange thing, knowing what had happened to them.

"I don't want to talk about that tonight," I reminded him.

His chin dipped in acknowledgement. I knew that wasn't the end of the conversation regarding my job and assignment, but he was letting it slide for now.

"What would you rather talk about, kitten?" he said, in a devilishly flippant voice that did things to me. Bad things. The way his sultry mouth curved up didn't help.

"Tell me about your tattoos. Why a dragon?" I jutted my

chin toward his chest. The beast's head ended on the left pec, the characters I couldn't read on the right.

"Dragons symbolize power in my culture. Sovereignty. Strength. When I was turned, I became the most powerful vampire in the world, and I was still just a kid at the time. I didn't want to forget who I was, so I had Kendrick put the dragon on me." He brushed his hand down one scaled side that slanted toward the V of his hips.

"And the characters? What do those mean?" I asked, swimming closer to get a better look in the bright pool lights.

Ezra stood at ease, letting me drift close while I reached out to touch one. "They're dates. Each of them was a life-changing event for me—for better or worse."

"So you don't forget," I surmised.

He nodded once. "Do you know how old I am?"

"A hundred and seventy?" It came out more like a question than an answer.

"Close enough. Do you know how old Dorian is?"

I let out a low whistle. "Old. Roughly fifteen hundred years was what the file said, but it could be more given how not-accurate those are."

"If it's not exact, that's close. Dorian is a supernatural who can't die. He's seen some shit, probably done some shit too. But instead of using his past to ground him, he's drifting aimlessly. The guy can pass weeks sitting in his study staring out the window. He's hollow."

My hand paused on his chest, fingertips just barely grazing his skin. "You worry that's your future," I murmured.

"I take steps to make sure it's not," he said. But that wasn't the same as saying no. He'd evaded answering. I couldn't blame him, knowing that I would ultimately use everything I learned to break them.

We had an agreement. No thinking. His thought whispered through my mind, deep and husky. I felt those phantom hands tug my chin up.

I was unprepared for the intensity I saw in his eyes. *I can't help it,* I thought back. *I told you that.*

He leaned forward, bare chest nearly touching mine. He twisted a lock of hair back behind my ear. I let out a shaky breath, trying not to let him rattle me.

Feather-soft lips brushed against my lobe.

"Let me help you," he rasped, his voice husky.

CHAPTER 32

The word "no" teetered on my tongue.

He sucked my earlobe between his teeth, and warmth shot through me. My core tightened. I drew in a sharp breath as my thoughts scattered.

"See?" he murmured against my skin. "I told you I could."

He grasped my hips, pulling me closer. The hard bulge of his cock pressed into my lower stomach. *Jesus, he's huge.*

"No Jesus here, kitten."

His fingers pressed into the bare flesh of my sides. My body moved through water at breakneck speed. My ass hit the deck in a wet smack and my legs parted of their own accord.

Meanwhile, everything was spinning.

"This isn't a good idea, Fangs," I said, drawing on the new nickname I'd made for him. "You're a target, *and* my mate. This," I motioned between us, "it's bound to just complicate things further."

Ezra gave me a few inches of space, opting to put his hands on either side of me instead—even if he still stood between my legs. "What you and I are feeling right now is lust—and because I can read your thoughts, I'm well aware of how much you are thinking about it. This doesn't have to be complicated if you don't make it that way. It's just sex. Hard, mind-blowing sex. We don't have to complete the bond. And maybe we'll both be able to think straight for two seconds if we get it out of our systems," he said. He was just close enough that his scent was intoxicating, drawing me in, but he toed the line, not getting close enough to be pushy and set me off. It was . . . unpredictable.

"And if it doesn't work?" I found myself asking. Instantly, I wanted to kick myself for being so weak when a big dick with a hot body came along.

Ezra snorted a laugh. "I haven't heard that one. That's new. But to answer your question, if it doesn't, we fuck again. And again. And again. We're both more than old enough to know how this works, Fury. You're here for a job. There won't be any of the messy complications afterward because I know what this is from the start. So why not indulge?" His voice was like warm honey flowing over me.

"And you think you can manage this without biting me?" I mused. I knew the only way to truly complete the bond was to bite and mark your mate. That was true for all three species of mine: vampires, werewolves, and fae. But we had even bigger problems if he bit me.

Ezra tilted his head to the side. "I'm not looking to lock you down when I know how this whole thing ends. I won't bite you unless you ask, but something tells me you won't have much to say once I'm balls deep in you. The choice is yours, but I've already kissed you. Teased you in the tub. Drawing the line at sex seems like punishing yourself, and I didn't take you for a masochist."

Well, when he put it that way . . .

Against my better judgement, I lifted three fingers.

"You don't bite me, *even* if I ask. I know how this mate bond shit works. The endorphins from skin-to-skin contact are meant to make the female laxer and more accepting of it. No bite."

He quirked an eyebrow. "We can still bite without completing the bond, Fury. Sometimes a little nip is just in good fun." He grazed the tip of his tongue over a fang.

I shook my head. "It's non-negotiable, Ezra. You *can't* bite me. What I am . . . biting won't change me the way you think it will. It's dangerous. Just trust that." I dropped the first finger and waited.

He observed me for a moment, surprising me when he chose not to probe at my thoughts. Then he nodded his understanding. "No biting. You have my word."

"No hitting, slapping, spanking, or using an object to do any of those things. You *will not* like the results if you do." I was very, very serious about this limit. It was a boundary I could not cross, and it was the one thing I told every man and woman I took into my bed. Raise your hand to me, and it was over. I wasn't into it, and I never would be.

"Understood," Ezra said solemnly, not asking why, though I suspected after the afternoon we'd had, he already knew. I dropped the second finger. "Your last condition?"

"I can be a Dom. I can be a sub. The second you tell me to call you Daddy, I'm out."

Ezra tilted his head back and let out a deep, rumbling laugh. "Kitten, on that, we're in complete agreement."

I lifted a dark red eyebrow. "Then what are you waiting for?"

In that moment, the skies opened, and rain poured down.

But when his lips crashed into mine, all I could think about was how I wanted *more*.

I moved forward to press against him and he pressed against me in return, crowding my space with his much larger body. My legs came up to wrap around his waist, drawing a groan from him.

He pushed me back, putting the bulk of his weight on his hands that were still on the deck. My back hit the cool stone tiles, and I stared up into a dark and stormy sky while he worked his lips down my neck. Kissing. Sucking. Nibbling—but not biting.

His fangs stayed clear of piercing my skin, true to his word.

He moved down my chest, pausing at my bra.

Slowly, he dragged his teeth down the slope of my right breast, fangs catching on the lacy fabric. He tugged it down over my hard nipple and under the curve of my breast, pushing it up more.

Then he turned to the other and did the same.

"Much better," Ezra purred.

I opened my mouth to tell him he hadn't fucking done anything yet, but that sly bastard heard it coming and ducked his head, taking my hardened nipple between his lips. The first long pull made my legs stiffen. The second made my back bow. When he released it with a pop just to whorl his tongue around the stiff peak, I let out a moan.

My legs became a vise grip around him. I lifted my lower half and pressed into the thick bulge beneath his boxer briefs.

"Such a needy little thing," he groaned, rolling his hips to meet mine. The friction was exactly what I needed to drive me even more wild as I chased that release.

"You're damn right," I breathed.

He wasn't even inside me, and I was on the verge of losing it.

"Not so fast," he murmured, giving my other nipple a quick suck before lowering himself back into the pool, forcing me to release my hold on him. He grasped my knees and spread my thighs as wide as they would go.

Then he grabbed the waistband of my shorts and pulled.

The storm overhead drowned out the rip of the fabric. Water poured down me, following every curve and contour of my body. Ezra threw the soaking wet fabric onto the deck, letting out a purr of approval for my lacy white thong.

"Dorian has good taste," he mused. Instead of ripping the thong off, he pushed the thin scrap of lace to the side. His nose dipped over my wet cunt, inhaling deeply.

"You scream when you come, or next time I'm not so nice. Understood?" His green eyes flashed. While he didn't have a wolf inside him like Roman, he was very much a predator in his own way. Arguably more of one because there was no separation between man and monster. He was one and the same.

I nodded once, mouth dry.

"I want to hear it," he said.

"Yes."

"Yes, what?" he prompted.

Part of me was tempted not to say it. Just to see what he would do.

His lips curved, amusement showing in his expression. "Try me. My body can go a lot longer and a lot harder than yours. See what happens when you don't play nice."

I swiped my tongue over the bottom of my teeth. I toyed with it but decided maybe next time—if there was one.

"Yes, Sir," I said.

Good, kitten.

He parted my folds, licking and pushing his tongue into me. Heat rushed through me, and then he pressed the flat of his tongue to my clit. The rough friction of it made me jump the first time he dragged it over me. The second time, I squirmed.

The third, I pushed back.

Overhead, thunder boomed, and lightning streaked the sky.

He switched to sucking on my clit while twisting his mouth. The sensation pulled a gasp from me.

Two blunt fingers pressed against my wet entrance. He thrust them in easily, curling to tap my G-spot.

Scream for me, he ordered.

Then he sucked me again.

I broke apart, and the next clap of thunder echoed my release. My channel tightened around him while my legs stiffened, then unlocked.

Heat rushed through me, engulfing everything. I was in a haze of wind and rain and stars. Lightning flickered behind my eyelids, but all I heard was that initial boom that went off as I did.

Ezra took me through the aftershocks, waiting until my vision cleared, and the tremors faded. I sagged in a puddle against the wet ground, only then realizing how hard the rain was coming down.

"As much as I want to fuck you right here in the middle of a thunderstorm, your body is human, and the wolf will never let me hear the end of it if you get sick. Let's do this inside."

I sat up as he hoisted himself out of the pool and then picked me up. He carried me with one forearm under my knees and the other banded around my back. I squinted up at him when we stepped inside. The lights flickered on, detecting motion.

"I can walk, you know."

"You can also fuck yourself, but instead I'm taking care of that."

I bit my tongue instead of telling him he'd yet to actually fuck me. Then again, there wasn't much point to biting your tongue when the person you're wanting to tell off can hear your every thought.

Ezra pulled his arm back, letting my legs drop to the floor abruptly. I'd barely caught my balance when he twirled me around, splaying a hand on my back and pushing me until I was bent over the kitchen table, my cheek forced against the surface, my arms spread on either side of my head.

"What was it you were just saying?" he asked, keeping his palm firmly pressed on me as he reached down with his other hand, lightly scraping the back of my leg. His fingers trailed toward my inner thigh, teasing dangerously close.

"That you'd yet to fuck me," I said, struggling to concentrate and form words as he touched me.

He curled his fingers around my thong, barely grazing my sensitive skin as he hooked the fabric.

"I fucked you with my fingers," he said, twisting his hand so his knuckles pressed into me but didn't give me what I so badly wanted. "I fucked you with my tongue, did I not?"

I groaned, trying to get the contact I needed for friction. It was so deliciously close.

Not the same, I thought.

He nudged my legs apart with his knee, and I spread them willingly.

"So tell me, kitten. I fucked you with my fingers," he

said, slipping a finger from his grip on my thong to run along the wet seam of my pussy.

I moaned.

"And I fucked you with my tongue," he continued, leaning over, and grazing his tongue over my skin, following the trail with his teeth.

I hummed in response, and he fisted the fabric, ripping it from my body in one swift move.

With one hand still pressing into my back, he used his other to rip his boxer briefs off.

"What do you want me to fuck you with now?" he asked, sliding his tip against my entrance, teasing me.

"I want you to fuck me," I growled impatiently, trying to push myself back into him, but he held me firm.

Say it, he whispered in my mind. *Say what you want. I want to hear you.*

"I want you to fuck me with your cock," I said, my voice hoarse and my frustration leaking through.

Ezra rumbled a growl of approval, pushing himself into me fully. A loud moan of pleasure and pain escaped me as his impressive girth stretched me out. I could've sworn my eyes crossed.

"Yessss," I hissed as I tightened around him in anticipation.

He slid himself in and out slowly, coating himself in my wetness as I adjusted to his size. I ground against him, encouraging him to give me more. God, I wanted more.

He moved faster, pacing himself as he picked up speed. With each thrust, I groaned, scratching my nails into the wood. He pounded into me from behind, reaching down and hooking his arm under my right leg, giving him deeper access, filling me more than I would've thought possible.

The pressure built in my core, and a thin sheen of sweat

covered my body, my cheek sliding over the tabletop as he slammed into me. I clawed at the table as his fingertips pressed into my flesh, holding me in place.

"Do you want to come again?" he asked between ragged breaths.

"Don't stop," I said, my voice strained. "I'm so close."

Ezra took his hand off my back, scooping his arm under my torso and lifting me up. I threw my arms out, supporting my weight. He never broke his rhythm. With one foot on the floor, half bent over a table, and the other leg held up, he gripped my hip and fucked me, just like I wanted him to.

Heat pooled in me, and I felt the telltale tingling flutters of an oncoming orgasm. I closed my eyes, dipping my head back, the pressure building—

He let go of my hip, reaching around to rub my clit in harsh, fast circles. My eyes flew open and my mouth opened in a silent scream as he thrust into me harder.

No longer a slow and steady climax, the intensity of the combined movements pushed me over. I screamed, a deep, guttural moan echoing in the kitchen. I squeezed my eyes shut and my inner walls clenched around him, pulling him in deeper as I came. Ezra pressed against my clit, and the muscles in my legs tightened and my body trembled as white dots exploded behind my eyes.

A wave of aftershocks rode through my system as Ezra pounded into me, finding his release.

My arms gave out, and I slid forward on the table. I tried to calm my breathing, but it was heavy and uneven as my heart thundered in my chest.

My mind raced at the strength of my orgasm. I wasn't sure I'd ever felt one so acutely. It had left me a trembling mess . . . but I wanted more. If they were like that, I wanted so much more.

Ezra ran his fingers through my hair, pulling the strands away from my eyes. The side of my face was exposed, and I could see him in my peripheral vision as I rested on the cold, flat surface.

He looked at me with a devilish smile, and I wondered what he was thinking.

Leaning forward, he grazed my ear lobe with his fang, then purred, "I told you I'd make you see stars."

CHAPTER 33
ROMAN

I listened outside Ezra's door as he flirted with her. No doubt he could hear when I'd arrived, and he was tormenting me on purpose.

I heard her laugh, and my wolf stirred. He'd been agitated at our distance from her, but there was nothing we could do about it.

She'd been at Ezra's for five days. I hadn't expected her to stay that long. For five days I'd been itching to see her. Talk to her. Smell her. I wanted more than anything to touch her.

My wolf nodded in approval.

I breathed in deeply then reached out to knock on the door.

Moments later, Ezra opened it wearing nothing but jeans.

I glared at him, knowing his game. "It's five in the afternoon. Can't find it in you to wear a shirt, or were you hoping to put on a show just for me?"

Leaning against the doorframe with an arm overhead,

he winked at me. "Hey, Roman. Didn't know you'd be here this early."

I sighed, looking past him to see Fury. Her jeans hugged her body, and she had a small backpack. She walked up to me, smirking . . . until she saw my motorcycle jacket and her face fell. I tossed her a helmet, and she caught it.

"Nice reflexes," I said, and pointed to it. "You'll want to wear that."

"Great," she mumbled, walking out the door.

Ezra cleared his throat. "She's feisty, but she's a fun one. Be careful."

Fury and I groaned at the same time, but she spoke first. "Try not to piss on each other, will you?"

Ezra chuckled. "Not my kink, but I'm not one to judge."

"Ugh, really?" she said to him, walking out the door and waving at him over her shoulder in dismissal. "See you later."

"You really are a dick," I told him.

"She likes it," he said knowingly.

"Mmm." Time to change the topic and get out of here. "Call if you learn anything new. My rangers are still looking for anything out of the ordinary. There are packs running the borders in all directions."

His eyes darkened, and he nodded. "I have six crews out. Nothing yet."

He was just as unhappy as I was about it. "I'll update if we find something." I turned to leave.

We silently rode the elevators to the parking garage. When the doors opened, we stepped off, and she tensed in hesitation as she took in my motorcycle.

"Roxanne said you get motion sickness, but I don't think you'll have a problem here."

She swallowed thickly. "What makes you so sure? To be

honest, I'm a little worried about puking inside my helmet. I can't die, so how about I don't wear the helmet, and if I throw up, whichever car it hits, it's their problem."

I couldn't help the small laugh that escaped me. The mental image was too much. "Just wear it. I'll feel better about it. You'll also appreciate not getting pelted in the face with a loose piece of gravel. It'll get better once we're out of the city."

I straddled the bike, putting on my own helmet. No, I couldn't die either, but she didn't know that. Aside from the possibility of shredding my face to pieces and having to heal from it, I also didn't care for pebbles or gravel, and with the number of cars on the interstate it was bound to happen.

"Wait, we're leaving Houston? Where are we going?"

I grinned at her apprehension. It was a nice change to be the calmer one. Usually, I felt as though I were pulled too tight, like a cord about to snap. From the moment we'd first seen her beating the shit out of the Dawsons in Rox's bar, my wolf had been right beneath the surface, testing my limits of control, desperately trying to rip the binds I held him with. The power struggle had taken some time to even out. Longer than I would've liked, given she'd opted to stay with the fucking vampire a few extra days.

The desire to protect her and be close to her was ever-present. But the reality of it was she wasn't Maya. For one, she couldn't die. For another, I was more likely to lose her by treating her like they were the same.

"I don't live here," I answered. "I sleep in the office if I have to stay for some reason. On the rare occasion, I'll stay at Rox's, but she stays with me more often. I keep a house on a lake, away from the city."

She grumbled incoherently and put the helmet on, straddling the bike behind me.

"Tap me twice if you're going to throw up. Otherwise, hold on." I didn't give her a chance to respond. I turned the bike over, and a loud rumbling filled the garage. It was awful in such an enclosed space, but to a wolf, everything about being in the city was too overwhelming. Sensory overload to the extreme.

She wrapped her arms around my waist the best she could and turned her head, putting one side against my back.

Everything about riding was exhilarating. The wind was so loud, it somehow made things peaceful and quiet. It was a strange combination. Like how sound disappeared under water and things felt calm.

Usually, my mind ran with a million thoughts, twenty-four seven. It never slowed down. I had to find ways to calm the storm inside and keep my sanity. I didn't want to end up like Ezra, a loner detached from anyone and everyone.

She kept her arms wrapped tightly around me as I sped like a bat out of hell, seemingly content to watch the scenery change as we left the city. Multi-laned gray concrete morphed to double lanes surrounded by tall trees. The air changed, no longer feeling so dense, but rather thick with the scent of nature. Cleaner.

After an hour, I pulled up to the house and cut the engine, taking off my helmet. She threw her leg over and lost her balance, but I grabbed her quickly and let her use me for support.

"Thanks," she mumbled, taking her helmet off too. "I just need to get my bearings. My legs feel numb from vibrating for so long. It's bizarre."

"But you don't feel nauseous, do you?" I asked her, curious to see if riding a bike helped her motion sickness.

She smiled, and it reached her eyes. "Surprisingly, no, I don't. That's a nice change," she mused. She tilted her head up, but she was looking behind me. "So, uh, Ezra said you had a log cabin by the lake. That's not a log cabin." She pointed to the house.

"No, not in the traditional sense," I said, getting off the bike.

"Then in what sense would it be?" she asked.

"It's a luxury log cabin, if you want to give it a name." I pointed south. "Houston is that way. This is Lake Conroe." I held my hand out to the nature surrounding us.

"Fancy," she said, but I didn't miss the snark. How could she go to *Dorian's* and then snark at me that I was fancy?

I frowned, feeling like I'd missed something. "I'll show you to your room."

I walked up the steps and through the door, wondering what she was thinking. I wasn't trying to impress her with *fancy*. I just wanted to get her away from the city. Have a minute to think around her. Breathe a little deeper with her near me.

"Why are you grumbling?" she asked from behind me as we walked up the main stairs in the house, heading to the second floor.

"What? I'm not grumbling." I looked at her over my shoulder.

She gave me a flat look. "You weren't saying words, no, but you're grumbling about something."

I grunted, going down the hall to a door, and turning the handle to open it. "It's Roxanne's room when she stays here, but if you don't like it, you can have my room across the hall."

Her lips turned up, and she quirked an eyebrow. "Was that a sly way to offer to share a bed, Roman?"

The wolf inside me went still at the thought. My cock twitched, and a rush of adrenaline swept through me at the thought of claiming her. The rest of me shoved it away, flustered that she thought I was trying to bed her instantly. "That's not what I—"

"Relax. The room is fine. Lighten up, Roman," she said, a smile on her face. "I'm just giving you a hard time. I don't know if you can tell or not, but I kind of enjoy it."

I looked at my feet and cleared my throat. "Right . . ." I grabbed the back of my neck, rubbing. I had no plans. No idea what to do. Aside from being mated, what was there between us? Nothing. I had nothing to offer her. I knew nothing about her. "Well, the sun hasn't gone down yet. Would you like to take a walk around the lake?"

She scrunched her nose at me, and I hated how adorable it looked. "Have you seen what nature does to my hair? Or my sweat glands, for that matter?"

"So that's a no. Got it."

"I'm not very naturey," she said.

I nodded. Okay. No walks in nature. Noted.

"I like baths . . . but you already knew that," she said, winking at me.

Didn't I know it. The first day we'd met, when she stared at me while fingering herself in the tub . . . it had been in the back of my mind since. The thought of her dark red hair wrapped in my fist while I fucked her from behind had started to replace the image of Maya's blonde locks. When the nights were empty and I woke up hard, it was her lips I started to envision moaning around my cock. Her dark eyes watching me.

Her.

A loud, thunderous sound interrupted my thoughts. Fury looked at me in confusion and moved to the window. Over her shoulder, I could see that seven motorcycles were pulling into the long driveway. "Were you expecting company?"

"Frequently," I said, hovering nearby. I could smell her shampoo. And she smelled entirely too much of the vampire. "We're shifters. Wolves. We run in packs. I usually have company. There's comfort in it."

She spun on her heel, moving to the bed, and tossing her bag on it. "Yeah, I think I'll stick to the bath, then." She bent over to take off her boots. "I don't much like crowds."

Her words clicked. A piece of information about her she hadn't given to me before. Had she given it to Dorian or Ezra? I didn't know, and I wasn't going to ask. What I did know was that she kept secrets. Secrets she wasn't willing to share yet. Secrets about who she was, and more importantly, *what* she was. I wouldn't find the answer easily, but if she left me enough breadcrumbs, I would figure it out.

I walked toward her, slowly, my skin buzzing with awareness. My voice went dark, and low. "What is it that you aren't telling me?"

"Hmm?" she asked, looking up to find me closer to her.

"I find it an odd choice, coming to Houston, when you don't much like crowds. But then, by your own admission, you also don't like nature. So, I have to ask: what is it that you *do* like, Fury?"

CHAPTER 34

He towered over me, imposing in my space bubble. His voice had gone dark, and his eyes glittered. His proximity and the husky tone in his voice had made something inside me stir.

I did my best to school my features. He wouldn't trap me in this.

"Jumping to conclusions, Roman?" I asked, tilting my head. "I honestly can't even figure out which direction you're heading with that. But to answer your questions, a person can like cities without liking crowds. I like convenience, for one. And cities have that. I also like solitude, but solitude doesn't have to equate to nature. Furthermore, nature around here is a whole different ball game. You can't argue that with me. You roam up north. I know you know there's a difference."

I could tell by the way his posture didn't change that he didn't believe me one bit. That was okay, as long as he dropped it. He couldn't dispute what I'd said.

He shifted his weight and crossed his arms. "The pack is making dinner tonight. You'll join us. Take a bath before or after, I don't care which. You're here. Try to enjoy yourself." He turned and walked out the door. It closed with a loud thud.

I sighed. Well, that had gone okay for about five seconds. I scrubbed my hands down my face in frustration.

Dorian was cold and distant, but he had moments of clarity where I felt a connection with him, even if it was only in short bursts. Ezra was the easiest. It was nice to have someone to talk to. And someone who let me not think about things in too much depth.

But Roman? How did I find a way to connect with him? It was hot and cold, and I didn't know what to do with it. How could I when I was certain part of the shift in his hot and cold attitude had to do with his wolf? Sure, we had attraction, but I didn't understand him, nor did he understand me. Not yet.

I looked toward the bathroom, thinking about ignoring him completely. He'd busted in on me taking a bath once before, so he wouldn't hesitate to do it again. Last time, he'd been on edge, desperate to find me and keep me safe. This time, he'd just be pissed off. Really, if I wanted to get away, a bathtub wasn't my best choice. It would just end with a relaxing soak being ruined.

I looked out the window again, watching the shifters gather around and greet each other. They all looked happy. Like family. It wasn't something I could relate to.

And there it was. A piece of the puzzle. That thing about each other we didn't understand. Or one of them, at least. If I was going to get the job done, I had to learn more about him, and this was a step in the right direction.

I leaned down, retying my boots, committing myself to socializing with wolves for the night.

Leaving my room, I could hear voices downstairs. I took

the steps slowly, gauging the response as some of the voices trailed off when they saw me.

At the bottom step, I surveyed my surroundings. A familiar face caught my attention.

"Caitlin," I said, somewhat surprised. "Good to see you again."

"Is it?" She laughed, standing in the doorway unmoving. "Last time I saw you, it was before you crawled out a window on my watch."

I lifted my shoulder in a shrug, putting my hands out in mock surrender. "Nothing personal. Just, well, it was a weird day. Besides, you look like you came out of it okay. It wasn't your apartment he burst into later."

"No, I'm the one who got my ass chewed out for losing my alpha's mate." She crossed her arms and looked me up and down. "You plan on sticking around this time? Or are you having another weird day?"

I gazed through the large windows, taking in the wooded area, listening to some birds chirping. "Oh, it's weird, all right. But I'll stick around. Besides, judging by the ride to get here, it's a long walk to Houston." I pointed down at my boots. "Plus, wrong shoes."

She huffed, moving aside, and throwing her arm out to let me by, several pairs of shifter eyes following me.

What was with the cold reception? I snuck out a window *one time*.

I made my way outside, where a bonfire was being lit and several shifters were moving seating around.

I realized Roman was behind me, and he'd been watching the entire exchange between Caitlin and me. "She's not that bad, you know," he said. "But she does hold grudges pretty well."

I sniffed. "I'll get over it." I held grudges too. Long ones.

I was a pro. I'd been holding grudges longer than they'd been alive. I snickered at the thought.

He put his hands in the pockets of his dark jeans. The black T-shirt he wore was tight and showed the contours of his chest and abs. It was such a different look than his suits. It was nice. Down to earth. "I'm sorry if I was too aggressive earlier. I—"

I turned to face him, putting my fingers over his lips. "Don't. Let's not do this, okay? Let's just do this thing you wanted to do with your pack, and I'm here to just . . . hang out, so let's not get serious with this. I think the last thing you or I need is too much serious."

He smiled. "Fair enough."

I clapped my hands. "Good. Now what?"

He barked a laugh. "Good speech, but no follow-up, I see?"

"I'm new here. Aren't you the host?"

Seeing someone over my shoulder, he yelled for one of the shifters to come over. A young shifter with tanned skin and jet-black hair followed orders, stopping in front of me and Roman.

"Sir?"

"Fury, this is Andy. Andy is going to be cooking the steaks tonight. How would you like yours?"

"Oh, um, medium rare, but closer to rare if you can. There's this sweet spot that's perfectly in the middle of the two if you can find it," I said to the kid. He couldn't have been a day older than nineteen.

He smiled and nodded. "That's easy enough."

"Is it? I thought I was being difficult."

"It's the same as Roman's, ma'am, so—"

"Mmm, none of that. Just call me Fury."

His fearful eyes shifted to Roman, who nodded to give him the okay.

After the kid ran off, I walked over to the bonfire and sat, Roman following in my shadow. He sat next to me, and I had to comment on the exchange.

"I approve of your temperature choice in steak. But I have to ask, is that how it always works with you? It's my preference, but they need your permission to call me by my name?"

He shook his head. "No, I imagine you caught Andy off guard. No one needs my permission for a choice you're going to make about how you want to be addressed, or anything else like that. But to have a woman say she doesn't want to be recognized and respected by title, especially the alpha's mate, I think you scared the kid. He probably thought he was being tested."

I laughed at the thought. "Testing the members of your pack is definitely not on my agenda."

As I said it, several of them looked my way, and I suddenly realized why there'd been such a cold reception in the house earlier. They were testing *me*. Sizing me up. I was the intruder. I hadn't had that with the few fae that were at Dorian's, and no one had been at Ezra's house.

I see.

Caitlin chose that moment to come up to me and Roman. "Mind if I steal her away, sir?"

He shook his head, gesturing for us to go on.

I shot him a look, but I got up and took a walk with her.

"Look, if you're going to give me the 'best friend' talk, don't bother. I got the sister talk from Roxanne, or some version of it," I said, hearing the icy tone in my voice.

She shook her head. "Nope. I was going to apologize

about earlier in the house, but now I'm reconsidering my decision."

"Wise choice. If you apologize to me, I'll remember it and hold it over you for eternity, never letting you forget the time you told me you were wrong," I said, walking slowly to who knew where in the woods.

She laughed and stopped in her tracks, causing me to do the same. When I faced her, she looked relieved, somehow. "You have an honest streak about you that I can appreciate. You might be pretty rough around the edges, but you don't beat around the bush."

"Why is that comforting to you?"

"Because you aren't going to bullshit him. He likes honesty. I mean, who doesn't? But some people value certain traits more than others. Roman values honesty. To him, honesty and loyalty go hand in hand. It's hard to find that once, but twice? He's lucky."

It seemed that Roman and I valued the same things. I hated being lied to. It made me want to stab things. But then the comparison hit me. Maya. She was honest. She was probably kinder about her honesty, but Caitlin still believed Maya and I shared that trait. That stung more than I wanted to admit.

I wasn't as honest as she thought, and there was some guilt lingering inside me as I heard her words. I didn't want to hurt him, I just wanted him to not hurt others.

We hadn't walked far; I could still see the bonfire in the distance. Roman wasn't hard to spot. The massive wall of muscle, his smooth, dark skin, and his long, clean dreads. He stuck out in a crowd. I could've found him anywhere.

A chill went down my spine, reminding me where I was. If Caitlin wanted to go deep, she needed to pick another night. So I did what I did best. Deflected. "Well, Second, to tell you the truth, I'm not sorry I climbed out a window. You don't have to be sorry for being mad at me for it. You had every right to. But we can move on. I'm not crawling out any windows tonight, and you aren't on babysitting duty, so we're square. I'll even let you find me a drink," I said, winking at her.

She laughed, and the tightness in her shoulders eased slightly. "C'mon. I'll get you a whiskey. That's what I drink, so that's what you'll have too."

I could see the smirk on her face as she said it.

Size me up all you want.

"Four fingers, no ice," I told her.

She raised her eyebrows in appraisal, then nodded once.

A flapping of wings caught my attention, and I slowed my pace. "Go on ahead. I'll be right there," I called out. She turned and looked at me in question, and I smiled. "I'm good. Just not used to big crowds. I'll walk a little slower."

She looked unsure, but I gathered she didn't sense anything out of the ordinary and she went on ahead, occasionally turning her head to keep me in sight.

As Caitlin went into the house to get our drinks, I took slow steps, waiting. I couldn't see him, but I knew he was there.

"I wondered if you'd find me out here," I whispered.

"Please," he scoffed. "Unlike you, I actually do my job."

I rolled my eyes. "Keep your voice down. Shifters have remarkable hearing." He clicked his beak in what I assumed was acknowledgment. "I haven't seen you for five days. Did you find anything?"

Hades flew down from a tree, and I stuck my arm out for him to land. He cocked his head to the side and squawked at me. "Five days, huh? I wonder why you haven't heard from me in five days. What is it about five days?" he mused.

"Oh my god, what is it you want to say, Hades?" I motioned for him to get on with it.

His feathers poofed up, and he shook his head. "Forgive me if I didn't want to interrupt your fuckfest with Ezra. Which reminds me, close the curtains. No one needs to see that side of you."

I couldn't help but laugh. "He lives in the penthouse. We didn't need to close the curtains."

"I assure you, you do," he said dryly.

I sighed. "Fine, get to the point. You know how to track Roman and give him my keycard, but you couldn't find a way to peck on a window or sneak through the door when we were in the pool. You can get anywhere you want to, Hades. I have no doubts about that. So why haven't I heard from you in five days?"

He stretched his wings out then pulled them back in, shifting his weight. "Nothing of consequence to report. I went to Duke, and he was clearly upset. He's looking into how anyone in this realm could possibly know your name."

"That's not—"

He let out a shrill squawk, cutting me off.

I shushed him.

"Don't be obstinate. It *was* your name. Duke doesn't want you here anymore, but he knows why you're staying. Supernaturals are flooding into Houston for the summit, but I haven't caught wind of any plans or conversations that explain what happened in the warehouse. No one even knows about it, as far as I can tell."

I frowned. That wasn't good. "Okay. Keep me posted. The guys haven't found anything either. I listen in when they talk about updates, whether they know it or not. I'll be here for a few days, I think."

"What about them?" he asked.

I sighed. "Nothing yet. I know what the vision said, but they just don't seem like they'll end the world."

He snapped his beak at me twice. "That isn't for you to decide."

"Fuck off, pigeon, I know that. I'm making a point. I haven't figured it out, but I'm working on it. If I don't know what's broken, I can't fix it."

"Tick tock."

"No 'tick tock', asshole. Aren't you listening? The visions have always shown the three of them combined ending things. I'll be more concerned for our timeline here when they finally start showing me something that indicates they're going to blow."

Hades puffed up his feathers again, reaching his leg up to scratch his neck. "Fine. I'll relay that message."

I rolled my eyes. "Tell Duke hi. And let me know if you see anything with those annoying and beady little eyes of yours. You know where to find me. Tap on a window."

He glared at me. "Which window?"

"Look for closed curtains." I grinned at him, letting him think whatever he wanted.

He grumbled, and I held my arm away from my body so he could flap his wings and get enough air to take flight.

I picked up my pace and made my way back toward the bonfire, crossing several small groups of shifters that were deep in conversation. I was heading toward Roman so I could sit next to him when I heard a familiar voice. I couldn't help but smile.

Roxanne had a beer in her hand and was telling a story when she caught sight of me. "Fury," she yelled. "There you are. Roman said you were off with Caitlin, but I saw her go inside alone." She ran up to me and embraced me.

The icy parts of me that wanted to keep a wall up were hard to maintain when Roxanne hugged me. She managed to knock my guard down when I least expected it, and I'd known her for less than two weeks.

I hugged her back. "Caitlin is off getting me a drink now. I was headed this way when I got a visit from the crow. He's hard to shake," I supplied, assuming I'd been seen with a bird on my arm. She snorted, but before she could question me about him, I asked, "When did you get here?"

"I've been here for a while. Just visiting a friend at another cabin that way," she said, jutting her thumb in a random direction.

"You're friends with Roman's neighbors? Are they shifters too?"

Roxanne scrunched her eyebrows at me, turning to her brother and then back to me. "He didn't tell you?"

I frowned and shook my head.

"He owns about sixty percent of the land surrounding the lake. Part of it is investment. The rest is a place for the pack to live. There are houses scattered all over the place. There's easily a dozen cabins nearby on this piece of property alone."

A lot of shifters had shown up to the bonfire. Now I knew why. It wasn't a party. It was their neighborhood. Family.

"I hadn't realized," I admitted, looking over to him. He was watching us, but his face remained neutral.

She waved her hand. "It's not a big deal. I just figured he explained the setup around here." She took a drink of her beer, tossed it in a green bin, and grabbed a bottle of water from one of the coolers. "Anyway, I wanted to tell you that we're going shopping tomorrow."

I cringed. "Shopping?"

She looked at me, confused. "Yeah, shopping. You have something against shopping?"

"Sometimes, yeah. What kind of shopping are we doing now?"

Her eyes widened, then she looked past me, and I could tell she was glaring at her brother. When I had her attention again, she said, "Dress shopping. For the summit."

"We wear dresses to the summit?" I asked.

The truth of it was, I'd read about the purpose of the summit. The frequency. The duration. The politics. But nothing more. And there was a good chance everything I'd read in my files was crap, anyway.

She looked at me incredulously. "You've spent time with all three guys, and not one of them has told you anything, have they?"

"Not really, no. Certainly not about what I should be wearing."

"Night one is a black-tie dinner, so we dress to impress," she said, winking at me. "Though you'll be on the arm of three, so I don't know how to coordinate that."

I stared at her blankly. "If they're wearing tuxedos, why does it matter? Aren't they all the same?"

The look of admonishment said I was wrong. I mouthed, 'Okay.'

"I made an appointment at a custom dress shop that serves supernaturals, so—"

"We need an appointment to buy clothes?" I asked in genuine shock and curiosity.

"Sometimes, yeah." She took a deep drink from her

bottle. "So, shopping tomorrow. Dresses. You and me. It'll be fun."

"I don't know about fun, but okay. Dress shopping it is," I mumbled. I knew she heard me. The wolf ears all around probably heard me.

Pulling me from my internal grumbling, Roxanne grabbed my hand, and tugged me along with her, walking around trees. "Let's go throw some shit."

I allowed her to drag me along. "I'm sorry, what? What are we throwing?"

As we came to a small clearing that was marked off by reflective tape, she stopped short, picking up a weapon off the ground.

"Axes," she said, with a wicked grin on her face.

I smiled. "Okay, now we're talking."

I grabbed one and observed the setup in the forest. Two wide oak trees had massive boards in front of them. The boards looked heavily reinforced with multiple layers to take the impact of a shifter's throw. The tree was simply to hold up the board.

Each board was marked and painted for points, and each board had a measured distance from the throwing line to the target.

"You first," I said to Roxanne.

She walked up to the line, drink in hand, and called out, "Third line." She threw, the axe making a whooshing sound as it sailed through the air and hit the third ring from the middle. "Ha!"

"Not bad, not bad," I said, picking up one of my own. "Third line." I threw, my axe hitting my board on the same spot as hers.

Caitlin came with my whiskey, along with one of her own.

"Nicely done," she commented, handing me the glass. "Can I watch?"

"If you keep the drinks coming, you can do whatever you want," I said, taking a heavy drink and swallowing, savoring the burn. It was spicy on my tongue and warmth bloomed in my chest.

"Bullseye," Roxanne shouted before releasing the axe. It smacked into the board, slightly off center, marking both the bullseye and the first line. "Damn it."

I repeated her call for my board, sending my axe flying and hitting the bullseye clear in the middle. "Oooh," I called out. I slammed back the rest of my drink and told Roxanne she was up.

Before long, we'd developed a crowd, and I hadn't paid much attention to how large it had truly gotten. I wasn't sure how long we'd been going for.

"Kill shot," she yelled. Behind her, money was exchanging hands and bets were being made.

"Not a chance," I mocked her, egging her on. I secretly wanted her to get it. She was a badass, and every single guy here needed to know it if they didn't already.

Thwack.

Kill shot.

Roxanne tossed her hands up in the air in victory then pointed at me as she walked in my direction. "You're up, buttercup."

I bowed to her, chuckling. "Gladly. Step aside, milady. I have a kill shot to make."

She returned the laughter and bowed out of my way. There was more murmuring in the crowd, and more money changing hands.

I lined up my aim and threw.

Kill shot.

I whooped, and Roxanne high-fived me. I met Roman's eyes at that moment, and I felt a tightness in my belly I couldn't explain.

As she picked up another axe, someone whistled and caught the attention of all the shifters surrounding us. Which, now that I was looking, was a lot. Then a call for dinner came, and the crowd dispersed, heading back to the bonfire.

We dropped our weapons, grinning from ear to ear. "I'm starving," I said, as I picked up my glass and she picked up her water bottle.

"Me too." She wiped her forehead with her wrist. "And I am sweating like a farm animal."

I belted out a laugh. "I'm sweating in places I didn't know could sweat."

I looked around the ground, stopping when I realized I hadn't had another drink.

Roxanne must've realized what I was looking for. "You only had the one," she said, casually.

"Yeah," I said, trailing off. "I just wanted to make sure I cleaned up after myself. Thought I had . . . two." *Or more.*

We walked side by side as we headed back. "Caitlin brought you one, but you never drank it. So she did." Roxanne shrugged.

Oh. Was she sure? That didn't sound like me at all. I scanned the ground and replayed the sequence of events in my head.

"Hey . . ." she started.

"Hmm?" I answered, mildly distracted.

"Thanks for throwing with me. I had a lot of fun."

I saw her out the corner of my eye, and she looked happy. "I did too. I haven't had that much fun in . . ." I trailed off. "Well, it's been a long time."

"You're the only one who throws with me and doesn't keep track of points."

"There was a point system?" I said, looking shocked. When she looked at me in surprise, I added, "I'm joking. I know there was."

"I mean it, though, Fury. I don't think you understand how much that means to me. Shifters are competitive by nature. *Everything* is a competition. Sometimes a girl just wants to have fun without it being a pissing contest."

"I think there's a pop song about that first part." I snickered, and she side-eyed me and laughed. "Well, then I'm glad you finally had someone to throw with who wasn't trying to make it about who comes out on top."

"You and Roman," she said.

"Me and Roman what?"

"I meant that you and Roman are the only other people that throw for the enjoyment you get from it. No one else does." She sighed. "What can you do? C'mon. Let's get dinner. Then I'm crashing in my room with you. I'm beat."

She looped her arm through mine and we made our way to the gathering.

Roman watched me walking with his sister. I couldn't read his expression, and I couldn't help but wonder what he was thinking. There was so much about him I didn't know, and so much about him I couldn't figure out how to reach.

What I did realize was that I'd seen more of him through other people's eyes, and that wasn't something I'd expected.

CHAPTER 35

I nhale.

Exhale.

Inhale.

Exhale.

Deep breaths, Fury.

I could do this. It was just a car ride. While I sat in the backseat. And some really nice shifter named Owen drove. Roxanne had called a car company for black car service. Whatever that meant. What I knew was that I was in a fancy car, it was black, it wasn't hers, and death felt better than motion sickness. How did I not have a hangover, but driving in a car made it feel like I did?

She patted my thigh. "We're almost there."

I mumbled incoherently in response as she looked at her phone. The idea of looking at something like that made my stomach roil again.

I didn't even want to go dress shopping. I could dress as a waiter for the summit and be content. For the love of anything they considered sacred in the realm of the living, I just wanted the car to stop.

Owen pulled into a spot, and as he put it in park, I flung myself out of the vehicle and onto solid ground. I landed on my knees, and the concrete scraped my skin. I ignored the burn, focusing on taking steady gulps of air.

"Ma'am, you're going to get burns from the concrete. It's too hot here," Owen said.

"Ugh, don't call me ma'am," I groaned.

"Uh, I'm sorry, Miss . . . um—"

"You're fine, Owen. Just call her Fury," Roxanne whispered to him. "You didn't do anything wrong; she just doesn't like it."

I grunted as I put my hands on my thighs and pushed myself up, wiping my palms on my shorts. I smoothed my hair out of my face and looked at the two shifters waiting for me. Roxanne was leaning against the car, calm as ever. Owen looked worried that his driving had caused a problem for me, and that he might suffer the wrath of my mate.

"It's not your fault, dude," I said to him, holding my stomach. It felt tender and far too sensitive. "I don't do well in cars at all. Doesn't matter who's driving."

Roxanne looked up, meeting his worried eyes. "It's true, and it isn't a secret. Roman knows." She clapped him on the back. "You're good. Give us some time to shop. We'll be here for a couple of hours. There's a café right there," she said, pointing to a tiny restaurant a block down the street. "I made you a reservation so you'd be comfortable. I'll call you when we're wrapping up."

The kid beamed at her. "Thank you, Ms. Mikaelson," he said, nodding and looking at me. I waved him off with a forced smile.

When he was out of a normal range of hearing, though he probably heard me anyway, I hissed, "A couple of hours,

Rox? Don't people just pick out a dress and buy the damn thing? How does that take two hours?"

"Oh, stop complaining. It won't be that bad," she said, turning on her heel to walk up to the storefront.

I looked up but there was no signage to attract customers from the street. Barely any indication of where we were. Lettering on the door read *Kelly Lee Boutique*, but other than that, it was a nice building that no one would have a reason to stop by and visit.

Roxanne opened the door, and I followed her, standing in the entry with my arms crossed and feeling incredibly uncomfortable from the moment I walked in.

I didn't belong here. At all. I hadn't felt so out of place in a hundred years. Not only was everything pristine, but it also looked like someone else should be wearing these clothes. They were frilled and feminine. Pretty. Flawless.

"Don't be intimidated, Fury," Roxanne whispered, reading me like an open book. "You could rock any number of these dresses."

Taking in a pale pink ball gown with its billowing skirt, I said, "I'm not so sure about that."

"Roxanne," a woman said as she walked up to us. "I heard you come in. I was so glad to see you on the books today. I was wondering when you'd be in. I almost thought you were having someone else dress you this year." A tall woman with creamy skin and long black hair leaned in to kiss Roxanne's cheek, and I took a step back in case she tried to do that to me.

"You know I wouldn't dream of it, Kelly." Roxanne kissed her cheek in greeting. "A lot's been happening lately." The knowing look they shared told me that Miss Dress here knew all about Roman Mikaelson finding his second-chance mate. "I'm sorry we're cutting it close, and I imagine you've been busy fitting people for the summit, but I knew you'd be able to take care of us."

Kelly's gaze shifted to me—my posture tight, arms crossed, knees skinned and bleeding—and she didn't turn her nose up at me. "Fury, it's a pleasure," she said, holding out her hand. I uncrossed my arms to shake her hand, surprised to find her genuinely kind and unassuming. "I'm happy to dress you both. But first, your knees. What happened? Did you fall outside?"

"I tripped getting out of the car. Lucky the ground was there to break my fall," I said.

"Well, let's get you cleaned up first." She ran to the back before I could say anything.

I looked at Roxanne, and she shook her head before I could argue my case about not needing a Band-Aid. "Don't get blood on her dresses. Just let her clean you up."

"Fine," I mumbled, sarcastically. "I suppose that makes sense."

"You can't die, Fury," she whispered, pointing to my knees, "but you can still get hurt. Even if it's a little blood, you haven't healed yet. So your healing powers are slower than mine, it would seem."

"Okay, stop being all logical," I said under my breath.

"Shopping really brings out the best in you, did you know that?"

I glared at her as Kelly came back out, waving at us.

"Come on back to the room. I have you all set up," she called from an archway.

I followed Roxanne through a rainbow sea of dresses and silky fabrics, still certain I would do better as a waiter at this shindig.

We entered a room with a plush couch and other seating. On a carved wooden table sat a tray of hors d'oeuvres and two flutes of what I assumed by the bubbles to be champagne.

"What kind of dress shopping is this?" I whispered to Roxanne.

She huffed a laugh. "The best kind."

I looked at the spread of food that had been laid out. Tiny sandwiches, a fruit salad, and a dish of pastries. Real dishes and linen napkins. I went over to the table to pick up a glass. "Is it free?"

She looked at me wide-eyed and shushed me.

I threw my hands up at her. "I'm new to this," I hissed at her. "And I feel really weird right now, okay? I like my jeans and Docs. They're comfortable. I like your brother's leather jacket. I wouldn't have thought it at first, but Dorian has pretty good taste in loose-fitting, comfy clothes too." I took the champagne and drank it down.

Roxanne sighed and smiled at me. "I know he does."

Before I could comment, Kelly returned to the room with someone. "Roxanne, Fury, this is my assistant, Jovie." A remarkably beautiful girl with high cheekbones and flawless skin waved at us. Vampire. Her pant suit was feminine, but sharp, and her eyes were focused. "She has keen taste when it comes to fashion and design. You should see what she's been working on. This fabulous spread she's called Evening through the Ages. It's simply stunning."

Jovie smiled and dipped her head. "I appreciate you saying so." She looked at Roxanne. "I have something special for you that Kelly thinks you'll like. I'll be back in a moment with a selection for you to try on." She left, and I sat on the chaise longue, propping my legs up and crossing my ankles.

Kelly came to sit next to me, and I tensed. She saw my hesitation and pointed at my knees. "May I?"

"Oh yeah, I forgot about that," I said, moving to make room for her.

She waved her hand over my knees and her eyes glowed silver for a brief second. She whispered a few words under her breath, and I looked down at my scrapes. They were gone. She moved away, pleased with herself.

"Thank you," I said, realizing the sting was gone and inspecting her handiwork. "Roxanne didn't mention that you're a witch."

"Oh?" she asked, looking to Roxanne for clarification.

She shrugged at me, unapologetic. Looking at Kelly, she said, "Fury lost a bet with a witch once, and she got stuck with a mouthy talking crow as a result. She sounded sour about it, so I didn't want her to toss you in the same pool."

Kelly laughed, nodding. "Was it my sister? Because that honestly sounds like something she would do. But seriously, it's okay. We aren't all that awful. We get a bad rap, but I suppose every supernatural does to an extent."

Speaking of the crow . . . I needed to figure out a better way to keep track of him. He was my link to Duke, but that only worked if he was with me. Now I had him on a mission looking for anyone who knew about the two fuckers in the warehouse. He knew I was at Roman's now, but where could I find him? It wouldn't surprise me if he were sitting in a tree waiting to shit on my head, to be honest.

"Fury?" Roxanne's voice pulled me from my thoughts.

"I'm sorry, what?" I asked, refocusing on my surroundings.

Both women looked at me with concern. "Kelly was just asking you about your style," she prompted, taking a piece of shortbread and eating it.

"Oh . . ." I trailed off. "My style?"

"Yes, your style. What fabrics do you like? Will you be

dancing? Here, stand up and let me look at your shoulders and frame. We wouldn't want to put the wrong cut on you. It's important we accentuate and work with your bone structure and your features, not against them."

"Uh . . ." I looked to Roxanne for help.

"Yes, I imagine she will dance. Something that moves easily. Nothing too tight or stiff. Nothing with a corset," Roxanne offered. "Oh, and the guys will be wearing Ralph Lauren."

"Which one?" she asked.

"Black Gregory Handmade Shawl," she answered.

I looked at her with my brows furrowed. What was she even talking about?

"Good. Yes." Kelly held her fist under her chin, humming and nodding as she took in the information. "Is there anything you've seen before that you like? From a movie or an award show?"

A switch flipped. I met her eyes. "Yes. *The Great Gatsby*."

"Gatsby?" She tapped her lips, her eyes twinkling. "Give me a moment. I have some ideas." She shuffled out of the room.

Roxanne gave me a look of surprise. "I didn't picture you going that classic. *The Great Gatsby*. That's the 1920s, right?"

"I'm an old soul, what can I say?" I shrugged. "You can't deny that the look would fit me though. Loose fitting. Not tight or stiff. Just enough edge to be dark, and just enough class to be sexy." I smiled, no longer hating the idea of a dress.

She smiled at me and shook her head. "I won't disagree with you. I just didn't picture it." She took a sip of her champagne, then said, "Dorian probably did. He has an eye for things like that."

My interest was piqued. "What, fashion?"

"No, not fashion. Just . . . reading people, I suppose."

I looked at her knowingly. "What happened between you two? You had a thing with him, that much is clear."

She threw her hands up. "Oh, no you don't. I am not falling in that trap. This is weird enough already on so many levels. I'm not going to kiss and tell."

Just then, Jovie came around the corner, holding a selection of dresses for Roxanne. "Kelly told me you love long skirts and form-fitting bodices. I have some here for you, but I think you may find this one to your liking. I have some standard go-tos, and a phenomenal two-tone trench gown. But this one here," she said, pulling out a shiny black number, "this is the one I see on you. Square neck, duchesse satin, classic black. I say we add pink pumps for a splash of color."

Roxanne ran her hand over the gown Jovie had suggested. "Oh, this one . . . it's beautiful," she whispered.

I smiled at the way she lit up. I nodded to her. "Go try it on. I want to see you in it."

She grinned, taking the dress, and walking into a changing suite right as Kelly came back with a little surprise of her own.

She held up a gown of liquid silver dotted with tiny beads in an intricate pattern. She began to fill me in on the details I could already see. "Yes," I breathed, as she talked up the cap sleeves and floor-length material. It would hug the body then drape loosely starting at about mid-thigh.

"It's the closest I have to hitting that Gatsby, 1920s era you were looking for. Jovie was working on it, but with a few touches, I can have it in time for the summit without a problem. It's not ready to try on," she said, pointing to some pinned areas and unfinished beadwork, "but we can get your measurements, and have it done before you leave."

Witches worked quickly, but not as fast as fae, apparently. Dorian could've just made the dress appear finished with a single thought. But I wouldn't complain. Not one bit.

"Done," I said, as Roxanne opened the door from her suite and came out in her black dress. She poked her foot out, clad in pink high-heeled shoes that looked like they were meant to be the death of someone. I pointed to them. "Can you walk in those?"

She smirked and strutted across the room, her curves and figure showing they were made for the way that dress clung to her every move. She stopped in front of Kelly and me, then looked at the beaded beauty hanging over the shop owner's arms.

"Is this yours?" she asked in awe. I nodded. "This is so . . . it's you. You were right. I haven't even seen you in this and I can tell it's meant for you."

I winked at her. "I know. It's like I know what I like, or something weird like that."

She whacked my arm and looked at Kelly. "Can I look at clutches and accessories?"

Kelly's eyes sparkled. "You always know how to make me smile. C'mon, this is my favorite part." Jovie came to take the dress from Kelly, but she held on to it. "I'll take this up front. We're going to take some measurements and get this one tidied up for Fury. Will you take care of that while I pick out a clutch with Roxanne?"

She dipped her head. "Of course."

Roxanne put her hand on her hip, jutting it out like a model. She spun on her heel, shaking her wild hair, and making sure to accentuate the swing of her hips. "Too much?"

"Go pick out a purse," I told her, rolling my eyes.

She laughed, walking out of the room, calling over her shoulder, "It's a clutch."

I huffed, and muttered under my breath, wondering if she heard me mocking her. The distinct lack of shouting said she either didn't or chose to ignore it.

"If you'd like to step over here, I can get your measurements," Jovie said, pointing to an area in front of a wall of mirrors.

"Yeah, sure," I said, making my way over to her. "What am I supposed to do?"

"Just stand here." She pointed to a circle on the floor.

I did as I was told, and she stretched a measuring tape from my shoulders to the floor, making a mental note, I assumed. She didn't write anything down.

"Arms out," she said, and I held them out, parallel to the ground.

She first measured across my back, and then from shoulder to fingertip. I scrunched my eyebrows together, catching our reflection in the mirrors.

"Why did you do that?" I asked, cautiously.

"Hmm?" she hummed, looking up into the mirror to meet my gaze.

"You measured the length of my arm." She stared at me blankly. "For a dress that has cap sleeves."

For a moment, she didn't respond. Then she laughed, looking down at the floor. She put her hands on her hips before looking up at me again. Jovie's eyes darkened and the pleasant smile fell away. A look of blind hatred stared back at me.

She opened her jacket, revealing a small bomb wrapped around her waist.

This wasn't happening again. Really? Was one day

without death threats too much to ask? I took two steps back, putting distance between me and the kamikaze vampire. My back bumped up against the heavy changing suite door.

"Time's up, Sunny," she said, a feral grin on her face.

I heard that name, and her choice of words echoed the vampires in the warehouse, and my mind was torn as I processed them. I stared at her for what felt like entirely too long, though it couldn't have been more than a second. "What the fuck did you just call me?"

At that moment, I heard Roxanne's voice on the other side of the main door. "Fury? What do you think of this clutch and these earrings?" she called, getting closer to us.

I made a snap decision when I saw Jovie's lip curl slightly, revealing a touch of her fang. Time was indeed up.

I turned around and ripped the heavy door off its hinges, shouting to Roxanne to run and get out. I'd be back soon, and this vampire bitch would be dead, but Rox needed to be as far away from the blast as I could get her. I swung the heavy wood into Jovie, sending her crashing into the wall in the far corner.

The room exploded, and my body flew back, crashing through something hard.

I landed with a thud, a heavy object on top of me, my head slamming into the ground.

The wind was knocked out of my lungs and my entire body hurt from the impact.

Time crawled in slow motion.

From a distance, I heard muffled screaming. Voices that were far away and calling my name.

Whatever was on top of me was pulled off. My vision was blurred, as if a haze filled the room. Roxanne's panicked look didn't register as real, and I could barely hear her screaming my name. I groaned, reaching up to touch my ears and pulling away fingertips wet with blood.

I tried to move, but my muscles protested, and my bones cracked.

"Kill me now," I muttered to Roxanne, and I was dead serious.

"Shut up, Fury, I'm not going to kill you," she said, yelling something I couldn't understand to Kelly.

Was Kelly a traitor too? Was Rox still in danger? I couldn't even get up to help. Ugh, this human body sucked so bad.

Roxanne hovered over me, pressing something to my leg, and dialing on her phone with one hand. She put it to her ear, and the last thing heard before I faded out completely was the sound of her voice.

"Dorian? I need you now."

CHAPTER 36
EZRA

Roman sat on a couch in his living room with his elbows resting on his knees and his hands running over his dreads. He was struggling to keep his temper in check. Keep the wolf down.

Dorian stood next to a large window overlooking the lake, his arms crossed, lost in thought. Who knew how he was actually handling it? The fae was made of marble ninety-five percent of the time.

I sat in a high-backed chair, my head tilted back.

"I don't understand how the witch knew nothing of that vampire," Roman said to no one in particular.

"Kelly," Dorian said. "Her name is Kelly. Both Ezra and I interrogated her. She was completely unaware of the motives, and distraught that it had even happened. When I arrived, she had Rox and Fury shielded in an effort to protect them until she realized it was me." He sighed, still gazing out the window. "She's working on some of Fury's wounds right now."

Indeed she was. Which was why Fury was rambling and

cursing up a storm, directing her angry thoughts at me through our connection.

"How did this happen?" Roman asked, looking in my direction.

"I have no idea. Jovie wasn't one of mine—"

"But she's under your jurisdiction. She is your faction, your responsibility—"

"Don't lecture me, wolf. I'm well aware of my roles and responsibilities. Before you rudely interrupted me, I was going to say she wasn't one of mine, but nothing about her lines up. We keep track of every vampire who comes in and out of here. None of my men knew of her, didn't recognize the picture Kelly had of her, nothing. It's as though she appeared out of thin air."

Roman added, "What I don't understand is why the vampires are suddenly willing to just bleed out or strap a bomb to themselves. For what purpose? What's the point of trying to kill Fury?"

"Fae," Dorian interjected. "We could potentially be looking at fae. I had thought witches, but it could be fae. Spells or compulsion could be what's pushing them. These suicidal vampires don't necessarily have to believe in the cause, they just have to be controlled."

I held my hand out, gesturing to Dorian. "See? He doesn't know the motives either, and he has nothing better to do in life than stare out windows and think shit up." I craned my neck, stretching the muscles. "This involves more than vampires. We just don't know who else quite yet."

"Are we looking at a small cult, an army, a group of extremists? Who fucking knows anymore?" Roman started to shake, his eyes burning an icy blue.

"Rein it in, Roman. She's upstairs. She can't die. She's fine," I reminded him.

I'd be fine if you let me die, Fangs.

I believe the general consensus was no. I voted to kill you if that makes you happy.

She whined in frustration. *This witch is knitting muscle back together. My skin is on fire. It's painful to breathe—*

Pull up your big girl pants, demon. I thought she gave you something for the pain. You have a low pain tolerance for someone who—

I haven't been in pain for over a century, you hemorrhoid. I forgot what it feels like, but if you would. Just. Kill. Me, I could be back in a flash. No problem.

I broke our connection, shutting her out as much as I could until it sounded like a loud, angry whisper that was just a touch too far away. I refocused on the conversation between the fae and the wolf.

"What suggestions do you have?" Dorian asked, looking between us.

"Suggestions for?" I said, not having heard the topic we'd moved on to.

"Pay attention, Ezra," Roman growled, his fingers gripping the edge of his seat cushion.

I narrowed my gaze. "I'm thinking about a multitude of things, and I don't have time to coddle your temperamental alter ego there, youngling. Watch it."

Roman stood up, but I didn't budge. I moved faster than he did. He could bring it.

"Sit down. Now," Dorian roared, his voice booming. "This isn't between us. This just includes us, or have you forgotten? All three of us are on equal footing, and all three of us are mated to her."

I smirked, turning my head to Dorian, taking my eyes

off Roman to remind him I was in no way intimidated by his show of power. "I voted to kill her and let her come back, but you two and Roxanne outnumbered me." I shrugged. "I put in my two cents."

Dorian pinched the bridge of his nose. "We've moved past that. The answer was no. It's not worth the risk. We don't need another one of her bodies to dispose of. We can't draw any more attention to ourselves than we already have, especially not the week of the summit. The bomb was at a public place. Human first responders are involved. Kelly is healing her to the best of her ability. Drop it."

No such luck, kitten. Tough it out, I said to her mentally.

A string of curses and creative ways to insult us bombarded my thoughts, causing me to almost laugh at her.

I exhaled loudly. "What was the other question?"

"The summit," Roman answered, his voice terse. "How do we keep her safe?"

"I don't know," I said, shrugging slightly. "I haven't really put much thought into it."

Roman looked at me incredulously, then looked to Dorian for help. "I know you don't care about mates, but this is callous, even for you," he growled, turning in my direction. "If you don't want the bond, reject her and move along. Just get it over with and get back to your club and endless, meaningless fucks. No one here's going to throw you a farewell party, but not caring about whether she lives or dies—"

"She can't die," I shouted, leaning forward in my chair, gripping the arms. "For fuck's sake, this has nothing to do with rejecting or having been rejected, you sanctimonious dickhead. Fury can't die, so excuse the fuck out of me for not running myself into the ground over how to protect her from *dying*."

"Yet," Dorian interjected, turning his head slightly before looking back out the window.

"What?" Roman and I said in unison.

"You said she can't die. Yet. She can't die *yet*," Dorian answered.

I sat back, massaging a temple. "Wait, what are you saying, Dorian? You saw what happens when she dies. You were there."

Roman groaned and scraped his hands down his face as if realizing something. I looked between them, waiting for an answer.

Roman looked up. "How many times should *you* have died in your lifetime? What about Dorian? And me?"

"We're only alive because nothing has killed us *yet*, and there's been no shortage of accidents or what should have been fatal encounters over the ages. We've questioned it before on how many occasions?" Dorian argued, looking over his shoulder.

I sighed. I knew more about her than they did. They couldn't understand. "It's not the same, though. We just regenerate and heal. She died and then *came back in a new body*."

"And when does that stop?" Dorian asked.

I stared at him blankly. "What'd you say?"

"I said, when does it stop? She can't die now. At what point does she?" He turned his head to look at us again. "Every supernatural has something that can kill them. It would stand to reason she does too."

"We don't," I said stubbornly. She wasn't the same as us, and I had no way of explaining it to them.

"Not *yet*," Roman said quietly. "But over the years,

there've been enough attempts on us to know our enemies have certainly tried to find out what does kill us, right? It's only a matter of time before someone gets us with something we can't heal from."

A realization washed over me, and for the first time I acknowledged there could be a deeper truth to what they were saying. I didn't need them to understand her like I did. It was good they didn't. Where I had arrogance leading me to a false sense of security, they were able to see more clearly.

I leaned forward, running my fingers through my hair. Killing her body was easy. Could someone stop the demon from coming back? I didn't know the answer. She would tell me no, but their logic . . .

"You're right." I exhaled deeply then nodded. "It's always only been a matter of time for us. Now she's in the same place. We don't know anything about her enemy, but we know they want her dead."

"They're not going to stop either," Roman said, his elbows resting on his thighs as he clasped his hands together. "It could be tomorrow or a hundred years from now, but whoever is after her won't stop until they succeed, and they don't care about collateral damage at all."

Somehow, figuring this out had put him in more control of his wolf. I didn't understand that in the slightest. Now that *I* saw the bigger picture, a part of me was fighting against an unnamed emotion deep in my chest.

"What do we do?" I asked.

Dorian moved from the window, coming to sit in another chair near me. He crossed his legs, rubbing his thumb over his fingers repeatedly while thinking. When he finally spoke, he said, "She has to stay here until the summit. Roxanne said she isn't leaving the house, and that she is going to stay here as well. I have too much to do in preparation for the summit itself, in addition to jumping between here and Avalon while I deal with something." He looked at me, anticipating an argument. "Ezra—"

"I don't disagree. She needs to stay here. We don't know if fae or witches are involved. And seeing that we've had three vampires try to kill her, I don't know how far the betrayal runs or who I can trust. Kendrick's the only one I can say with certainty." I shifted my focus to Roman. "It pains me greatly to say it, but right now, the shifters are the most trustworthy."

Even the shifter driver, Owen, had shown his loyalty. Not only had I listened to his thoughts, but he too had been guarding Roxanne and Fury when Dorian had arrived. A witch and a shifter, protecting a demon. It would've been laughable only minutes ago. Now? Concern and hesitation washed over me, and I pushed the new feelings aside, trying to focus.

Dorian dipped his head in thanks for my agreement.

I watched Roman. He'd been teetering on the edge of sanity since she'd arrived. I'd seen flashes and hints of icy blue in his eyes, the dormant wolf demanding to come out. Though he seemed more in control once he had a better understanding of the situation, I knew it would be short-lived. I only wondered how long before his wolf showed himself? It had been a long time . . .

"That brings us to the summit itself," Dorian said. "I can come get Roxanne and Fury. I'll sift and bring them to the summit directly. No driving, no go-betweens."

"Who do we have that we trust implicitly?" I asked, holding out my hand and raising my index finger. "Kendrick, that's one. Roxanne, and Caitlin . . ." I held up my second and third fingers, and Roman nodded.

"James and Tristan, for certain," Dorian said. "That's five. We have to move around and socialize. We don't want anyone to suspect there's something going on in the background. Roxanne can keep an eye on Fury when we aren't with her."

Thinking about the layout of the grand ballroom where we would have our first night of the summit, I said, "It'll be tough to limit entrances. We don't have enough people. James can be in the kitchen, watching what happens in that area. He'll blend in well."

"Put Tristan at the front door. Less likely to draw attention to himself," Roman added, sitting back in his chair.

"Put Kendrick on a side entrance. He's good at lurking in the shadows. Would Roxanne work best at the back? We can make our rounds, bringing Fury to her after we arrive," I said.

Dorian nodded. "That works well. They can alternate posts if they need to. Fury and Roxanne will inevitably move around the room, but we can limit their movement. Caitlin, Tristan, and Kendrick can rotate their assigned locations as needed."

Roman cracked his neck and sighed. "It's not enough."

"It has to be," I said. "It's what we've got. We keep close, and we can work out how to manage each day moving forward."

Dorian gazed between Roman and me, looking for signs of agreement. "Let's get through the summit. Then we figure out what the hell is going on. In the meantime, we keep her safe."

CHAPTER 37

I stuffed the last of the french fries into my mouth as Roxanne ran the rules by me one more time.

"I got it," I said through a mouthful of food.

"Repeat it, then," she said, hands resting on her hips. She was already dressed, with her hair styled and makeup done. She was just waiting on me to finish eating so I could get dressed. Why was I eating now and not at this grand dinner that was going to be held at the summit? Why was I eating a chicken burger—not that it didn't taste good—instead of indulging in a six-course French fusion discovery?

I recited the rules. "Don't eat the food in case they try to poison me. Again. Don't let anyone else get me a drink. If I set my drink down, don't drink from it again. Always have a babysitter with me," I mocked in a bored tone. "I heard you, Rox. For three days, I've heard you. And Roman. And Dorian—"

She held her hands up in surrender and blew out a deep breath. "Okay, okay. I'm sorry. I'm just worried. Feeling a little anxious."

I wiped my mouth off and stood, patting the little bulge on my belly. "Good thing my dress isn't as form fitting as yours, am I right?"

She huffed a laugh, but I could still hear her anxiety riding her.

"It's going to be fine. Of all the places to try something, you really think anyone in their right mind would try tonight?"

She glared at me. "Thinking like that will get you into trouble."

I shrugged, moving to the walk-in closet where my dress hung. "Yeah, but I can get out of trouble, so I'm really not all that concerned about it."

"You'll be the death of me, I swear," she mumbled.

I laughed, getting undressed and stepping into my new gown.

That psycho vamp had only blown up the back of the store where the changing rooms were. It was just enough to take us both out. Or it should've been, had that door not held up as a shield. Kelly had recreated Roxanne's dress and finished mine the day before, checking with Roman to see if she could hand deliver it.

I shimmied into the silky fabric, letting it glide across my skin as it settled in place. I slipped on the low, t-strap heels and walked into the bedroom. Roxanne let out a low whistle.

"You're going to knock them dead tonight," she breathed. "That looks stunning on you."

Warmth bloomed in my chest. It felt right, wearing this dress, even though the closest I'd come to something so luxurious when I was alive was in catalogs.

"Can I ask you a question?"

Roxanne looked at me in confusion. "I'm surprised you had to ask that question. I think we've been through a lot, yeah? After almost being blown up together, and all. I figured you knew you could ask me anything."

I cocked an eyebrow at her. "I asked you about your fling with Dorian, and you flat out refused to answer," I said, pointing out the contradiction.

"Mmm hmm." She nodded. "You can ask me anything. I just may not answer."

"Right." It was my turn to glare at her. "Anyway . . . Roman's your brother and you clearly had some sort of *thing* with Dorian you won't talk about. Doesn't it, I don't know . . . bother you that the three of them are my mates, especially when two of them mean something important to you? Does it bother you that your brother has to share me, and you have to watch it?"

Roxanne gave me a small smile. "No. It doesn't. It's not like you're playing the field. Bonds are . . . well, you don't get to make the rules. If you choose to accept or reject it, that's still on you, but can anyone force a bond? No." She walked over to me, straightening my dress, and smoothing out any areas that needed it. "Dorian and I weren't made to last, but that doesn't mean we didn't have fun. We were together so long ago. It was at the last summit. I love him, but not in the way you think. We made much better friends than lovers, and neither of us look at each other that way anymore."

I exhaled, not realizing my breathing had been slightly tense. I nodded. "Okay."

"Relax. There isn't one bit of anger or jealousy here. You won't get that from me. Ever." She smiled, but then frowned like she was thinking otherwise. "Well, maybe a little jealous that you can pull off that dress so well." She winked at me.

She was moving away from the emotional direction of our conversation, and I went with it. Relieved. I appreciated the deflection. "Please. If we want to discuss that kind of jealousy, I wish my skin tone looked as good with every color. You could wear something bile-colored and you'd still manage to make it look radiant."

"Ew," she laughed, "really? You went there?"

I shrugged, walking over to the dresser and grabbing the long, pearl necklaces each guy had bought me to match my outfit. I don't know who bought the first strand, but no doubt, when that was learned, the other two wouldn't be outdone. They couldn't claim me yet, but they found subtle ways to put their mark on me.

"Tell me about this hotel again. I honestly shut down when the guys were talking about it because we were on round two or three of the rules by that point." I hid my grin. Roman had to repeat it. Couldn't help himself. His desire to keep me safe was overwhelming.

"Of course you did." She snorted. "It's at one of Dorian's historic hotels downtown. It's supernatural staff only, but since this all happened, there hasn't been enough time to check everyone's background, whereabouts, dealings, and credentials again. Either way. First night of the summit is always the opening soiree."

"The meet and greet," I supplied.

"No, smart-ass, it's not a meet and greet. You aren't joining a glee club tonight. This is a big deal. This is the kickoff. The summit is tense and political. It really matters to supernaturals. This is our one night where we're all on even ground. We eat and drink—"

"I don't get to eat and drink," I grumbled, wondering where I could hide a flask in my dress. "Not unless an assigned babysitter provides me with said drink."

"Oh, look, you were listening," she mocked. "Anyway, as I was saying, we eat, drink, dance, have conversations. Schmoozing. It's political, in a way. Like sizing up opponents, but it's clean. I'll walk you through each day. Just stand with me, and you'll do fine."

I fixed my earring, thinking quietly about the job I'd been sent to do. Get through tonight and then learn more at the summit. If they were going to take it one day at a time, so would I.

Roxanne came and fixed the pin in my hair, sweeping up one side. It fell around my shoulder in loose waves. She wore a headband scarf in duchesse satin to match her dress, and it held the tight curls of her afro away from her face. Her lips were painted with a berry-colored lipstick, complementing the shade of her new shoes.

I held my arms out. "I'm as ready as I'll ever be."

We walked downstairs to find Dorian waiting for us. He was watching the sunset over the lake, adjusting his crystal cuff links, when he heard us and looked over.

For a split second, my heart stuttered in my chest.

We drank each other in, and I took back what I'd said about tuxedos looking the same. The way it was cut to his body was like magic. It had to have been. He wore a vest underneath the jacket, in a dark silver that matched the fabric beneath my beaded masterpiece.

Dorian's eyes traveled the length of my body, his lips parted slightly as his mouth hung open for a brief moment.

He cleared his throat, his voice taking on a husky tenor as he said, "Fury, you look . . ."

"Stunning?" Roxanne offered. "That's what I said."

"Breathtaking," he finished.

Never having received compliments like this, I had no idea how to respond. The best I could do was give a small smile and thank them both.

As we stared at each other silently, Roxanne eventually piped up, "So . . ."

"Yes," Dorian said, walking toward us. "Fury, we're arriving outside in case you feel sick."

My stomach twisted, knowing the sift was coming. "Oh, I'll feel sick, all right." I just wanted to keep the food down this time.

As soon as we arrived, my heart was beating faster, and my stomach threatened to empty itself. I held on to Dorian's arm as he steadied me, and I took a breath.

"Maybe we need to look into some motion sickness medicine or something," Roxanne suggested.

That would have been better to bring up earlier, and I would make sure we'd have that discussion at a later time.

"Shall we?" Dorian said, holding out his arms for each of us to wrap ours through.

We walked up the steps to the historic hotel and entered the lobby. It almost felt like a flashback. It wasn't quite 1920s, but maybe the 30s. It was old-fashioned, and I loved it. When I spotted Tristan's familiar face, I dipped my head slightly in greeting. He kept his features neutral upon seeing me, but I saw the tiny spark of acknowledgment in his eye.

We entered a room to the right of the entrance, and my mouth fell open. It had been called the grand ballroom in their discussions, but I hadn't understood why until that moment. I let go of Dorian's arm and looked around in awe.

The space was expansive, more so than the outside of the building had suggested. The floor was a beautiful cherry-stained hardwood. The windows were floor to ceiling, and warded, from what I was told. Cream drapes in a heavy, luxurious fabric hung, framing the glass. What must've been a hundred tables filled the room. Fine china and crystal glasses, gold cutlery, and opulent floral centerpieces. It was a lot to take in.

In all my life, I've never seen anyone look as beautiful as you do right now, a voice lightly touched my mind.

Smooth line for a player. I smiled and scanned the room, looking for Ezra. *Where are you?*

A hand lightly touched my waist, slid around my stomach, and pressed me to the hard body behind me. "Right here," he breathed in my ear.

My legs quaked, and a shiver of desire crept up my spine.

I turned around, and he kissed me on the cheek softly, still holding my waist, but only grazing his fingertips over me. The beads on my dress clattered together.

He stepped back, never taking his eyes off me. His tuxedo looked like Dorian's, but he had no vest and wore black on black. He kept me under his gaze for a moment longer before he turned to Roxanne, taking her hand in his, bringing it to his lips and kissing her fingers. "Roxanne, you look radiant, as always."

She winked at him. "I know."

"Rox, would you like to join me for a drink? Ezra and Fury can meet up with you in a minute, I'm sure," Dorian said. His voice wasn't cold, nor was it genuine. They were moving Roxanne to the back, where she'd keep her post, and where I would eventually follow.

Ezra nodded to Dorian knowingly, then put his attention back on me as they walked away.

He took my hand and placed it flat on his chest. I wasn't sure what his intent was until I felt a flask in his tuxedo pocket. His eyes sparkled with mirth, and I grinned at him.

"Sometimes we need a little bit to warm us up," he said, taking it out of his coat and unscrewing the top. He handed it to me, and I took a swig, feeling the burn of bourbon as it hit me.

"I appreciate the gesture," I said, taking one more and screwing the cap back on. He took a swig of his own then tucked it back into the lining.

He winked at me, his lips curling up in a grin, the tiniest point of a fang extending. Taking my hand, he laced his fingers through mine, walking me to the dance floor.

String music played, nothing too fast. Simple melodies to get the night started as people were arriving.

Ezra put his hand on the small of my back, pulling me close, swaying and moving our bodies in time with the music.

"I could get used to this," I said quietly, remembering what it felt like to be pressed against him in bed.

"I'd prefer it, honestly. But you'll be passed between us tonight," he said, looking around the room as we danced.

I cocked an eyebrow at him. "I knew you were willing to share, I just didn't realize you were so blasé about it."

His fingertips pressed into my back, and his eyes glittered with hunger. "You've been with the wolf for five days. I hate it."

I shrugged. "Do something about it," I challenged.

He opened his mouth when a deep voice came from behind me. "May I?"

Ezra grunted, seeing Roman. I turned around and had to catch my breath.

Roman's dreads were pulled back, showing off his cheekbones and amber eyes. Up close, I could see flecks of icy blue within. His ever-present wolf on the watch.

He wore the same tuxedo as Ezra and Dorian, choosing to go for the classic styling. It hugged his muscles, but the cut was tailored to him and flowed naturally with his movements.

"Roman," I breathed. "You look handsome."

He smiled and reached out, tucking a stray wave behind my ear. "You look . . . beyond comparison." He looked over at Ezra, nodding knowingly, and Ezra returned the gesture.

To be continued, he said as he walked away, mingling with supernaturals I didn't know.

I took Roman's hand in mine, and his other rested around my waist as we danced toward Roxanne's assigned corner.

"Thank you," he said.

I looked at him, confused. "For what?"

"For giving us the illusion of control with you tonight. For letting us keep you safe," he murmured.

When his normally deep voice whispered, it vibrated over my skin and through my bones. I breathed him in, taking in his scent as I closed my eyes and he led me across the floor.

"What do I smell like?" he asked me.

My eyes flew open. "What?"

"You smell like storms and chaos. I want to know what you think I smell like," he answered.

My stomach tightened at his heated gaze. I cleared my throat. "Like . . . wind. The trees. Earth," I said, closing my eyes as I spoke.

"Ahem," Ezra said, "hate to interrupt."

Roman glared at him. "And yet, here you are instead of my sister," he grumbled.

"She said you took too long and went to the bathroom," he said. "I told her I would wait here."

"I doubt she said that first part," I said. "But I'll go to the bathroom too." They shared a look, and I saw the hesitation. "Guys, she just went to the bathroom. I'll only be walking alone until I get in there then I'm with her. It's okay."

"Ezra, you stay until they're back?" Roman asked, and he nodded in agreement. A small smile gracing his lips, he squeezed my hand before letting go and disappearing into the crowd.

"I'll be right back," I said, heading down the hall to the women's restroom, feeling Ezra's eyes on me.

I pushed the door open and walked in. A sitting area where women could touch up their makeup was empty, the plush couches untouched.

"Rox?" I called, walking into a stall, and shutting the door as I heard a toilet flush. I started to carefully pull my skirt up. "Rox?"

No answer.

A chill crept up my spine. This was wrong.

The skirt material fell out of my hands, back down to the floor.

I slowly opened the stall door, listening for sounds in the bathroom and hearing nothing.

I stepped out, checking the periphery first and only then looking forward.

A piece of folded white paper was on the counter. A tube of lipstick sat on top.

I rushed over to it, picking up the tube, seeing it

smeared with blood. My breath hitched. My heart started pounding in my ears.

Carefully unfolding the note, I read the words written in a familiar berry color.

EAST SIDE EXIT. A car is waiting. Get in. Alone. Or Roxanne dies, and she doesn't come back.

CHAPTER 38

I read it three times.

Shock pulsed through me before resolve set in. I calculated my odds if I simply defied them and told the alphas. After all, there was strength in numbers, right?

That very logic made me hesitate. I suspected whoever was behind this had to have numbers too. A lot of them, by the looks of it. If they saw me make my way out of the bathroom and go tell Dorian or Roman—that would be it. I had little doubt they'd kill her to make a point. Then they'd wait to steal someone else or find some other plan to lure me out.

At least I couldn't die. Not permanently.

I could tell Ezra. Keep him updated. Let him tell the guys once I was wherever that car would take me. If they didn't release Roxanne, though . . .

Best-case scenario, I could play my cards right and find a way to save her.

Worst-case scenario, Roxanne died.

That wasn't an acceptable outcome. Emotion flooded

me. Losing her . . . it would haunt me. She deserved so much more. I would do anything to get her back.

I swiped the bloody lipstick off the counter, folded up the paper, and tossed them both in the trash.

Ezra brushed against my mind. *Everything all right?*

There's been a change of plans, I thought back, turning for the bathroom door. I peeked my head out then exited and turned down the hall—for the back door that would lead to my getaway car.

Change? His mental voice took on a different quality. Sharper. More perceptive. *Fury, what the actual fuck are you doing?*

They took Roxanne. I was told to take the east exit where she was posted and head out back. A car will be waiting for me there.

"Fury?" a light voice called. I paused mid-step, stomach sinking.

"Yes?" I turned, plastering a smile on my face for Caitlin.

She smiled too, but the slight narrowing of her eyes told me she wasn't buying it. "Where are you going?" she asked, starting toward me at a still somewhat casual pace. "We were very clear on everything before we came—"

I lifted my hands in mock surrender, letting the tension ease from my shoulders. "I know, I know. It's just, I really don't do great with parties. Or crowds. Or people, for that matter. I just need a couple minutes of fresh air without one of the guys or one of their people breathing down my neck, ya know?"

I'm getting Dorian and we are coming to you, Ezra said, and it was a real effort not to let the annoyance show on my face. Caitlin's suspicions had lowered, and I didn't want to give it away.

If you get Dorian, you can kiss my ass and our deal goodbye.

I'm a hundred-and-twenty-six-year-old demon that can't fucking die, Ezra. Roxanne can, and unlike me, she doesn't get to come back. You know this. I'll keep in contact with you, but we do things my way. I felt his hesitation, a mental pause as he considered it, and Caitlin caught up with me.

"Mind if I go with you, then? I could use some air myself." Instead of waiting for an answer, she continued past me and out the double doors.

I sighed. Just great. Exactly what I needed. Another fucking complication when I was trying to save Roxanne.

Ezra? I thought as I started for the door. *Are you with me?*

His answer was immediate. *I think this is a rash plan. You . . . There are things we don't understand about what's after you. You—*

They will kill Roxanne, Ezra. I won't let her take the fall. Are you with me, or am I alone in this?

You're never alone. I'll play along for now. For Roxanne. But the second I lose contact with you, I'm telling them, and we give chase. Do you understand?

That was a decent compromise and probably the best I was going to get, given I was his mate and all. *Understood. Now keep them distracted because I have to take out Caitlin.*

I shoved at the door a little harder than necessary and stepped out into the sticky embrace of the night air. It was thick with humidity, trapped by the clouds that told of a coming storm. It made my dress cling to me even more, and not in a good way.

"So," Caitlin said as the door shut behind me. She had a cigarette in hand and a lighter in the other. She flicked the top, and a small flame came to life. She touched it to the end, and it turned a burnt orange and began to glow. "Is this really about the party and your role as their mate being overwhelming, or were the last few days with us just an act? I can't quite tell, but I know you're a good actor."

Aw shit. That made me feel even worse about what I was going to have to do. I casually stepped toward her, scanning the street.

A black Honda Civic was parked down at the end. The lights were on, but the car wasn't moving. If I had to bet, that was my driver.

"Color me surprised. You don't seem the type to smoke," I said, coming up beside her at an angle.

She took a long draw then blew it out. "Working for Roman isn't always easy. There are a lot of shifters to be managed, and someone has to take care of the things he can't. I picked up the habit after Maya died and haven't quite been able to stop." She tilted her head to look at me out of the corner of her eyes. "You didn't answer my question."

I sighed. "No, it isn't an act."

The edge of her mouth tugged up. "I'm happy to hear it. I worried when I saw you heading for the door."

Normally, I would've asked for a cigarette and mentally taken a seat. Maybe even enjoyed the conversation. I liked her better when she was more direct and less uptight. Which made this suck that much more.

I moved closer until I could sling my arm over her shoulders. She gave me a strange look but didn't shrug me off. "Unfortunately for us both, the truth is I care a little too much." Her eyebrows drew together in confusion. I curled my arm inward, cutting off her air supply in an instant. "I'm sorry about this, really."

She tried to take in a breath and gagged.

I'd already maneuvered my position to be somewhat behind her so that when she reared back, trying to stab me with the burning end of the cigarette, I caught her wrist and twisted it. She hissed in pain, letting out more of her precious air supply. I was careful not to break it though, just bruise. I wouldn't hurt her any more than necessary. I just needed to get away.

They're starting to wonder. Need to hurry up, Ezra chimed in as Caitlin tried to stomp on my foot.

"I'm going as fast as I can," I grunted.

She used her free hand to reach behind her and grab a fistful of my hair.

Motherfucker.

"The hair?" I winced as she threatened to rip it out of my scalp. "That's a low blow."

She grumbled in reply. I took that to mean she wouldn't have if I weren't strangling her. It was a good point. Unfortunately, it wouldn't save Roxanne.

She doesn't want to hurt you, but she's going to shift to protect herself. Hit her in the side of the head and be done with it, Ezra said.

I pressed harder against her throat and the thrashing increased. "I'm trying not to hurt her. Turns out that's a lot harder than trying to cause pain," I groaned.

She's a wolf. She'll heal. Do it now.

Her body began vibrating, and her chest rumbled. Her wolf was coming out. I tightened my arm over her throat in a lock that would've killed a human. The shifting halted. Her thrashing movements slowed, becoming weak. Languid. Only when they stopped altogether did I start to relieve the pressure.

She didn't gasp or jerk to life. Her legs gave out, and she started to crumple. I let her down gently, hoping that he was right about her healing. Her pant suit was ripped, and her hair was a sweaty mess.

A sliver of guilt ate at me even as I saw the slight rise and fall of her chest.

Take care of her, I told him.

I didn't have time to stick around and keep an eye on her.

There was a car waiting for me.

All I had to do was take it.

I started down the street, walking as fast as I could in my heels. When I got to the end of the sidewalk, the blacked-out window rolled down.

"Get in the back," a man's voice said. I didn't recognize it, or him.

I reached for the handle then paused. "How do I know she's alive?"

He lifted a gloved hand, holding a cellphone. A few taps on the screen and Roxanne's face lit up. He turned it around to show me.

Her dress was torn, and her left eye was swollen and blackened. She had a split lip and heavily bruised jaw. She must've put up a fight. I couldn't figure out why she hadn't shifted.

"Rox?" I asked in a terse voice, noticing the rise and fall of her chest. She blinked a couple times with her good eye. "I'm coming to get you. Just hang tight."

"No," she rasped. Her vocal cords sounded shot to hell. They must've really done a number on her. She moved her mouth, trying to form words. What she could say came out in a slur. "Roman needs you. You're his last chance—"

"All right, chat time is over. Are you going to get in the car, or we gonna do this the hard way?" my driver asked in a deep voice. Given how rough Roxanne already looked, I wasn't sure she could handle the hard way.

"Nope, that's proof enough." I opened the back door of the car and slipped in.

His eyes met mine in the rearview mirror, cold and unflinching. At first glance I'd thought they were brown, but they were a dark shade of purple. He wore a hat that covered his ears, but I suspected fae. No one else had eyes like that.

He lifted his hand, holding a vial between his forefinger and thumb. "Drink this."

"Do I have a choice?" I asked, knowing it was a drug of some kind and doubting I'd get lucky enough for it to be poison.

"Do you want to see the she-wolf live? Or have you reconsidered the hard way? I don't believe wolves can regrow fingers and toes very fast. Pretty painful."

I sighed.

This is a bad idea, Fury. I don't trust it.

No shit, I thought back to him. *The point isn't to trust them. It's to make sure Roxanne comes out alive. Just stick to the plan.*

"Times up, Devil. Drink it or I have my friend get his pliers out and we can watch her lose them one by one."

I reached out and took the bottle in my hand. It was cool to the touch, but not cold. The liquid inside glowed a faint green, which meant magic was at play here. Not science.

"Bottoms up," I murmured, popping the cap with my thumb.

I pressed the rim to my lips. There was only enough for two swallows, but one swallow was all it took.

My head started to spin. My vision blurred. I expected to lose consciousness, but when I didn't immediately pass out, alarm bells clanged in my head.

My driver turned around in his seat, another object in hand. Even cross-eyed and seeing double, there was no mistaking the syringe.

"I really hate being drugged," I groaned. "Can't we do this the easy way where I just sit here—"

He moved faster than I'd anticipated, though in all honesty, I probably wouldn't have stopped him, anyway. I'd already come this far and swallowed the weird green potion. There was no turning back now.

The needle disappeared into my thigh. The twinge of pain that followed was so slight I wouldn't have noticed if I hadn't watched him push the stopper down.

"Time to take a nap," he said.

My eyelids fluttered. My thoughts wavered as Ezra shouted in my head. I counted the seconds, only getting to eight before blackness closed in.

CHAPTER 39

Carnival music played softly in the background.

I tried to open my eyelids, but they didn't seem to be working right. The darkness still surrounded me, but that damning music grounded me in reality. I tugged at my arms, but they didn't seem to be working either. Neither were my legs. I tried to wiggle a single toe, but I wasn't sure if I actually did or if it was just my mind playing tricks on me.

The music continued to play all around me.

Left. Right. It went round and round and—

A wave of vertigo hit me. Or maybe it already had, and I was only now registering what it was. Vomit fought its way up my throat. The acid burned as it climbed.

The music kept playing.

And I kept spinning.

My lips broke apart as my body's natural aversion to movement sent the contents of my dinner spewing everywhere.

My eyes flew open.

Suddenly, the darkness was gone. Instead, bright lights

assaulted me. They were everywhere. Red and white. Gold and blue. My head lolled as the spinning continued. My neck rolled and my head followed like a bobble, unable to stop itself.

My wrists were tied together over a golden metal pole that was moving up and down in a rhythmic motion in time with the music. I tried to regain control of my body, but that was a lost cause. My legs were strapped to stirrups. I was riding an animatronic metal horse.

Carousel.

I was on a carousel.

Ezra? I called out mentally.

My hope was already fizzling, but the silence dashed it.

Looked like backup wouldn't be coming.

I had to save Rox all on my own and figure out who the fuck was behind this nonsense.

My stomach turned again. With my dinner already gone, I retched up bile, dripping down my chin and onto the beautifully beaded dress.

I had to get off this fucking ride.

"The devil lives," a mocking voice announced like a loudspeaker at a show.

I tried to peer past the bright lights, but the spinning prevented me from truly seeing anything beyond the painted horses from Hell.

"What? No snappy comeback this time?"

I tested my mouth, and found myself able to open and close it, though my control was still weak. "Kill . . . you . . ." I ground out. Not the most terrifying, but it was the best I had.

"You're going to kill me?" the voice asked.

My head rolled, and I used the momentum to nod.

He let out a condescending laugh. "You hear this? Even

drugged, covered in her own vomit, and completely at our mercy, she's still making threats." Several grunts followed. I had an audience. Great.

"Weak fucker," I replied, sounding surer. Whatever the asshole driver had given me was wearing off, and these dumbasses were just letting it.

"Weak?" he asked quietly. All the mocking was gone, replaced by utter seriousness. "Turn it off. I think it's time we send this bitch back to Hell once and for all."

The carousel slowed. I thanked my lucky stars. If they'd hurry up and kill me, I could come back not drugged and ready to rumble.

A loud mechanical clunking echoed in the night, and my horse finally came to a stop. Now that I wasn't moving, I could finally make out the silhouette standing at the edge of the ride.

He lifted an eyebrow. "Surprised to see me?"

"Tyler?" I asked, knowing that wasn't his name but wanting to egg him on. "Teagen? Travis?"

"Taylor," he said in a dark voice, stepping up onto the shiny metallic floor. "Taylor Dawson. I was the alpha of the Dawson pack. Until you came onto me and pissed off your *mate*." He pointed at the darkened skin of his forehead. A brand if I ever saw one. The elaborate R was placed on top of a crest I recognized but couldn't place. "He branded me a rogue because of you. I can't shift *because of you*."

I tried again to move my arms, and while I could, I definitely couldn't break my bonds yet. I needed more time.

"I tried to walk away. You tried to take something that wasn't yours. You only have yourself to blame," I mumbled. At least I was able to speak a little better than before. The rest would come. It had to.

Taylor's face hardened. "Untie her. It's time."

Time? Time for what?

A fae and another vampire came up from behind him. The vampire undid the bindings, and the fae grabbed my shoulders then roughly yanked me off the horse. I still couldn't fully walk. My legs were jerky, my limbs not complying when my body told them to hold me up. I started to fall to the ground, and he grabbed a fistful of hair, dragging me off the carousel.

Pain erupted in my scalp, making me hiss. My back arched when my ass dropped two feet and hit pavement, tailbone first. A searing pain lit that bone on fire, spreading outward.

Shit. I was pretty sure he'd just broken it.

Motherfucker.

"She's moving too much. Give her another hit," Taylor commanded.

A needle jabbed me in the arm courtesy of another nameless asshole.

I blinked while I still could and found there were a lot of them hovering near me. Easily several dozen.

The drug soared through my veins, quickly taking effect, causing my stupid human body to betray me.

"Where's Rox?" I forced the words out while I could still talk.

Taylor snapped his fingers. "I knew I was forgetting something. Thank you." He grabbed the attention of another minion, raising his voice as he asked, "Where's the bitch? She should get a front-row seat to this."

My body went completely limp and my eyes stayed wide open, frozen in place. I was trapped inside myself, unable to do anything.

The fae guy dragging me stopped, and I fell back on the concrete. The lights of the Ferris wheel and other carnival rides lit up the edges of my vision. Thick storm clouds sat heavy over us, watching ominously and waiting to open the floodgates. Not a single sliver of the moon was in sight.

"Get your hands off me, you fucking traitors," Rox said in a slurred, husky growl.

They'd suppressed her wolf somehow, and she had to be pissed. I couldn't actually see her. Just the lights against the dark. I really wished he would get on with the killing.

Knees smacked against the pavement near me. I recognized the sound as they popped.

"Fury?" Her voice changed. "Fury, what happened—"

Crack.

"Gag her," Taylor said gruffly. "I don't want to hear her bullshit."

Sounds of a scuffle followed, but it was short lived. Then it was just Roxanne's grunts, the carnival music, and Taylor talking.

"Wolf boy, can we get on with it? Her mates are looking for her, and I don't want to be here when they find the body. I get that you got a bone to pick, but this is about stopping her—not your petty fucking grudge."

Well, at least my driver was an asshole to everyone.

"Have you forgotten what her supposed mates have done to us?" Taylor replied in a low voice.

"No," driver man replied. "I'm well aware. We all are. That doesn't change the fact that I don't want to be here when they find her. The angel came to *us*. He showed us what happens. Get it over with."

The angel.

My mind was spinning like it was still on the damned carousel.

How could an *angel* have done this? Why? It didn't make sense.

Someone had to have told them the name Sunny, though. They couldn't have pulled that out of thin air.

So maybe there was something to it. Maybe an angel had betrayed me . . .

But why? I didn't know the angels. We had different jobs, but we worked for the same purpose.

Was this about the job? That they had failed, and I wouldn't?

That seemed extreme given what would happen if no one succeeded.

None of it added up.

I waited, hoping they'd drop more breadcrumbs. Maybe a name. A face. Could my mysterious angel be here right now?

I wasn't sure, but I needed to find out.

There was just one little problem.

I was faceup and unable to move.

Taylor leaned over me, a twisted grin on his smug fucking face. Behind him, something broke the pattern of the clouds. I focused on it. Trying to will myself to see.

It happened again.

Then again.

And on the fourth time, I was able to make out what it was.

A crow. Hades was here.

He turned in the sky and stared down at me with beady black eyes that I really hoped were saying he was going to get the guys. Then he twisted and flapped away.

"Are you ready to die, Devil?" Taylor asked me, as if I could answer. He knelt down, his face looming closer. He had a twisted streak in him, and for that alone I was happy we had an audience. I had little doubt he would drag this out if left to his own devices, but they wanted him to get on with it.

I could handle whatever pain he would throw at me. It would be temporary, and then I would die. I would come back, and I was going to question every single mother-fucker here tonight because I wanted to know who this 'angel' was. They were dead supes walking.

"Our angel told us your secret," he said after a moment. "He told us the only way to actually end you."

Given they'd already tried poison and blowing me up, I wasn't exactly terrified.

"Goodbye, Sunny Adams."

Then he did the only thing I hadn't expected.

He bit me.

CHAPTER 40
DORIAN

I was going to fucking kill that vampire.

Then when he was dead, I was going to kill every other fucking person that even knew someone who was involved. I was going to wipe this little cult from existence.

And once I finished doing that, I was going to lock Fury up on the Isle of Glass until I got some fucking answers from her about who and what she was, and why so many people wanted her dead.

But first I had to find her.

Vampires were scouring the east of the city. Shifters the north and west. The other fae and I had taken the south, but I also sent half my men to the other sections of Houston because I didn't trust anyone. I had to hope more of my people were less corrupt than theirs.

I sifted mile by mile, searching the streets of south Houston for my mate, but Fury was gone. Ezra had told us about the trap they'd laid, but the driver wasn't actually a driver at all. The car was still sitting there when we started the search. It appeared that whoever it was had sifted her out. Which meant she could technically be anywhere.

Most fae weren't powerful enough to take another person outside Houston, and our attackers always seemed more interested in killing her than anything. I wasn't certain if she was even here, but I kept looking because it was all I could do.

The feeling of being helpless for the first time in over a thousand years was unsettling. Deeply disturbing. Panic inducing.

I wasn't familiar with those emotions. I hadn't felt them since Morvain died and Lyra fell into her downward spiral. But here and now, I felt them again.

Anger rode on their heels.

I sifted again, going closer to the shore. I scanned the horizon, listening for anything that would lead me in the right direction. But there were no screams. No fires. No dying or dead people are far as I could tell. Everything was seemingly the same.

"Dorian," a voice said, sounding breathless. I turned, but no one was there. "Up here," it said again.

My head tilted back.

It was the crow from the warehouse.

"Where is she?" I demanded. "Where is your master?"

The beast cocked its head, flapping its wings. "First, she's not my master," the crow smarted off, wasting my time. He had seconds to live if he didn't tell me what he was clearly here to say. "Second, she was taken by an angry group of supernaturals. They've been brainwashed into thinking she'll end the world. They have her at King's Pier."

"Where's that?" Not the most familiar with the area given I never stayed longer than absolutely necessary.

The bird turned as an explosion rattled the street.

I sifted toward the noise and reappeared in front of a tacky arch that read *King's Pier*. It was an amusement park.

And the Ferris wheel was currently falling out of the sky.

I pulled out my phone and hit speed dial as I walked into the park.

Ezra picked up on the first ring.

"King's Pier. Tell the wolf."

I didn't wait for a response before disconnecting our call.

Supernaturals were sifting away and running in my direction, but they didn't seem to notice me. They were too busy fleeing something . . .

I picked up my pace.

"Fury!" I shouted.

The boom of the carousel exploding was my answer.

CHAPTER 41

My limbs felt like they were being torn from my body.

My skin was on fire.

My very being was breaking down because of one little detail I hadn't anticipated.

The dead can't be turned. We're already dead. The magic that we gained upon entering the Afterlife wasn't meant to mix with the magic in the living world.

Over the millennia, a few had made the attempt. Tried to return to life on Earth. Return to the living realm permanently. Each time, the angel, poltergeist, or whatever else that did so ended up dying a horrible, painful death—a true death—as the magic that was their soul literally tore apart.

That was my future.

My ending.

Taylor Dawson was right when he said he'd kill me. Now that I understood just how much they knew, I was certain there was a traitor in our midst. Someone in the Afterlife didn't want me to succeed. For an unknown reason, someone wanted the world to end.

And someone had picked the wrong fucking demon to come after.

I wasn't *The* Fury simply because I knew how to break and fix people the right way.

I was *The* fucking Fury because I was the last person you wanted to piss off if you wanted to live, dead or not.

And if I was going down, I was taking these sons of bitches with me.

I had just enough clarity. Barely enough focus. I teetered on the edge of losing myself in the pain when an electric current tingled through my arms. It couldn't burn off the drugs, but it could kill the pieces of shit who'd given them to me.

"Look at that. Doesn't look so tough now, does—" Taylor didn't get to finish before his entire body exploded.

The people gathered around went quiet, only just beginning to realize their mistake.

I didn't need my demonic strength to end them.

I didn't need my cunning or hard-earned combat skills.

I was one of the most powerful demons the Afterlife had seen because of one little fact.

No one knew how or why, but I made shit go boom.

And one by one, they did.

I knew the general direction they'd taken Roxanne. I hoped what little control I had was enough to save her from my wrath. But the rest of them? They could die. I was going to, so it only seemed fair they joined me.

The most excruciating pain I'd ever experienced consumed me, flesh and soul. I felt like my cells were being ripped apart. It was worse than burning, or drowning, or even being beaten to death.

As the werewolf bite from Taylor Dawson infected me

with venom meant to change me into a wolf, my soul began to die.

And my magic rose in response.

The control was gone.

Explosions went off left and right.

Shaking the ground. Rattling the stars.

Water rained down on me as I started to lose consciousness.

And that awful music cut out as wherever it was coming from detonated in a shower of flame and ash. Each explosion was bigger. Deeper. It was my soul crying out in a way that my body couldn't because of the drugs they'd pumped into me.

Tears leaked out of the corner of my eyes, mixing with the rain.

This was the end.

Whatever it was that I'd found both here and in the Afterlife was over.

It wasn't the end of the world that saddened me the most in my final moments. I hadn't felt true fear in so long that it took me by surprise. The thing I was most sad about was that I couldn't say goodbye—to Duke, the father figure who'd watched over me for a century. To Roxanne, my first best friend. To Roman, who just wanted to protect me. To Dorian, who would never have the truth he deserved. And to Ezra, who was unexpectedly my greatest confidant.

I hoped they realized I wasn't trying to be the stupid, self-sacrificing hero.

I'd just gotten played.

It could've happened to any of us.

Even the best, the strongest, and the most infallible had a flaw.

Unfortunately for me, my greatest strength and weakness were one and the same.

No matter how hard I tried not to, I cared too much.

And this time, it had gotten me.

CHAPTER 42

ROMAN

I ran like my life depended on it.

In a way, it did.

King's Pier was forty-five minutes by car.

Thirty on my motorcycle.

But only ten if I let the wolf out.

I knew the consequences if he was in charge. I knew what was at risk. If we found her dead, if whoever was after her had succeeded, the last bits of sanity would splinter. We'd go feral. Rogue.

So I ran.

Rain poured down, filling my coat with water. It slowed me, but not by much, because I ran without caring who saw me.

My paws ate the distance, a fast and rhythmic sound as they pounded the pavement.

Lights were the first thing my wolf picked up on.

An illuminating blast lit up the sky like a firework show, except the boom that followed rumbled the earth. Explosions rocked the ground the closer I got. Tremors vibrated the streets, shaking anything in its path.

I extended my claws, tearing up gravel in an effort to keep myself grounded despite the quaking pavement and thunderstorm raging around me.

I closed in on the pier.

I burst through the entrance, muscles burning and mind so hyper-focused on getting to my mate that the ground breaking apart beneath me didn't deter me. Not one bit.

I leapt over the ten-foot hole in the pier where churning waters thrashed underneath. The closer I got, the worse the destruction was.

Until I reached her.

Everything in me clenched tight.

My sister, Dorian, and Ezra all knelt around an unmoving body.

I padded up to them, and Roxanne was the only one to lift her head.

My sister's icy blue eyes said it all. "Something's wrong."

I shifted in an instant and went to her side.

Rain poured down on us, dirt and gravel mixing as it sloshed against Fury's pale skin. Her eyes were wide open, but she didn't move.

I would've thought her dead if not for the slight rise and fall of her chest.

"What happened to her?" I demanded, my voice more animal than man.

"She was drugged," Roxanna started. "Then Taylor bit her—"

A thunderous growl built in my chest. I should've killed him when I'd had the chance. I should've—

"She killed him. She killed all of them. The explosions . . ."

"I think she's dying," Ezra said after a moment. "Actually dying. What she is, it's not meant to cross with our kind."

"What the fuck—"

"You know what she is?" Dorian said, lifting his head. He looked like he was already feral. His amber eyes wide. The cat-slitted pupil dilated.

Ezra nodded. "I can't tell you—"

"Tell me how to *fix* her," he growled. It resonated with the wolf.

Ezra lifted his hand to Fury's cheek. Beneath the pale skin, lights were dancing. Her normally black eyes were bright shades of yellow and orange, swirling like the colors under her skin.

"I don't know how," he yelled back. "All I know is she's not from here. Her magic is different. Her body is different. This body should die so she can go to another one, but it was bitten by a wolf and she's dying inside it."

"We could suck the venom out," I said.

"It's too integrated already," Dorian said. "We suck it out and we'll likely kill her in the process, but she may not come back from it."

"She's not coming back from this either," Ezra argued.

"What if all three of you changed her?" Roxanne said softly.

I didn't think it was possible for me to go more still.

"Rox, if this is how she's reacting to a wolf bite from a mid-tiered wolf, I can't imagine she could survive transitioning into a three-way hybrid at once," I said.

"Normally, I'd agree. But there's magic here we don't understand, and you're her *mates*. Some part of her resides in each of you. Use that," Roxanne said, running her hand over a purple-splotched wound on Fury's thigh. "Before it's too late."

"Would it work?" Dorian said, staring straight at Ezra with an intensity that made me fairly certain if it didn't, Ezra might wish he could die.

"I don't know," the vampire said honestly. "I can't reach her, even now. If I could, we wouldn't even be having this discussion."

Dorian clenched his hands into fists. Meanwhile, the lights within Fury were growing brighter, moving under her skin like lightning. The pier shook harder.

"Do you *think* it will?"

Ezra went quiet for a moment. We all stared at her face, hoping for some sort of answer. But she lay as unmoving as before.

"I truly don't know, but we don't have a better idea, and that glowing light beneath her skin looks an awful lot like the explosions that are happening. I think we should try."

"Then we try," Dorian said.

"Wait," I interrupted. "This could kill her instantly—"

"Do you have a better idea, wolf?" Dorian snapped.

"No—"

"And are you prepared to let her die *permanently* because you're too scared to try anything?" Dorian continued.

His accusation stopped me in my tracks.

This whole time I'd been terrified that I wouldn't be able to keep her safe. I hadn't, and now there was a chance that she could die.

I could do nothing. Wait and see. But in all reality, what was happening right now was beyond explanation. It was unlike anything any of us had ever seen. Something was horribly wrong with my mate, and it had been set in motion by Taylor's bite.

And maybe, just maybe, the three of us could save her if we tried.

Or kill her, a small voice in my mind whispered.

I knew enough now to realize that voice was fear, and I couldn't listen to it any longer.

"No," I said solemnly. "I'm not."

"Good," the fae replied. He reached beneath his tux for a chain he kept underneath. He lifted it over his head, revealing a slender vial at the end. "Because I intended to try either way."

He whispered ancient words under his breath that I couldn't make out. The vial glowed. He twisted the top off and then grabbed Fury's jaw to part her lips.

As he dumped the contents into her mouth, Dorian said, "If any of you ever breathe a word of how the fae are made, you'll wish for death by the time I am finished with you."

I lifted Fury's wrist to my lips.

Then I bit her.

Her body jerked once and the lights within her turned brighter. Blinding. It hurt to watch, but I couldn't look away. I wouldn't.

"I hope this works, kitten," Ezra murmured. The vampire sank his fangs into his wrist, pulling and ripping open a gaping wound. The blood flowed heavily. He pressed it to her lips, letting it drip into her mouth. Her heartbeat thundered like a racehorse's hooves. It beat heavily against its cage of blood and muscle and bone.

On a broken and crumbling pier, I sat at my mate's side and prayed this wasn't it. That we weren't making the greatest mistake of our lives.

Ezra cupped her cheeks, and both Dorian and I tensed. My wolf screamed inside, clawing at my mind. I swallowed thickly.

We knew what was coming, but we agreed to do this, we had to let it happen. We had to let her die.

Ezra snapped her neck.

A crack echoed as lightning struck.

Her heart stopped.

The storm continued to rage.

Time went on.

Seconds passed as all four of us held our collective breaths.

"It didn't work," Dorian growled. He stood up and kicked a hole through a building so quickly that I hadn't realized he'd moved until it was too late. "It didn't fucking work!"

My breathing grew ragged. That thin tether of control I held began to fray as my anger and fear and emotion took over.

I'd thought it was just the wolf that wanted her. I still loved Maya. I still missed her . . . but I could have loved Fury. I could have built something with her. I could have done a million things differently. Been less guilt-ridden and less focused on betraying Maya's memory. Less overprotective. Less wishy washy. I could've tried harder. I could have. I could have. I could have—

A single thump stopped me.

I looked at her face. She hadn't blinked, but there, beneath her skin—the light started to fade.

Dorian turned his head to look at her, and Ezra froze.

Her chest rose and fell once.

Then she gasped.

I stared in stunned silence, torn between grabbing her,

kissing her, and wringing her neck for dying on me to begin with.

She blinked a couple of times and reached to her face to wipe her eyes. Then she stared at her hands like they belonged to someone else. Another second passed, and she slowly lifted a hand to brush her hair back and feel the now-pointed tip of her ear.

Her eyes, still yellow, went wide.

"You're fae now," Dorian said, standing closer than before.

"And a vampire," Ezra added.

"As well as a shifter," Roxanne said softly, speaking when I couldn't.

Fury dropped her hand. A quiet laugh bubbled up on her lips. She tilted her head back in the rain, and all I could think was that she was the most beautiful, enigmatic creature I'd ever seen.

And I was so fucking lucky that I had a second chance.

"I should've died," she said.

"Technically, you did," Ezra said grimly.

"You don't understand." She shook her head. "What I am . . . what I was . . . we can't become supes. We die whenever someone tries. This shouldn't be possible."

"Neither should having three mates, but here we are," Roxanne said. She hugged Fury tightly, and Fury hugged her back. "You had me worried," my sister continued. When they pulled apart, she punched her in the arm. "And don't you dare ever try to save me again."

Despite the atmosphere, I couldn't help but chuckle. So did Fury when Roxanne shook out her hand.

"Damn, what are you made of now?" She looked her up and down.

Fury did the same. "I don't know. This defies everything I know."

"Speaking of," Dorian interrupted. He crouched down, coming face-to-face with her. "You have some explaining to do."

She sighed. "I suppose me almost dying from being bitten gave it away..."

"Who are you? *What* are you?" Dorian asked, recovering rather quickly for a guy who'd been on the edge only moments ago.

"My name is Fury. Just Fury. I'm a demon sent from the Afterlife."

My lips parted, but credit where it was due, Dorian didn't react one bit.

"Why?" Dorian asked.

"Wait, the vampires trying to kill you were telling the truth?" I looked up and narrowed my eyes on Ezra.

He averted his gaze. He'd known about it, and still he'd tried gaslighting me into believing I was a horrible mate for questioning the things they'd told us about her.

I looked back at Fury. "Are you going to end the world?"

She blew out a tight breath.

"No." She shook her head. "You are. I was sent here to stop you."

CHAPTER 43
AN ANGEL

The Isle of Glass was dreary, as always. Cold. Brutal. Though not unpleasant.

Most of the guards had been called away to deal with the search for Sunny, and those who hadn't were now dead. The isle was near empty. But not completely.

There was still one who slept within these halls.

One who'd witnessed divinity and lived.

Deep within the castle on the cliff overlooking the ocean lay a maiden so old she was near ancient. A woman who'd been forced to sleep for over a thousand years. Trapped in a tomb. Imprisoned in her mind.

While many believed her father to be more powerful than all, they were mistaken.

I took the stone steps that circled down several levels. So deep that if the rock were to fail, we'd both be buried down here for eternity. There were no windows. No light.

It would've been utterly silent, if not for the softest sigh of breathing.

I reached the bottom step and entered the chamber.

The floor and ceiling were crafted from the finest

marble. Precious gems lost to the world ages ago were inlaid in the walls, framed by gold designs. It was as if he'd tried to cleanse himself of the guilt, adorning her prison with treasures and bestowing on her more riches than one could spend in a lifetime.

In the center of the room was a single stone tomb with a glass lid.

I approached it, taking in the veil of white hair that splayed across the silk pillow. Blonde eyelashes fanned out over her closed eyes. Her skin was unnaturally pallid, not having seen the sun in over a millennium.

I remembered what she'd once looked like, though.

How her light pink lips curled into a smile. How beautifully red had stained her pale skin, and how the angels who looked down had wondered if it would ever lose its taint.

She was a sleeping beast.

A monster.

She was the daughter of the man I wished to punish for touching what was mine. For saving what was mine.

He had no right to take her from me.

Now I was going to take something in return.

My hands touched the cool glass, and I pushed it off the tomb in a single motion. It hit the floor, shattering like a thousand crystals as the sound broke through the silence and reverberated off the stone walls.

"Lyra," I said, speaking in her mother tongue. "It's time to wake up."

AN ALPHA WOLF, a seductive vampire, and a dominant fae all walk into a bar. What do they have in common?

Being mated to me, apparently.

My dreams of retirement crashed and burned when the

rogue shifter bit me. Not only have I changed into something neither world has ever seen before, but my mission just became even more impossible. To find the answers about what I am, I enlist the help of an infamous ex-poltergeist, a shifter freak, and my least favorite pigeon.

What a team we make.

Oh, and did I forget to mention that my mate's bloodthirsty daughter is awake and hunting my ass now? Because that's a thing too.

Why?

I have no idea, but we have every intention of finding out.

An angel is playing games with me, but little do they know—I've got three alphas by my side, and this dark horse plays for keeps.

ONE CLICK WHITE RAVEN NOW!

Join Kel's Newsletter: www.kelcarpenter.com

AUTHOR'S NOTE

Fury is a demon, and she can get away with a lot. While she and those around her can joke about how much she drinks, her guys are concerned for her. Sooner than she'd like, she will have to face this head on.

While she is fictional, the reality of her past and why she drinks is far from fantasy.

If you or someone you love needs help, please reach out to a friend, a family member, a counselor, or one of the resources below.

Alcoholics Anonymous
   https://www.aa.org

The Substance Abuse and Mental Health Services Administration
   https://www.samhsa.gov/find-help/atod

The National Domestic Violence Hotline

https://www.thehotline.org
800-799-SAFE (7233)

United Nations Domestic Abuse
https://www.un.org/en/coronavirus/what-is-domestic-abuse

ACKNOWLEDGMENTS

These are weird to write, aren't they? They feel weird. Is this what award speeches feel like, when you stand up and say you'd like to thank the academy?

In all seriousness, this journey started as something else between us. We didn't set out to write a book together. That wasn't the plan. (No, I'm not telling you the plan.) But what we did start morphed into a joke that we should just write a book. (Haha.) That changed into a casual sugges-tion. (Yeah, right. Okay.) Then the poking and prodding and strongarming started. (Wait, are we really doing this?)

Now here we are.

Maegan, without you, Hades wouldn't exist. A promise delivered. Thanks for being the best damn PA we could ask for. You seriously keep the show running behind the scenes.

Graceley Knox, Amanda Pillar, Courtney Lummus; you've each contributed to our plans in different ways, and you're awesome for it. We appreciate you more than you know. Having friends to listen to us and provide guidance when we need them the most is invaluable.

Dom, our proofreader, we were lost without you on this one. Thank you times a million.

Matt, thanks for watering me. Love you lots.

AJ's little demons, thanks for upping the difficulty level in getting some of these chapters written. Stop trying to stand behind me when I am writing. I appreciate a good challenge, but I'm not ready to answer those questions yet.

Basically, don't ever read what I write. You're both tiny tyrants, and you're both my world.

Mr. Jane, thank you for supporting me, listening to me, feeding me when I get cranky, and encouraging my endeavors. You get me the way no one else can.

And finally, to you, our readers. Without you, this journey wouldn't be possible. We can't wait to share more of Fury's story with you.